When Dani Smiled

Published By

RockHill Publishing LLC
PO Box 62241
Virginia Beach, VA 23466-2241
www.rockhillpublishing.com

When Dani Smiled

Athina Paris

Dedication

This book is dedicated to all the women who have survived abuse, be it physical, psychological, or emotional.

And to all the good men who stood by them, believed them, and did what was right, even when under threat to themselves, you make the world a better place.

Like cancer, may this scourge be eradicated from civilization; soon.

CHAPTER ONE

Dani clutched the portfolio pages tightly to her chest as she stepped out the door and glanced at the January sky. It was clear in the east but ominous clouds gathered in the west, broadcasting a possible downpour—typical Johannesburg summer weather, surprises at every turn. She held the drawings closer, not prepared to lose years of hard work to potential torrents. Better rush too, if she planned to make it to the art shop before ten; had to look professional at the interview.

She gazed at her Jack Russell on Mrs. Brown's windowsill, glad the kind woman had offered to look after the little rascal whenever she was out. She tapped the glass and there was an instant pricking of ears and wagging of tail. She smiled at the furry face staring back at her, 'Coco, go play.' Instead, Coco hopped around, pawed the pane, and licked it. Poor Mrs. Brown, another slobbered window to clean.

Coco had been a gift from Sams, and generally, she regretted accepting anything from him, because every time she did, he felt entitled to some part of her life. She was convinced Sams was a freak of nature, because he was that one thing so many men wanted to be but were not, and she could not remember a time when he had not been number one at just about everything he had put his mind to throughout their school years. As far back as she could recall he had always been good-looking, smart, charming, and excelled at sports, especially rugby. A lot of idolatry had flown around that school. He thrived on it, she found it exceedingly disturbing.

Her heart dropped as she reached her car, there was a deep dent and crack on the Beetle's front bumper. She peered at it, poked it, gave it a kick then looked around; trying to find someone who might explain this; as per standard calamity manual, no one in sight. Now, when exactly did this happen, here, or at some parking lot? Her father had bought it just two months previously.

'Ugh,' she uttered. It was a new car with a scar and she with no idea how it had been inflicted. She felt like crying but what would that accomplish? She should have known then that this was not to be a normal day but ever the eternal optimist she set forth into it as if it were an adventure.

The damaged bumper returned her thoughts to Sams. Once, when they were still learning how to drive, he had taken his mother's car without permission and gone over to her house. She hated it when he turned up unexpectedly because he was constantly looking for things she did not intend giving him.

He sort of kissed her... She labelled it sort of, because she had been unresponsive. However, when he forced his tongue into her mouth, she became responsive, by pushing him away and locking herself in her bedroom. Sams did not understand or accept rejection easily and left in a huff. She should rephrase that, he tried to leave in a huff but proceeded to scratch a long ugly line all the way down the car's side as he drove past the gate, so instead, he left in a furious mood.

Something curious happened to Sams that particular January morning. Just as he was about to sit down to write an exam, he had the overwhelming urge to call Dani, not a mere flicker of an idea, but a burning anxiety to contact her.

He glanced at the time. Nothing doing, that call had to wait until he was done here, and that was at least two hours away. Yet, the urgency persisted. He glanced at the clock again then shrugged; there was nothing he could do about it now. Slowly, the feeling waned then vanished, having lasted a total of two minutes.

Sams was not to know that two powerful forces were at work that morning; the first conspired to give him another chance at attaining what he wanted, and the second endeavoured to give Dani what she needed.

He was not to know that had he given up writing that exam and called her, the selfless gesture would have finally shown him in the light he wished to be seen, and worked favourably in his pursuit of Dani Marie Creswell. For at that very moment, she stood on the side of a highway, cursing the damaged bumper that had come off completely. She had ridden over the mangled mess and it was now stubbornly stuck under the Beetle, with a sharp edge dug deep into the front right tyre, which leaned at a strange angle in shreds to the right.

Now, did she call to announce that she would be late for her interview, a tow-truck, the insurance, or her father? Safe was probably the best way to go about this.

'Galfrey's, good morning,' said a prim and proper voice.

After a quick greeting, she stated her business. 'My name is Dani Creswell and I have an interview with Mr. Ridley at eleven, but I would like to speak with him first, if possible.'

'One moment please.' Prim and proper checked the schedule. 'Are you sure it's today?'

'Yes.'

'Why are you calling?'

Did people not listen? 'I have an interview but I'm in a bit of a situation.'

Prim and proper glanced at the schedule on the computer screen. She was here a few days and did not yet understand all the lists, rolls, rosters, schedules, appointments, interviews, and consultations. And the name Ridley... now what was it that she was she forgetting? 'Miss Creswell, what are you coming in for? I don't have a Mr. Ridley on my register.'

'I'm coming for...' What was that absurd title? 'Creative Virtual Assistant,' she did not think it had anything to do with fashion, but Mr. Ridley had called because her former lecturer, Julia Morris, had referred her. He had not divulged much else either, except to mention that he was from Galfrey's IT Department, as he had been in a rush to get somewhere. The mere fact that he was from Galfrey's was exciting enough, but she would have preferred it if one of the designing department heads had called.

'Now I know where to look.' Prim and proper said, but she didn't. Removing the earpiece, she pressed speakerphone on, so she could talk as she wheeled herself to the other computer.

A man sauntered over to the workstation and stopped, obviously having something of importance to impart.

Becoming aware of his presence, prim and proper blushed. Who could concentrate with a man like him standing around? Besides, she had no clue what to tell the young woman at the other end where her interview was, or where to find Mr. Ridley. She pressed a few keys, but unable to find the required information, glanced towards the man.

Seeing she was flustered and in some quandary, Nicholas decided to step in. 'Is there something I can help you with?' He asked and focused on the name tag on her breast. 'Simone.'

'Sorry sir, but I can't find Mr. Ridley on my roster.'

For a moment he didn't know if he should find it funny or simply a lack of professionalism, then realising this was the new receptionist, who had started three days ago—without receiving much training as the previous one had simply left for who knew where or what reason—he accepted that she was probably not aware of much yet. 'Simone, Mr. Ridley is in the hospital, he was involved in a serious car accident five days ago.'

Prim and proper gasped, that's what she had forgotten. But she heard of it on her very first day, while trying to assimilate all that was going on and, well... 'Miss Creswell, I have terrible news.'

Dani caught prim and proper's gasp loud and clear, just been unable to catch the discussion that preceded it, so resigned to disaster for the rest of the day, she retorted annoyed. 'Well, what can you do, just give them to me. Can't be worse than what I'm looking at.'

Nicholas grinned at the sarcasm and leaned against the granite counter. Now this he had to hear.

'Mr. Ridley had an accident and is in hospital. When his PA called to ask for the list, I emailed it back, so I don't...' She opened a file on the PC and clicked a few times. 'Oh bother, there were three pages, the first only had two names, the second was blank, so I didn't see yours on the third.' She muttered. 'I'm sorry.'

Dani was upset. If they had checked their appointments properly, they could have called and avoided all of this. 'What am I supposed to do now? I'm stuck, and alone. Are you coming to keep me company?'

Prim and proper's face turned red. 'Excuse me?'

'I am stuck on the side of the highway, on my way to a place I shouldn't have been on my way to, some careless person damaged the front bumper, so it has now fallen off and become lodged under the car, there is a punctured and destroyed tyre, and I can't do anything until a tow-truck gets here. I also need to call the insurance. I just thought I should let Mr. Ridley know first.'

Intrigued by venting lungs, Nicholas decided to step in again. 'Who is that?'

'Please hold,' Simone muted the line. 'Miss Creswell, sir. She was supposed to see Mr. Ridley today, but her interview wasn't cancelled, so this...' She made an apologetic gesture and pointed to the phone.

'Ask her where she is and we will send someone to pick her up and take her home. It's the least we can do. Then, check with Mr. Ridley's PA to reschedule the interview.' He advised.

'Miss Creswell,' she repeated Nicholas' message.

'But... you don't understand. When will they come, before or after the tow-truck gets here? And what if I have to wait until dark? You know people do whatever they want, when they feel like it nowadays. I do not want to waste anyone's time, I can't take the chance of someone stealing my car, and I definitely cannot loiter around here, alone, for an entire day either. I need to call my father. Ugh daddy, you are so busy... Drat it.' Dani continued talking to herself.

Nicholas smiled. When last had he heard such a mild curse, or a woman who wanted to call her father? And now that anger had transformed into worry, he could hear the warm tones in her voice. Without thinking and forgetting why he had stopped there, he asked for a connection to another phone. 'Let me take care of this.'

'Thank you, sir.' Simone sighed with relief.

'Miss Creswell,' Nicholas began.

'Yes,' the male voice surprised her.

'Where are you?'

'Huh.' Dani looked around. 'Almost across Melrose Arch, facing south. I came down Grayston Avenue.' Why she had gone to Benmore Gardens for the few items that were hardly necessary then headed for the highway, she did not know either.

At least she knows directions. 'I know where that is. Are you safely off the yellow line, cones set out, hazards on, etc,'

'Yes. What a horrible morning.' She sighed deeply. 'But wait, it could be getting worse.'

'What is wrong now?'

'There are three men walking towards me, and they are waving sticks.'

'Miss Creswell, get into your car and lock yourself in, I'm on my way.'

'But...'

'Give me your cell number, and I'll call you right back.' He wrote quickly, grabbed the paper, and dialled from his own phone, as he made his way back to the lift.

'Hello,' Dani answered.

'There you are. Where are the men?'

'Still walking.'

'Are you safe?'

'I think so.'

Reaching his floor, he went into the office, grabbed his jacket, and car keys. 'Are you scared?'

'Not really.'

Thank goodness. It would be so much worse dealing with a fearful or hysterical woman. 'So, how long have we been chatting and we still haven't been properly introduced?'

'Ten.'

'Excuse me?'

'You asked how long, ten minutes.'

'Miss Creswell, are you trying not to give me your name?' He grinned, thinking he felt her smile.

'But you have been calling me Miss Creswell all this time.' She pointed out.

'Yes,' he agreed, but the point was to make her feel at ease until he got to her. 'I meant your name. We don't have to continue so formally.'

'It's Dani.'

He liked it instantly and imagined a tomboy. She probably loved pants, short hair, male sports, and had climbed trees as a child. 'Short for?' He asked as he got into his car.

'Nothing, it's Dani Marie Creswell. Mom liked Kylie and Dannii Minogue when she was younger. I think she said she flipped a coin, so there it is.'

He laughed, a happy laugh, as if he were having a conversation with an old friend. 'I like it.'

'Thanks.' She couldn't see him but she also liked the way he sounded.

'Marie?'

'My grandmother's name. What's yours?'

'Nicholas.'

Her first image was of Saint Nicholas, and she wanted to giggle as she imagined a man in a red suit pulling over on the side of the road in a sleigh. 'Do you like it like that, or another version?'

'You mean Nick or something? No, just plain Nicholas.'

'Oh no...'

'What?'

'The men stopped to see what is happening.' She opened the window. 'Thank you, but I'm okay,' she told them. 'I'm waiting for...'

She must have either dropped the phone onto her lap or muted it because he couldn't hear the rest. He might not know her but suddenly, he was concerned for her safety.

She took a few seconds to get back. 'I'm back,'

'Dani,' he exhaled with relief and realised that saying her name gave him a rush. He wondered if this was what men felt when they called those hotlines late at night, where the voices held so much more promise than looks ever would. 'Are you okay?'

'Yes. They were just concerned about me sitting here alone, and offered to change the tyre, until they saw what it really looks like. They moved on when I told them someone is on their way.'

'Nevertheless, stay alert. By the way, what do you drive?'

'A Beetle,'

In his mind's eye, he saw fading yellow, a brighter hue on a door, pink daisies on the bonnet and side, and an accompanying incredible racket. No wonder the thing was falling apart.

'Nicholas,'

It felt as if she had wrapped his name in silk and slowly unwrapped it again. He couldn't wait to see what she looked like. A silence followed.

'I forgot what I was going to say.' She admitted. 'Oh yes, what car should I expect?'

'A white Audi,' he gauged traffic, trying to figure out how long it would take to get to her. 'Are the men gone?'

'Yes. Have you ever been stuck?'

'I think twice.'

'Recently?'

'No, when I was a student.'

'Who helped you?'

'My friends,'

'Are they still your friends?'

He could not understand why this felt like the best conversation in the world. 'Two of them are, Andrew and Leon,'

'It's funny how that happens. Nicholas,'

She had to stop doing that. 'Yes,'

'About the insurance and tow-truck—'

'Just hang on, I don't want to disconnect. And we'll decide what to do when I get there.'

'That thing is wedged tight and I'll damage much more if I ride over it again. Never mind that, the tyre is not only flat, but beyond repair. Do you know how much longer you will be?'

He glanced around, getting his bearings. 'I'm on Katherine Street; so it could take fifteen or fifty minutes. It's not as if I can drive at two-twenty.'

'No, you can't do that.'

'Did you ever get a speeding fine?'

'Not for speeding. But I did get a ticket for failing to stop at a stop sign.'

'Why on earth would you do that? Was anyone else at the intersection at the time?' He asked curiously.

'Not driving. But the van that made me get the trick ticket.'

'The what?'

'There was never a stop there. So in the morning I drive, nothing. In the afternoon, I never saw the new painted line or the sign because of the parked van.'

He grinned. 'Oh, I see. Did you complain?'

'I did, but paying less wasn't what I was after. I wanted to explain that it was unfair to catch people like that.'

'And you know where fair lives.' Goodness, but he was enjoying himself. 'Sorry about your day, it shouldn't have turned out like this.'

'I needed to know the thing was going to fall off, so I guess today was as good a day as any other.'

'How did that happen?'

'I don't know. When I got to the car, I noticed someone had bashed it. I just didn't realise it was that loose. I have no idea if it happened where I live or somewhere else.'

'Was there a note?'

'No, and that is what really upset me. Whether they can pay or not is beside the point, I have insurance. I just wanted someone to say sorry.'

'Are you big on apologies?'

'Sorry is a wonderful word, it fixes many things, especially when meant sincerely.'

'And people lie all the time.'

'A cynic, huh?'

'Not about everything, but I know many liars.'

'Sadly, so do I,' and how was it possible that she was having such a natural conversation with a complete stranger? 'Ugh, imagine this on Oxford, Corlett, or Nelson Mandela Drive... during rush hour. The nightmare I'd have caused then.'

'You would be famous, but more likely infamous,' he grinned. 'During the traffic report. And get a couple evil eyes.'

She laughed. Looking in the rear-view mirror, she noticed the lanes emptying of traffic, except for a white spec in the distance. 'I see a car coming towards me, is that you?'

'Yes, that's me.'

Her face scrunched up in surprise as the vehicle approached. That was no sleigh. What were people earning at Galfrey's?

'Oh,' he said as he peered into the distance and realised it was a recent model Beetle, not a 1960 battered jalopy.

'Do you want to wait in the car or get out and stretch your legs?' What nonsense, he was debating how he wanted to meet her.

Dani decide. Getting out quickly, she then ducked back for her handbag. *Say he's a weirdo, pervert, or psycho?* She wondered, but somehow, she didn't think so. Taking a deep breath, she readied herself to meet her rescuer.

Nicholas turned the Audi's hazards on and pulled up behind the Beetle. All he could see as she leaned into the car was a long pretty summer dress, dainty flat sandals, and light brown hair tumbling over her left side, so much for the tomboy. Alighting from the car, he grinned and took a few steps.

She straightened her back, turned and smiled. She had learned early but specifically around her teenage years, that she possessed two smiles. One was a plastered grin for complete strangers and two... there was something about that smile that made people, but especially men, lose their heads. Now, relieved that he was here, she forgot about such things and simply expressed her gratitude.

The grin disappeared from Nicholas' face. What was this walking towards him? He could half-see and the rest imagine as a breeze toyed with the delicate fabric and long light brown hair. She was on the short side, but had the nearest to perfect face he had ever seen. He gulped as his heartbeat scaled a wall, must be an erotic hallucination because he had never seen anything as... a bunch of adjectives flew through his mind and he discarded every one. Somehow, he could just tell, she was neither a dish nor a possession, much less a sport. What she was, was perfect, and he felt like falling to his knees at her feet.

Dani was having a similar experience, just not as carnal. She had imagined Nicholas to be a regular office guy, and he might still be that guy, but there was nothing regular about him. His clothes were impeccable; light blue cotton shirt, well-cut blazer, and a pair of jeans, that sat perfectly. *That is why we designers bother,* she thought. But clothes were secondary, he was well-defined... Insipid word; he obviously looked after himself, had dark hair, an expressive face, brown eyes that danced, and a friendly smile. *How apt,* she thought. *Why shouldn't a knight rescuing a damsel in distress look like a knight in shining armour?* Now, how did they greet?

Nicholas made that decision. He offered his hand. 'Dani,'

She took it willingly and smiled again. 'Hello, Nicholas.'

He couldn't help himself and simply stared, then, shaking himself back into reality, he turned to look at the damage. 'So, this is the dilemma.' He walked the short distance, bent down, and peered under her car. 'Yep, you have it quite right.' Then he went to the front of the Beetle. 'Bummer,'

'Don't you mean bumper?'

He laughed.

'So, what do we do?'

'As you said, we can't touch this car again. Okay, so, what's the tow-truck's number? I'll call them and you deal with the insurance.'

She searched for a card and gave him a reference number to quote.

'Right,' he walked towards the embankment, then returned a few minutes later. 'They'll be here shortly.' He announced. 'Or so they said. Grab your things and put them in my car.'

She realised then that she had not thought this thing out properly, because now, she was at his mercy. Perhaps she should have called Sams... Her eyes returned to Nicholas immediately, willing to take her chances with him.

Besides, he didn't look dangerous. Actually, he did, but it was a different kind of danger that he presented.

Seeing her expression, he knew where her thoughts had gone. 'I'm not going to attack you.'

A blush rushed up her face.

When last had he seen one of those? Then again, the women he mixed with were world wise, sophisticated, and classy. This... this was a wondrous woman child who was doing strange things to his senses. He wondered how old she was. 'Can I help you?'

'There is only my portfolio.' Returning to the Beetle, she realised that she had been holding her breath. Was it even normal to get butterflies when looking into a strange man's eyes? Glancing at him through the rear-view mirror, she wondered what he was thinking, or feeling because he seemed to be going through something himself.

Never in his thirty years of life had he imagined that he would meet someone who looked like her, and for him, there were no two ways about it. Who cared about magazine perfect? That she wasn't tall enough? In his eyes, she was perfect. And those green eyes... forget about blue ponds, lakes, rivers, and seas where men drowned themselves. These were a meadow, soft and gentle, with the promise of life.

She clutched the loose pages carefully. 'Drat,' she said, half talking to herself, and half to him. 'Now, I can't go to the art shop.'

'Is that where you were headed?' He asked as he opened his car's door.

She nodded as she placed her things neatly down. 'Coco, my dog, ate my folder and I wanted to go get a new one before the interview. To look professional. Not arrive with piles of stuff in my hands.'

'Your dog ate your bag?' He asked amused.

'And it's a little dog. Well, she didn't eat it all at one go, but she sure chewed every corner, handle, and strap. Which is funny as she never touched anything at home.'

He didn't understand something, if she was seeing Adam Ridley, who was in IT, why was she carrying her portfolio around? 'Right,' he said as he glanced at the top page of her work, which was an interesting take on the military look. 'You mentioned dad before, is there also mom, boyfriend, anyone?'

She was probably in the presence of the fastest moving playboy in Johannesburg, or... sneakily she darted her gaze to his left hand. Okay, no ring, but that didn't mean he was single. 'Yes.' She told him ambiguously and hid a smile.

'Then pick a number and let someone know you are safe.'

She was travelling in the clouds, better come down fast. 'Thank you for reminding me.' She dialled.

'Hi honey, how did it go?'

'It has been postponed.' She imagined they would do that much since Mr. Ridley was in hospital. 'Mom, something happened to my car...' and she explained.

'Then what are you doing now?' Carol asked concerned.

'Waiting for a tow-truck,'

'Alone, on the side of the road... do you know where you are?'

'Mom, I'm fine.' Dani assuaged as she noticed Nicholas watching her. 'And a friend is here with me.'

'Sams?'

'No, Nicholas.'

Carol's interest was instantly pricked. 'Who is Nicholas?'

Dani pressed the mute button and asked. 'Who are you? My mom wants to know.'

He had wondered whom she would call. 'May I speak to her?'

Dani was surprised but said, 'sure,' and gave him the phone.

'Mrs. Creswell,' he began politely and walked away for a few minutes, then came towards her again. 'Don't worry Mrs. Creswell, and I'll see that she is not stuck without transport. And if she needs to see you before her car is repaired, I will either take her myself or let her borrow mine.'

Dani stared at him. Was he serious? Then she stared at the car. Was he mad? She did not have to know much about cars to know that that model was obscenely expensive. She definitely could not chance getting anything stuck under there. So it seemed as if there was only one way she was seeing her parents if she wanted to. She looked at him again. Was it okay to like the idea so much?

'Goodbye,' he handed the phone back. 'I think she's okay about me. I don't blame her, so many ugly things can happen on the side of a road.' He shivered, relieved that he was the one here. 'Are we going to stand outside until we bake, or can we at least sit in my car while we wait?'

She turned to get in.

Right behind her, he opened the door and as he did, she turned around and it was as if she were in his arms. He restrained himself from reaching out.

'Thank you, Nicholas.'

He could smell her; perhaps jasmine, but subtly diluted. He leaned in to test if the scent became stronger, but no, it stayed in that alluring plane. Suddenly, he felt lecherous, but imagine some other creepy man here... No, he couldn't leave her alone; especially while she was without a car.

Dani watched his face as something was obviously going through his mind, as if he were planning something quite complicated but also stunningly simple. And how was it possible that one could become attracted to a stranger in so short a time? She had never felt anything as acute as this. Was this what Sams felt? Then she felt very sorry for him because it would never be reciprocated. Her eyes found Nicholas', if he moved another inch, he could touch her. Her heartbeat accelerated, making her feel weak.

'Have we met before?' He asked suddenly.

She shrugged, uncertain, also thinking there was something vaguely familiar about him. 'Maybe we have walked past each other at a fashion show.' She suggested.

'Maybe,' he told her but was unconvinced. 'Oh, look, they actually kept their word. Then again, they are never far from calamities.' He said as a tow-truck rolled in front of the Beetle.

The man was helpful and friendly and had the car ready quickly. After having her sign the required papers, he climbed back into the tow-truck, waved at them, and drove away.

'So,' Nicholas said as they watched the Beetle disappear. 'Where to my lady?'

She smiled. 'Am I not holding you from something important?'

'You don't want me here?'

'You were busy at work and now you're not.'

'I was leaving the office when this exciting episode of Johannesburg life happened. I also heard you tell Simone to give you the bad news and then asked her if she wanted to come keep you company. It made me curious.'

'I spoke that loud?' She asked embarrassed.

'The entire reception area heard you.'

Colour suffused her cheeks.

He grinned. 'I'm teasing, the speakerphone was on and no one else was around. So, where is this art shop?'

'Is it really okay for you to be here?'

'Absolutely,'

CHAPTER TWO

At the art shop, he was fascinated as she walked through the full aisles. She was there to find a folder, but she couldn't resist touching everything else. He watched her fingers; it was as if she caressed brushes, pens, tubes of paint... He had never imagined art supplies could be so sensual.

'Dani,' the woman at the cash register hugged her excitedly. 'You're back. How was your year away?'

'Many new experiences, exciting, and informative.'

'I would say foreign can only take you so far. Did you pick up any of the accents?'

'I don't think so, or my mom would have said something already, but I did learn some French.'

Nicholas was a distance away, as there were a few customers hovering around the counter and he was not one for traffic jams, but he was following the conversation. She had recently returned from somewhere, somewhere where she had learnt French. Considering she was in fashion, it could have been Paris itself.

'I'm glad you had a good time,' the woman continued. 'And do come see us again.'

'Definitely, thank you.' Grabbing the new folder, she searched for Nicholas.

He went towards her immediately, and having to navigate art supplies and people, he stood behind her, almost pressed his body to hers, and placing hands on her waist, steered her through the maze. A delirious carnal desire filled him, further intensified as her scent enveloped his senses.

It was as if he transferred heat through his skin, suffocating her. Outside, she took a step away from him and refilled her lungs with fresh air.

'We need coffee.' He glanced at his watch. 'Or something substantial, it's lunchtime. Any particular place you would like?'

'Whichever is closest, they are all okay.'

'There is also the Grace.' What he was thinking was disturbing but he could not help himself. All he wanted to do was get a room at the hotel, get her naked, and have mind-blowing sex. His pulse raced.

'Light is good this time of day.' She was picking up some serious vibes between them and the last belief she wanted to foster was that girls were served on platters during the course of a day rescue. She was not going to aid and abet in what she was beginning to understand he wanted. Hotels, with easily accessible rooms, were not on the agenda today.

There were about a dozen men in the establishment she chose, but none seemed to notice her. Nicholas studied her, instinctively knowing she was doing something because she was a gorgeous girl. Her shoulders slouched, her head dropped, her hair hid her face, and she sat in the shadows, obviously, avoiding detection. His radar however, had tuned in and locked onto her from the first moment he heard her voice. A feeling of déjà vu filled him.

He discovered that her father was CEO of Creswell Enterprises—a giant in the car rental industry—which he knew about. Her mother gave most of her time to their church, where she helped run all sorts of charity and social programmes. Dani was an only child, but from the looks of it, it seemed she had never been a spoilt brat.

'What about you?' She asked. 'What is your family like?'

'It seems we already have a few things in common. My parents had problems conceiving so I am also an only child. Nowadays, dad plays golf most of the time and occasionally dabbles on the stock exchange.'

'Is there a wife?' She asked bluntly as she looked at his left hand.

He waved his hand. 'No, never been tempted yet.'

'What about your mom?'

'Mom tinkers in her garden, and goes into the office when she feels like it. That's what she says, but it's pretty much every day, after ten.' He smiled warmly. 'But twenty-five years ago, she and her sister-in-law started a company.' He added proudly.

'Speaking of companies, what is it you do at Galfrey's?'

Lie or tell the truth? He went for truth, just not directly. 'I am in the executive, pandering to Catherine and Samantha Galfrey's every whim, and make sure it all runs smoothly once they have issued their orders.'

Dani scrunched up her brow, trying to remember her notes on Galfrey's upper echelons. There were three designing departments; Rene Asher ran Haute Couture, Deborah Potts was in charge of department store designs, and Louis Wilson produced attire for sport stores. Adam Ridley handled IT, which was why she did not yet understand what he wanted with her. A bunch of names in Admin, HR, Financial, Legal, and then there was Samantha Galfrey, Catherine Galfrey, and Nicholas Galfrey. She fixed her gaze on the man across the table. 'Nicholas, is your surname Galfrey?'

He did not blink. 'Yes.'

'Why didn't you tell me when we were introducing ourselves?'

'Because that darn name makes people act peculiar. I wanted you to relax, not be all uptight and nervous, and I wanted you to know me, not my name. Is that such a bad thing?' He looked pleadingly at her.

Of course, this also explained why he could jump into his shiny expensive stallion during work hours to go rescue strange women. But now, that interview and job... depending on the outcome of this encounter, would Nicholas influence Mr. Ridley?

Nicholas watched her face, knowing exactly where her mind had gone. 'What are you thinking?' He encouraged.

'I need to do this on my own. Please tell me that you will not interfere, meddle, give a glowing report, or otherwise, about me. Assuming Mr. Ridley is allowed to choose his own staff.'

'Adam runs his department whichever way he sees fit. Everyone does. I have almost no say in hiring or firing. And this is precisely why I didn't want you to feel weird in my presence.'

'Which one is your mom?' She queried.

'Catherine is my mom and Samantha my aunt. She was married to my father's late brother. Are we okay with this?'

'No star for you today. And I will admit, it is not an outright lie, but you did covert operations.'

'Sorry?'

She curled her lips and nodded. 'You are learning. So, since you have no siblings, do you have cousins? I do, lots.'

'Two, and both older than me. Veronica is physically and mentally handicapped so I see her about once a week when I visit home, as my aunt also lives there. It's convenient and helpful with Veronica's care. Jethro joined the French Foreign Legion fifteen years ago and we haven't seen or heard from him since.'

'Not a happy child, huh?'

'No, not at all. How do you know that?'

'We had someone like that at school. Very troubled and unhappy boy, he also enlisted.'

Nicholas watched how she ate; the pace wasn't fast, or slow, just different and no one could doubt that she enjoyed food. He stared at her lips as she passed her tongue over them. He wanted to say something but got lost in her gaze. It came to him again. 'Please save my number and promise that you will call every day to tell me if you need to go somewhere, anytime.' But given a choice, most people never took it, so he wouldn't give her one. 'Never mind, I'll call you.'

'There is a bus route on my street.'

'But I'd like to take you around.'

'Please don't feel guilty about my predicament.'

'No, none of that, I just want to.'

'Okay.' She shrugged but her heart did a somersault. 'But now...'

'Now what?'

'I was so eager to impress Mr. Ridley, hoping that he would hire me on the spot. I am not being funny but I need to think of alternatives if this becomes a prolonged absence.'

'What position were you applying for?'

'I didn't, he called me because one of my lecturers told him I'd be good at it. It's called Creative Virtual Assistant.'

'What the hell is that?'

She rolled her eyes. 'That's what I said.'

'What if I...'

'You promised.'

'Let's make a deal. This is the first week in January, so, if Adam is not out of hospital by the end of the month and ready to interview you, you are sending your CV in. I'll bet there are a bunch of other people at Galfrey's who may need your help.'

She smiled. 'Thank you. But you promise that is all you will do?'

He nodded, as he crossed his fingers under the table. 'Which of your lecturers recommended you?'

'Julia Morris, do you know her?'

'As a matter of fact I do, she is a huge Galfrey supporter. But I would say of the work, not mine.' Considering he had dated two of her close friends and then sent them on their way, he supposed loyalty to friends played a part in her attitude.

'Why is that?'

She had an amazing openness about her, almost as if she had never been corrupted, so he wasn't about to tell her about his rather seedy past. 'Opinions, so let's just leave it at that.'

'Do you design?'

'Not fashion, but I can draw. I am more an ideas and numbers person.'

She started pushing food around on her plate. What would they do once they left here? Gazing up, she could tell he was thinking the same, but she could also see that he already had an activity in mind. She blushed as she visualised them entwined on a bed, and would swear he was seeing the same picture. The blush deepened.

This was interesting, and something he had not experienced before. They fed off each other's thoughts, because that blush had not appeared there for nothing. She could see what he was imagining. Okay, stop it right now and go do something. 'Since we are done, do you know of a place where...'

Her eyes were like green lasers. That he was awakening perplexing feelings was true, that she felt herself respond was true, that she would carry them wantonly out was not true.

He lifted a hand. 'Whoa. I'm thinking it, you are thinking it, but we hardly know each other. I like you, a lot, and from the looks of it you like me too, so for that reason, we are going to take this slow. We are not going to do stupid things, mess it all up, and then regret it. Although it is terribly exciting to start that way, I get the feeling that is not an option where we are concerned.' He was a liar, of course he wanted to start that way. The odd thing was; the other bit he had just said was also true. 'So, what do you say?' He encouraged.

'Thank you.' She said with relief. It was not hard to see he was a man of the world, who already knew all of this, perhaps too much, whereas she knew nothing. What chance would she stand against his charm and experience when her body and mind were already becoming increasingly traitorous?

From what he was witnessing, there were two possible scenarios. Either, she was putting on an act, and teasing him mercilessly, or, she was as innocent as she appeared. If she was playing at the first, she would soon trip herself up, but if she was the second... Hell, he should not fool around with that.

He studied her closely; never had he encountered anyone as adorable, and what was that incredible pull she was already exercising over him, because right now, there was not much he could do to resist it. He felt primitive, his blood at boiling point, as if he were on a hunt. Rising from the table, he offered his hand. 'I'm thinking Botanical Gardens.'

They walked up and down, left and right, sat on benches, ate ice cream, shared a bag of cashew nuts, and talked non-stop. He liked how this felt, and although noticing that self-consciousness filled her when he became personal, she answered straightforward, was amusingly smart, and witty.

It was one of those odd downpours that all Johannesburgers know so well; there is no thunder or lightning, the sky opens, pours down for about fifteen minutes and then the sun comes out, and starts drying everything again. It caught them just as they passed a gazebo so they returned there, wet, laughing.

'I forgot my umbrella in the car.' She realised.

'It wouldn't have done us much good even if it was in mine.' Noticing how the dress stuck to her chest, he leaned against a column.

'No,' she agreed. 'But now I don't have one.'

'There you go, we already have something to do tomorrow.'

'Umbrella shopping, imagine that.' She said with a grin, dug in her handbag for tissues, and gave him a handful.

There it was again. 'Dani, I know you from somewhere.'

She shrugged, took a few tissues, and started drying her face and hair. 'I admit, I also get a familiar sense around you but I don't recall.'

He flicked a few shimmering droplets from her hair then letting the hand descend, brushed the curve of her chin. Her face turned at once, wanting more. Encircling her waist with one arm, he pulled her to him. Her mouth was cold and tasted of vanilla ice cream, the combination sending his body into a spin. He could feel tremors, not only in her but also himself, as he drank her in. He had heard women say that they melted; he was doing the same, because he felt it everywhere.

She needed to press closer, to feel every caress, every heartbeat.

Moving from the column, he enfolded her with both arms. She took a sharp breath and buried her hands in his hair. He kissed her eyes, cheeks, and returned to her mouth. Heavens above, he teetered beyond a dangerous line, his body completely ablaze.

Now this was a kiss, one she was enjoying far too much, she was sure, she thought as her head travelled on some mysterious plane, and nothing like Sams' kiss. Sams had been pushy, demanding self-satisfaction. Nicholas... He gave, and took, even if she were no pro.

A shaft of sunlight hit their faces and Nicholas pushed her gently away.

'This is our cue to leave.' He dropped a kiss on her nose. 'Dani, have you ever had a boyfriend?'

She shook her head. 'I never saw the point.'

'And were you ever kissed like that before?'

She blushed, of course he could tell.

Now, how was he going to resist wanting to teach her everything she should know? However, did she need to know all of it right away? Oh but his head was in a muddle already.

'Sams did kiss me once, but it didn't feel anything like that.'

'Who is that?'

'Someone I went to school with. He says we are friends but I'm not so sure that's what he means. He kissed me and when I stopped him, he became upset, got into his mother's car and scratched a deep line down the side as he flew past our gate.' She shook her head. 'He never told her that he did it. That poor woman was lied to so many times.'

He tucked some stray hairs behind one ear and taking her hand started the walk back to the car. 'I'm guessing he's the one you wanted apologies from?'

'He did many times, but I didn't believe him.' She said cryptically. 'But I learnt years ago to never expect anything good from Sams.'

'Why is he called that?'

'Too many esses in his name. How would you like to be called Samuel Stevens Strauss?'

He nodded. 'Quite a mouthful. Do you still see him?'

'Sometimes, but not by choice. I didn't tell my parents because they like him, but I moved away because of him, not because I wanted to job hunt. I could do that just fine from home, but he's always around, which I don't like.'

'Why is that?'

'His persistence freaks me out, and I hate how he makes me feel.'

He certainly didn't like the sound of this Sams either. 'Does he know where you stay?'

'I've only been there about a week, so not yet. I do want to ask my parents to not tell him either, but how do I explain? Everyone thinks he is marvellous. He's good at everything, highly ambitious, well-to-do, an excellent rugby player, big, strong, some call him handsome. I have no clue.'

No, he didn't like Sams one bit.

'He did one nice thing though; he gave me Coco as a puppy. But I could swear there were so many strings attached that I wanted to refuse.'

'Where is this guy?'

'Still at University, but I try not to concern myself with his business.'

'Then restriction of information is imperative if you don't want him turning up on your doorstep.'

She nodded and stopped in a spot of sunlight. 'We should dry as much as possible before getting into the car.' Tilting her head back, she closed her eyes, opened her arms, and offered herself to the sun.

He smiled, loving her spontaneity. 'How about dinner and a movie?' He certainly didn't want the day to end.

She glanced at her dress. 'Has to be something casual.'

'Even a hot dog will do.'

The corners of her mouth crinkled. 'Okay,' she said and put her arm through his. 'Lead the way.'

After some deliberations, Cresta won the toss. Mainly because it was close-by and Dani seemed to use common sense. They compromised; he chose the movie, she the restaurant.

The movie... what did they watch? He had no idea if she remembered something, because he didn't. He was excruciatingly aware of her presence and every movement she made was an experience. She grabbed his arm, rested her face against his chest, and once, grabbed his thigh when something exploded on the screen, but mostly, she let him hold her hand or put his arm around her shoulders.

It was ten o'clock when they walked out into the parking lot and pressing her against the car, he kissed her, his hands adoring the feel of her face, ears, and hair. Oh, he pretty much was a goner. Of course, now he needed the experience of waking up beside her. 'Where are we going?' It was only fair he offered an option.

Clearly, this was his, *your place or mine* question. Did he believe everything was free, that there was no reckoning about anything? 'I'd like to go home.'

'How do we get there?'

She gave directions as she searched for her phone, and seeing the missed calls, dialled the number immediately. 'Hello daddy,'

'Sweetheart, what is this I hear about your car? And where were you? I was worried.'

She smiled. 'The car is sorted, and we were at the movies.'

'How will you get around? For goodness sake, I run a car rental company; I'll send you one tomorrow.'

Heat seared through the dress as Nicholas' hand rested on her leg. 'Hold on, daddy.' She muted the phone. 'What is it?'

'Please say no and let me take you around.'

'Are you sure?'

'Yes,' Nicholas nodded.

'I don't need a car, daddy. And I'll keep you informed about mine as soon as I hear from the garage.'

'Do you know who's responsible?'

'Not a clue.'

'Who's with you?'

'Nicholas.'

'Are you sur—'

'Yes daddy, I don't need any help.'

'I hate thinking about all the things that can go wrong because no matter your age, you are our baby and we want to protect you. But we also love you and have to let you go discover all the scary things on your own.'

Her voice became softer. 'I know, daddy, and I love you both for it, and I promise that I'm not in trouble or danger. It was just a mishap and I'd like to sort it out my way.'

'But you will call the minute you need something.'

'Yes daddy. Goodnight.'

Undoubtedly, she was attached to her parents, and having this happen mere days after moving into a new place was making her emotional. Reaching out, he wiped the single tear sliding down her cheek. Was it possible to fall in love in a day? He had always thought the concept of love at first sight a little suspect. But taking today into consideration, he hadn't suspected enough.

He glanced at the block of flats as they got out of the car. It was a nice looking place, but he had imagined something different. Taking her new portfolio bag and pages under one arm, he followed where she led.

When Dani put the key in the safety gate, there was a flurry of activity inside.

'Coco,' she grabbed the squirming animal. 'Meet Nicholas. Drop those on the table.'

He did and looked around curiously.

'Please sit.' She invited. 'Do you mind dog fur on everything?'

He smiled. 'I'll be fine.'

The instant Dani dropped Coco on the floor, she was against Nicholas' leg. He patted her, scratched her ears, and offered a finger for her to bite.

Dani went into the kitchen and put the kettle on. When she returned, she made a sweeping gesture at the room. 'What do you think?'

'Pleasing,' he noted. 'But it doesn't feel like you.'

It took her a second to understand. 'Oh, yes, well, that is an interesting observation. As it happens, it's Anya's, my best friend; I'm just babysitting it until she returns from London. She didn't want to let it go, put everything into storage, and then start all over again when she gets back in about a year. I offered to look after it, so all I have to do is pay the rent.'

'Is your friend also a fashion designer?'

'Oh yes, an amazing one actually, she got an internship with Gurggle.'

He nodded. 'Impressive, those are people with high expectations. But you are a bunch of talented people.'

'Are there others from my fashion school at Galfrey's?'

'Quite a few.'

'I want to make you coffee, tea, whatever, but I want you to come make the first one.'

He followed her to the small kitchen.

She took a couple of coffees, teas, and chocolate from a cupboard and placed them on the counter. 'If I don't have your brand, tell me which, or buy one and then I'll know how to replace it.'

He didn't know anyone like her. Taking one of the coffees, he made his own as she watched attentively. 'That's it, no bells, frills, or whistles.'

'Do you want something to eat, a sandwich, biscuits,' she glanced at the time. 'But it's late, maybe you shouldn't.'

'Would you mind me looking at your work?' He asked eagerly.

'I'm a designer, of course I want people to look at it.'

With mug in hand, he flipped through the loose pages. 'What was that atrocious job's title again?'

'Creative Virtual Assistant,'

'You may be qualified for whatever that is, but you are this first.' He pointed, meaning it sincerely. 'When did you do these?'

'Some are from my college days, but this,' she went to a page. 'Is from last week,'

'They are gorgeous, as are you.' Placing the mug on the table, he pulled her into his arms. This was the moment for his song and dance of seduction. The moment no woman had ever resisted. *Problem, this is no woman.* He thought. *What is the matter with you? You don't fool around with this, unless...* Had the M-word actually entered his mind? Thankfully, that always sobered him up. He let go of her mouth immediately but still kept her in his arms. 'What time do you get up?'

She just stared back at him.

He smiled. 'So I know when to call you.'

'Seven.'

'You do know that I don't want to leave.'

Her eyes deepened their green. 'I don't want you to go either.' She realised how dangerous the statement was. How did she back out of it now? 'Huh…'

She has no clue what she is doing, and hell, she needs protecting from me! 'No, Dani, you want me to go.' Without another word, he was out the door.

Leaning against the closed door, she exhaled deeply. How was it possible to feel this strongly about a man after only one day?

CHAPTER THREE

Nicholas awoke at six. No, he got out of bed at six, because he had barely slept. He lay sprawled on his bed, eyes fixed on the ceiling, then stretching his left arm out, he felt the empty space. He turned to look at the pillow.

Through the years, some interesting faces had reclined there, but this morning, there was only one on his mind. He thought back to how he had felt about those women. What had attracted him, how the relationships began, how they ended here, how long they lasted, and how they parted ways.

Nowhere, anywhere, ever, had these feelings been present. Sure, he had liked them, as all were fantastic people, and some he still ran into occasionally, but this... He closed his eyes, 'Dani,' his body responded. 'Liza, Maggie, Cynthia, Shelley,' and for good measure he added. 'Laura.' Who was gone only two months, but nothing stirred. 'Dani,' there it was again. He gave up on wasting time and went to the shower.

Dani groaned as the alarm went off. She had climbed into bed late, and taken forever to fall asleep. She had tossed and turned, trying to figure out if everything had been an accident, coincidence, a dream, or meant to be. How could anyone guess?

Embarrassment engulfed her. Was it proper to let go as she had, was it real, or had she simply been overwhelmed by unknown sensations? She touched her mouth, closed her eyes, and recalled how he made her feel. It was something that began in her core and awakened a delirious hunger. She wanted a repeat so badly, tremors ran through her body. She scrambled out of bed and ran to the bathroom, suspicious that he would be true to his word. Ten minutes later, the phone rang.

'Good morning, Dani,'

Something jumped in her breast. 'Good morning, Nicholas,'

He bit his bottom lip at the other end. She sounded so darn sexy. 'Are you still in bed?' Why was he asking, so he could suffer more?

'No, I'm up.' She told him but threw herself back onto the pillow.

'Did you think about me?'

Was it decent to admit that he was stuck in her head? 'Yes.' She told him shyly.

'As I did of you. Dani, I have to go to work, but I will come by after twelve. We'll get lunch and then it's umbrella hunting time, or do you need to do something else before?'

'No, that's fine.'

'Have a nice morning then.'

'Thank you.' She lay there a moment longer then went to the desk in the corner and opened her laptop.

She checked messages, posted pictures, and wrote about the previous day's mishap. Now, she was sorry she had forgotten to take pictures of the disaster. She chatted to a cousin in Australia, another in Canada and then closed the laptop. Going to the sitting room, she grabbed the drawing pad.

Her phone rang again and in a haze of creativity, she answered. 'Hello.'

'Hi Dani,'

She hesitated a few seconds. 'Hello, Sams.'

'I thought about you yesterday. But I was in an exam, so I couldn't talk then. How are you?'

'Fine, and you?'

'I've been swamped. Why didn't you tell me you left home?'

She stared at a point straight ahead. What did she say, ask, discuss? There was in fact something to talk about, but he dodged the subject every time she brought it up.

'It's actually great that you're closer now, I'd love to show you around town. Take you to all the hotspots.'

But these mindless activities he never forgot. Besides, she knew the place fairly well herself, she had spent four years driving up and down all these roads and streets. 'I'm job hunting and haven't got much time.'

'Surely not at night.'

And if going out solved the problem, she would have done so many moons ago. There was only one thing she wanted from him, but he was still obstinately refusing resolution after five years.

'Where do you stay, I'll come visit.'

She had to warn her parents to not divulge her whereabouts. And as Nicholas had mentioned, she did not want to find him on her doorstep. 'I have to go, but I'll let you know.'

'Make it soon; we have a lot to catch up.' He disconnected and stared at the phone. She might not know it, but he knew her well, and he knew that she was lying.

It all came back to the previous day, he simply wasted the chance he was given. If he had surrendered to the gut feeling, all he would have lost would have been the fee he paid for the exam, as he could have written it later in the year again. Instead, he carelessly postponed making that call. He remembered again in the afternoon, but then, he had been at rugby practice. Had Sams had an inkling, he would have realised that the second call was even more important to make, for it would have prevented further far-reaching consequences, for right then, Nicholas had taken Dani in his arms and imprinted his very essence onto her.

Here was the story of her life, a constant running and hiding from Sams. Annoyingly, he had always believed himself in love with her, but she had a dissimilar understanding of the relationship. She saw him as... perhaps a distant cousin, sometimes friend, or acquaintance, but never more.

The differing opinions had led to tense situations throughout high school, becoming worse during their final year, as his pursuit intensified, and eventually resulted in a blazing row, which took place days after she made the mistake of going to their graduation dance with him.

She hated it, knowing that her feelings would never change, he pressed on, willing that they did, and through the tug-of-war, she learnt that Sams was not as accommodating as others imagined. Because that day still rattled her, or rather, Sams had rattled her. She never told anyone about that fight, not even Anya, and wished to obliterate it from her own memory as well.

Dani looked up from the drawing pad and sighed, thankful Anya had given her the opportunity to be here, away from home, where Sams never said excuse me pardon me, and just pitched up at the front door whenever he pleased.

She had met Anya when both attended open day at Fashion School, connected immediately, and then discovered that they lived within five kilometres of each other. When their tertiary education began, they were already firm friends.

Providence placed them in the same class, so they shared the drive to college. Luck kept them together during the second year, but by the third, they were following different courses. Anya decided that a place closer to college was best and invited Dani to share. Dani considered it, discussed it with her parents, and elected against it. Yet, she spent many a day, and night, in this very flat, as both sat on the floor working on projects and patterns for their end of year shows.

After graduating, both did honours but even before Anya was qualified, a local label had already snapped her up. Dani got a call from a department store looking for fresh eyes; she declined, uncertain how to proceed into the future. And it was then her mother had the great sense to suggest she take a year off to travel as they had family on all continents. Dani grabbed the chance. Perhaps in the meantime Sams would find a girlfriend, a fiancée, no, better, a wife.

Her itinerary had been fifty days per country, as there were six to visit. She began in New Zealand, then Australia, following to the US, onto Canada, then UK, and finally France. She had visited distant and close uncles, aunts, and cousins, with whom she had forged wonderful friendships. Now, there was Skype, Facebook, twitter, and endless other communication channels.

As soon as she returned she realised Sams had not given up on his dream. Often, she felt more like a possession than a true love ideal, more like a goal he had decided on and couldn't care less if she wanted to participate or not. So every day, insomnia threatened to move in, and she racked her brain trying to figure out what to do next, to find an escape, short of moving away to another country. Then, Anya called.

Of course, that November day, as they celebrated Gurggle's offer, Dani did not disclose her personal reasons for volunteering to babysit a flat, or explain that she was looking for a way out of Bedfordview because of the misguided male. Her relationship with Sams was complicated and messy and she hated discussing it with anyone she cared about. And providentially, the block of flats allowed pets, so it was perfect, as she had missed Coco. And the rent was cheap in comparison to the price tag on the apartment she was eyeing in Rosebank. First, she needed to get this job so she could then afford that.

Her parents, David and Carol, had been nervous about the move, mentioning all the things that could happen to a young woman on her own in the city, but both had also always been supportive, encouraging flights, unsure steps, and new ventures. Besides, they told each other pragmatically, Dani was taking only her clothes, and Anya would not be gone forever.

The intercom buzzed and Nicholas heard his secretary's voice, 'Mr. Galfrey, Mr. Ridley's personal assistant is here.'

'Send her in.' He had asked to see her because he wanted clarification on what Adam was doing in his department. And Margot would definitely know, because Adam did nothing without her.

The attractive thirty-something woman entered his office and he felt her anxiety immediately. He motioned for her to take a seat. 'Margot, do you know why you're here?'

Margot Becker took something resembling a deep breath, but Nicholas doubted it would support the lungs of a canary. He understood her mood, she was not afraid of what he might say, she was upset that she had made a mistake.

'Simone told me. I am sorry, sir.'

'What is with you IT people and this sir thing? It's as if the entire department thinks I'm out to get them. Adam is the same, actually annoys me with all this formality, and he older than me. And we two,' he pointed to both of them. 'We have known each other a few years.'

Margot nodded. That they did, but never been close friends. For the simple reason that he was a womaniser, often created rumours, and possibly scandals, and she was happily married. She liked and respected him and therefore chose not to cause either any grief.

'So, back to why you are here.'

'Please don't be angry with Simone, she's new. I should have double-checked myself, and I take full responsibility. I apologise, Nicholas.'

'Cut the crap, Margot, you know you had nothing to do with that mistake. And I will bet anything that in the two years you have been here, you never had a name slip anywhere.'

'I take a lot of pride in what I do.'

'Good, because I know you are meticulous. And now, a favour. I know it's not part of your job description in any way, but I would appreciate it if you helped Simone become more focused, she's a little...' He made a hand gesture. 'Airy.'

That was certainly true. 'So you won't fire her?'

'Goodness no, everyone needs to make mistakes to learn something.'

Her sigh of relief was audible.

'Tell me, how long has this career opportunity of Creative Virtual Assistant been available at Galfrey's?' He asked with an amused look.

Margot looked surprised. 'That is what Miss Creswell is being interviewed for.'

'And that is exactly why I want to know what a Creative Virtual Assistant does.'

'They help brand and build online business.'

'Is there any type of design involved in this?'

'If they can create eye-catching websites, social media campaigns, consumer-targeted internet, and cutting-edge programming, it is design. They promote, manage, and maintain client marketing, they do customer surveys...' she stopped.

'Isn't that what you people in IT do already anyway?'

'Yes, but Adam is restructuring, creating, and redefining posts. We are also swamped, and all our ages are leaning towards or above the thirties, so we need a young expert to bring the new trends in.'

Nicholas' brows raised. 'An expert, you say? Then explain to me why he would hire a fashion designer for something like that?'

A smile crawled across Margo's lips. 'If the person is excellent at social networking, such as Facebook, Twitter, Pinterest, Instagram, Tumblr, etc., then that would be of interest to us. Adam has been led to believe that she is the best and ostensibly, quite a programming problem-solver as well.'

'Really,' he was exceedingly curious now, and sure wanted to know more, but he preferred to get the rest of the information from the horse's mouth.

Margot nodded. 'Apparently she is a whizz.'

'Well, isn't the world full of surprises. Have you seen this girl?'

Margot shook her head. 'No, and neither has Adam, he just wants her skills. Have you?'

Nicholas felt a shiver run down his spine as he saw Dani in his mind's eye. 'Yes, and she is the most ungeeky, unnerdy girl I've ever seen.'

'Thanks,' Margot said with affront.

He laughed as he looked at her. Margot was a beautiful woman by anyone's standards, so what he had just said was rather redundant. 'Sorry, but you know what I mean. Okay, then this is settled.' He had meant to be angry with someone but found he couldn't be. Because by making one simple mistake, Simone had inveigled for Dani to enter his life, something he was finding near hypnotic. 'Thanks Margot, that is all then. Now, let's hope Simone doesn't skip pages again.'

He knocked lightly, Coco answered, barking and jumping, and the door opened almost at once. Walking in, he pulled Dani into his arms.

'Nicholas,' her hands went into his hair.

Reluctantly, he let her go, and bent down to pat the little dog. 'Ready?'

'Yes, let me just take Coco to Mrs. Brown.'

Noticing the discarded drawing pad, he was curious to see what she had been working on, as her designs impressed him. The first two pages were wonderful, but the third... He glanced at the door quickly. Had Dani drawn it? All he could see was a pair of angry male eyes. He walked away and leaned against the wall closest to the door.

As soon as they sat down to lunch, he knew she was miserable. She was a happy girl, so he wanted to make it right immediately. Reaching across the table, he took one of her hands. 'Please tell me what's wrong.'

She looked up. 'Do you think that we invent problems?'

'You mean people,'

She nodded.

'I know some obsess, others are paranoid, but most follow instinct; which means, there are reasons for how we feel. So, what is upsetting you?' He encouraged.

'Sams called.'

'You really don't like this guy, do you?'

She shook her head.

'What did he want?'

She told him.

'It seems I don't like him either. And next time he calls,' his gaze intensified. 'Tell him he's wasting his time, because you are already in a relationship.'

Her eyes opened wide. 'I am?'

'Dani, what do we call this?' He opened his hands. 'Sure, we don't know much about each other or where it's going, but it is one.'

She felt shy and awkward but also happy.

'There you go,' he smiled as he noticed the mood change. 'And since neither of us seems to be hungry, let the hunt for umbrellas begin.'

They chose Sandton City to start their quest. As Nicholas pointed out, if they couldn't find an umbrella there then what was wrong with Johannesburg?

She caught him glancing at The Garden Court Hotel, made a tsk-tsk sound, and shook her head. He shrugged apologetically, dropped a kiss on her nose, and taking her hand, they began their search.

They bought three umbrellas, and all were unsuitable for rainy days. The first was a pert lacy thing with a frivolous frill. Nicholas took a liking to it and said something about going to the Botanical Gardens for she did not know what in the gazebo. Her face filled with heat as she recalled their first kiss. He nodded knowingly and winked.

Number two, was a disgusting puce pink, which Nicholas picked again. Why, she asked. Bending his head, he whispered something about a photo shoot where she should wear nothing but the umbrella, to just cover the strategic bits. She stared at him, feeling the blush run across her forehead. He giggled that time.

She chose number three. Why? She did not know either. It was a horrid white thing, with round plastic windows. Where did anyone look stylish with a thing like that, the middle of a freshly ploughed field? Alternatively, when used upside down it could pass for a fish bowl.

Nicholas was speechless, unable to think of any uses for it. He did however comment, 'for people in the fashion industry we sure know how to buy crap.'

The rest of the afternoon was spent between coffee shops and boutiques. Nicholas loved watching Dani as she studied the designs, felt the fabrics, and contemplated the garments' construction.

'Have you heard about your car?' He asked as they walked out of a store.

'They didn't say when they would call, so I'll give them a few days.'

Nicholas checked the time.

'Do you need to be somewhere?'

'No,' it was a lie, but he was not about to admit that he wanted to see Adam Ridley, because she would probably get upset. He wondered how they would fight, and how they would make up. Who would apologise first, and would she cry? Everything about her excited him.

'I have to get that.' She stopped in front of a florist's window.

Nicholas looked at the *that* she referred to. It was a pretty flowerpot with tulips.

She searched for a card and matching ribbons, and when satisfied, went to the counter with her purchases. 'You won't mind, will you?' She asked as they walked out. 'To take it to Simone, I owe her an apology for being rude.'

'You bought that, for someone you don't know?' He was mystified, she acted out of a place he did not understand.

'Well, I'm hoping to know her. Is she Miss or Mrs, and do you know her surname?'

No, he did not know anyone like her. Stopping, he placed a hand on her cheek. Her face moved closer. He adored how she did that, the gesture telling him that she loved being touched, especially by him. He forgot he was in the middle of a shopping centre and covering her mouth with his, kissed her.

At the flat, he sat on the sofa teasing Coco, while Dani was in the kitchen making sandwiches. They had decided not to eat out again as both were tired. He glanced at his watch, too late for hospital visits now.

Dani threw him a smile, and set the small dining table quickly. 'The bathroom is through there.' She pointed.

Walking past her, he pressed his body against hers, and pecked her lips.

He glanced around, curious about the products she used and how she kept everything. It was neat, clean, and the pleasant scent of jasmine permeated the air. As he walked past the bedroom again, he noticed the laptop on the corner desk, a sewing machine on the floor, and three beautifully crafted chocolate coloured dresses hanging in front of a closet. Finally, he glanced at the bed, imagining her lying in it; it wrenched his gut with desire.

They sat at the small table, as if they had been doing it for years, chatting about small things, nodding, and laughing.

'Pretty dresses,' He pointed towards the bedroom.

'Thank you. Two of my friends are getting married on Saturday and I'm one of the maids-of-honour. And naturally,' she smiled. 'I made them.'

'Oh,' he made a disappointed gesture. 'Is there any time in the weekend for me?'

'Sorry,' she scrunched her nose and lip. 'The wedding is in Pretoria, so I'm going on Friday, as there is always so much happening.'

'Can I take you, or was there another plan?'

'I need you to take me as I was supposed to drive myself. Without the car, my parents would have brought me back on Sunday, but you can come pick me up again if you want.'

'I'll be there. Just say the time.'

She gave him a gorgeous smile. 'Thank you.'

'So, what's tomorrow's itinerary?' He asked eagerly.

'I have to do some shopping. What time will you be done at work?'

'I have told them that I am leaving at twelve for a while.'

'No one can get upset with you?' A concerned furrow crossed her brow.

'No, they can't fire me.' He smiled, then asked. 'Dani, when is your birthday?'

'Is it my birth date you want to know or my age?'

'Both.'

'I'll be twenty-three next month.'

'An almost Valentine's Day baby?'

She shook her head. 'Missed it by quite a bit. And you?'

'I just had a birthday, turned thirty on the thirty-first of December.'

'Oh, not a New Year's day baby?' She teased.

'Am I too old for you?' He asked seriously.

She gazed at him for a second, then rising from the chair, went to him, and bending over his face, kissed him.

Her inexperienced mouth caused odd sensations, as if his heart were about to burst, along with every other body part. Automatically, he pulled her onto his lap and returned the kiss. But this would never do, he hungered for so much more; everything. Slipping a hand inside the blouse, he felt her breasts in the lace; firm, perfect, then, began a trail of kisses down her neck. She tilted back, instinctively knowing to push herself closer. He rose, picked her up into his arms, and took three steps.

Her eyes snapped open. 'Nicholas,'

In those green beauties, he saw two things, a call filled with desire, and the cry for mercy. It was up to him, which he heeded. Then he knew, knew that she was inching her way into his heart and that he could never hurt her. 'Dani,' he gulped and hugged her to his chest. 'On our second date, are we both insane?'

'Thank you,' she whispered against his face.

'Right,' he said in a good mood and put her down. 'Let's clear the table.'

'Mr. Galfrey,' Adam Ridley was taken aback when Nicholas entered the hospital room.

'Adam, are you ever going to call me Nicholas?'

'You are my boss, and it is habit. What are you doing here?'

'Checking up on you. So, what did you do to yourself?' Nicholas saw the neck brace, one leg in traction, and an arm dangling from a rope as if belonging to a marionette.

'I diced with two taxis.' Adam grinned. 'I'm kidding, it wasn't their fault either. Some guy on a motorbike decided that red robots were not for him. I'm just glad no one else got hurt.'

Nicholas nodded. 'Do you know when you will be discharged?'

'The neck and leg are getting on; it's the arm the doctor is concerned about. Is there chaos at the office?'

'Not from what I saw.' Nicholas walked to the window and leaned against it. 'Do you have everything you need, is your hospital plan adequate, medical aid doing what they are supposed to?'

'I think so and my wife has not said anything about problems. Do you know something?'

'No, I just wanted to make certain you're being looked after.'

'Thanks, I appreciate it.' Adam studied the other man for a moment. 'Nicholas, why do I get the feeling you are here for more than to just check on me?'

'Well, you're right, so here goes. When did we start employing Creative Virtual Assistants?'

The question surprised Adam. 'That's what you want to know?'

'Not exactly, but what is it?'

'There are two parts to that job. The one is very IT related and the other is into the social networks.'

Nicholas made a gesture. 'Okay, but what I really want to know is why Miss Creswell was chosen.'

Adam did some mental configurations. 'Ah, Julia's girl. She ran the school's Facebook page, Bebo, Twitter, blogs, plus a bunch of other things. I've seen her work, astounding.'

'But you do know that she's a fashion designer.'

'Oh yes, I understood that quite clearly. And Julia stressed rather strongly too that as good as she is at it, she will be wasted behind a computer.'

'I wonder where she learnt all that. That's years of practice and experience, right?'

'Definitely, and she seems to have plenty. And no, I don't know where she learnt it, as they certainly don't teach it at Fashion School. My aim is to get her to train others, and then I will send her to Asher's department.' Adam furrowed his brow. 'Has something happened to her?'

'Nothing physically, thank goodness, but there was a mix-up concerning her interview.' Nicholas decided to stick as closely as he could to Dani's wishes.

Adam did not like the sound of that. 'How do you mean?'

'Her original interview was on Monday. But with you here, it was supposed to be cancelled, it wasn't.'

'But…' Adam looked concerned. 'Margot never makes mistakes like that.'

'Adam, please relax. I'm not here to tell you Margot made a mistake, which she didn't.'

'I'm still confused.'

'Okay, this is what I really want to know. Did you need the interview or had you already made up your mind and she was going to be hired?'

'Nicholas, are you trying to tell me not to employ her?'

'No.' Nicholas said quickly. 'I want to know what your decision was before I walked in here.'

'The interview is a formality for paperwork. I was going to take her.'

'Good, that's all I needed to know. Should we wait for you to get out before she starts, or will you call her in?'

'I can.' Adam shrugged.

'Would she know what to do straight away?'

'Probably, she's exceptional. I think her lecturers were traumatised when she left college. She did a whole lot while she was there, they love her dearly.' Adam studied Nicholas. 'I also recall Julia saying something else.'

Nicholas saw mischief on the older man's face. 'And what was that?'

'It's actually quite funny, because in jest, I think she hit it right on the head.' A grin spread on Adam's face. 'Her precise words, *there she goes to the lion's den, but before he roars, she'll have his heart.* She does, doesn't she?'

'Julia said that?' Nicholas was near speechless.

Adam nodded seriously. 'Apart from her skills, she is apparently quite a gem, but you know that already, don't you? So, there is something you want me to do.'

Nicholas smiled. 'Oh no, you already did. I have my answer, and I promised. How did she put it? Not to interfere, meddle, give a glowing report, or otherwise. Therefore, you will do whatever you wish on your own, but she is not to start work until this date.' Nicholas scribbled on the back of a business card and placed it in Adam's hand. 'That is the one thing I am telling you, leave her free until then.'

'Why, wasn't she free already?' Adam asked sarcastically as he waved his dangling hand. 'I just want to get out of here.'

'Just hang on.'

Adam made a face. 'Wow, original and funny.'

'Jokes aside, I do hope you recover quickly, we need you.'

Adam's grimace turned into a disbelieving look. 'It seems all you need is Miss Creswell. How do you know each other?'

'Would you believe I only know her since Monday? We met because of the interview mix-up.'

'You're kidding.'

'Oh no, quite true, and it's mind-blowing.'

'I can see that. And now, I'll tell you another thing Julia said. She asked me, no, ordered me to look after her. Told me, rather sternly too that if anything happens to her little darling, she will personally wring my neck. So please, tread softly with this girl.'

Nicholas grinned. 'Well, that is exactly what I intend to do.' He waved and left.

It was an excruciatingly hot day and Dani wore denim shorts and a pretty top that exposed one shoulder. Nicholas could not resist placing a kiss there every time she stopped beside him. She was on the short side but he had guessed that she had good legs. It was more than that, her proportions were so perfect that a knot had found a permanent home under his Adam's apple.

He never imagined that shopping for groceries could be so enlightening. She leaned against his chest often, and read the ingredients on the bottles, boxes, and packets. She never took anything with preservatives, colours, or sweeteners, telling him that the point of eating was to preserve life, not destroy it with poisons. That she refused to consume rubbish because it looked attractive, and that she would rather eat a bag of brown sugar—although she barely touched it—than put unpronounceable sweeteners in her mouth. She even read the ingredients on the dog food and treats.

He peered at the sky as they left the parking lot. 'What would you like to do tonight?'

She turned to him. 'I've chosen twice, so tonight is your turn, whatever you want.'

'Really,' a brow lifted inquisitively.

'Yes,'

Right off the bat, he knew what he wanted, and if he looked at her, she would know it too, but that was not a consideration. He did not know how they had come to that decision because neither had said the words, but it was like a billboard in his mind, so he had to think of something else to occupy them. 'Do you like dancing?'

'I'm not very good at the all-over-the-place kind.'

He grinned. 'You mean rave, club, disco.'

'That phase apparently flew over my head.'

'I didn't mean that kind anyway. I'm taking you to ELLA's. It's a forties lounge and they play old and romantic. It's also very sumptuous and relaxing.'

She made a face of disappointment. 'I'd love to but I'm not dressed for it.'

'Fear not, we are on our way home.' He liked the sound of that, but wished they were going towards his place, not this one, which wasn't even hers.

They decided that he didn't have to change, so he sat on the sofa playing with Coco while she got ready. He was curious to see how long it would take her to get through the entire female ritual. But when she stood before him within half an hour, he thought he would never be able to get up as he gaped at her.

She smiled and did a little half-turn. 'Do you like?' She loved the way he looked at her, how he made her feel, as if she were the only woman in the world. Sure, she could also see the desire to pounce, but he had more scruples than even he was aware of.

'Dani,' was all he managed as he got to his feet and encircled her with his arms, his hands running up her bare back. Her scent enfolded him as he leaned in to kiss her and she did not complain about make-up. He loved her mouth; it was always soft, luscious, and inviting. She merely looked up with those green eyes and offered herself to him. He let her go, because if he didn't...

They dined in a red velvet-covered booth and he liked the contrast she made with the grey satin dress. Her hair was up, but in an informal way, with a pretty diamante flower peeking through where she had tied it together. She was wearing real diamond earring, and he wondered if she had bought them herself or if a man had given them to her. What kind of man; those did not look cheap. She had travelled; he still didn't know anything about that, so she could have met someone other than Sams… Jealousy raged.

He touched the earrings carefully. 'These are beautiful.' Which meant that whoever gave them, not only had taste and money, but also knew her well.

She smiled sweetly. 'Daddy's gift when I turned twenty-one.'

What a relief, he did not want other men giving her gifts like that. Three days he knew her and he could no longer imagine anyone else near her. 'I know you travelled a bit,' he might as well find out now. 'Where did you go?'

They laughed merrily as she told him about silly emus, demented kangaroos, rodeos, an insane episode with a Canadian Mountie, that she had worn beanies in England because the weather refused to cooperate with her hair, and that she had been unable to force herself to taste frogs' legs and snails in France, although it had been her favourite place. 'It was fun, but it's also true, there is no place like home. And I wouldn't have gone if it wasn't for Sams.'

'How do you mean?'

'He was pressing me again, so when mom made the suggestion I thought, goodbye Sams, and hoped that he would find a woman while I was gone. Sadly, it didn't happen.'

'It no longer matters now.' He turned to her, a hand going to her chin. 'We found each other.'

She smiled and leaned towards him.

He kissed her, tasting her deeply, then pulled her from the seat and led her to the dance floor, so he could wrap his arms around her and feel the whole of her pressed against him.

CHAPTER FOUR

'Aunty Carol,' Sams called as he stopped his car in the large driveway in front of the gate.

'Hello Sams.' Carol greeted and pressed the remote. 'I haven't seen you around for a while.'

He drove in, got out quickly, and kissed her cheek.

'How is your mother? I haven't seen her either.' Carol continued.

'She is well, but travelling a bit. She is doing a house in Pretoria.' His mother was an interior designer. 'And I have also been busy. Did you hear I got a job at Harris International?'

'Oh yes?' She looked impressed. 'So, you are finally going to practice making lots of money.'

'I don't only intend to practice; I want to be very rich.'

'You do know that money isn't everything.'

'Why do people who have money always say that?' He looked at the eyes that were so much like Dani's.

'Because it's true. And Sams, it's not as if you have ever been poor either.'

'No I haven't.' He admitted. 'But regardless that I will inherit a lot of money when I turn twenty-five, I want to build something amazing by myself.'

'And you can do that without being obsessed. All money does is give you options, not bring you happiness. Do you want something to drink?' Carol offered. 'It has been so hot lately.'

'That would be nice.' He followed her to the kitchen, the two Labradors traipsing behind and going to lie down near the back door. 'Gosh,' he said as he leaned towards a notice board and pointed at an old photograph.

A bunch of Grade Eights made faces at the camera. Peter was Superman, Leslie a ballerina, Ashley a cavewoman, Justin a policeman, Mark a racing car driver, Sams pretended he was the strongest man in the world, and Dani was crossing her eyes as she held a pair of scissors. All fourteen, except for Dani who had always been the youngest in the group, she was thirteen.

Carol didn't have to ask what he wanted to drink, she took a coke from the fridge and placed it in front of him. 'Justin and Ashley got married last Saturday.' She smiled. 'Some people just make things work. Dani designed and made the maids-of-honour dresses.'

He nodded. 'She will go far in fashion.'

'So, how is the working and studying at the same time working out for you?'

'It is a bit of a seesaw but I'm okay. Besides, it's actually part of the programme and I don't work every day.'

'Have you heard from your father lately?'

'Last month. I think he said he was in Frankfurt.'

An indiscernible look appeared on Carol's face. After ten years, she was still unable to reconcile what had happened to his parents, still regarding it as a freak occurrence. It had been the messiest divorce, both tearing at the child as if he were a bone between ravenous dogs, yet, both such wonderful people, who loved their son endlessly. And that was when Dani took matters into her own hands concerning the lonely boy and started bringing him home.

'I am also being considered for a national rugby team.'

Carol smiled. 'Congratulations, that was always your dream. Which one, or are you not at liberty to say just yet?'

He shook his head, grabbed a jar, and took a few biscuits out.

Sams had never been shy in this house. She poured herself an orange juice. 'Are you still at Res?'

He shook his head. 'I've had my own place for a while already.'

'Did your mother help you with it?'

'You mean decorating? No, I told her to let me try. I don't think she likes it, but I do.'

Carol studied him. He was a good-looking young man and seemed friendly enough, but she had often speculated as to why Dani had never welcomed his advances, because goodness, she knew he had tried, wanted, dreamt about dating her, and as far as she would guess, he was still trying. The fact that Dani never had, made her wonder, because Dani was an excellent judge of character.

She knew something had changed in the relationship around their final year of school, but the culmination had definitely been days after their Graduation dance. That had been a bust, sending up a huge red flag. Something had happened, making Dani apprehensive and very angry, and although she had always been close to her and David, she had chosen not to tell them about an incident that obviously distressed her a great deal.

Then she noticed how Dani started distancing herself from him, yet still spoke to him if only to keep some form of peace. But whatever Dani's standpoint, he still looked very much interested, so today, Carol knew he was not here to visit, but because he wanted something. Perhaps she should start a countdown.

'How is Dani?'

Carol almost laughed. 'She's okay.'

'Is she working yet?'

'There is a place interested in her, but something happened to the man who wants to see her. He's in hospital, so she has to wait.'

'Has she been home since she moved?'

'She hasn't been gone that long and last Saturday,' she turned and pointed to the picture on the wall. 'Was the wedding, so we were in Pretoria. I'm guessing you didn't keep in touch.'

'Not with them, or Leslie. The only two I see on a semi-regular basis is Peter and Mark, and only because they still live around here. Will she be coming this weekend?'

'No, she and I are going to visit my mother so I have to pick her up, as her car is in for repairs.'

'Why? She has a brand new car.' Deep wrinkles crossed his forehead.

'The front bumper fell off. The thing ended up all twisted under the carriage, did some damage to the bottom, and destroyed a tyre.'

'When was this?'

'Last Monday,'

'Did she get hurt?'

'No, she's fine.' Carol flicked a recipe book open.

'Did Mr. Creswell have to go to the city to sort it out or was the car brought here?'

'No, she did it all herself. Well, Nicholas helped her.'

'Nicholas?' The hairs at the back of Sams' neck stood up.

'A friend of hers, very polite, gorgeous voice,' Carol thought back to the phone call and how he had quickly dispelled her fears, 'I haven't met him yet, but he sounded decent.'

Well, he didn't think so. Now, who the hell was Nicholas, where in the blazes had Dani met him, and when? He had been right about her lying; she had mentioned nothing on Tuesday when he called her.

They heard a noise, the dogs got up and ran, a door opened, footsteps, and David entered the kitchen.

David kissed Carol then shook Sams' hand. 'Hello Sams, how is it going in the big city?'

'Okay I guess.' Sams was irritated. 'I was just hearing about Dani's accident.'

David smiled. 'Yes, all grown up, wanted no help from me. Not even a car.'

'Then how is she getting around, with the bus?' Sams said it as if the idea belonged in the dustbin.

'Maybe Nicholas lent her his car; he said she could borrow it.' Carol pulled a pot from a hook.

Sams was not getting a good feeling about Nicholas, and he wanted to know who this interloper was. 'I got a job with Harris International.' He announced the second time that afternoon, if only to get his thoughts together, because none of this was sounding good.

David patted his shoulder. 'Well done.' Then went to the fridge and grabbed a coke. 'I'm guessing they have you on your toes.'

'Quite,' He needed to stay here as long as it took to unravel this mystery.

'Sams, would you like to stay for dinner?' Carol asked as she opened a drawer.

'I don't want to imp—'

'What nonsense.' David laughed and then turned to Carol. 'Do you need help, honey?'

'No, I'm fine; you boys go do whatever.' She went into the pantry.

Coming out to an empty kitchen, she placed a rice container on the counter. As her hand rested there, the phone vibrated, announcing it was about to ring. She picked it up immediately and answered, 'Carol.'

'Hi mom,' Dani greeted.

'Hi,' Carol walked around the kitchen, gathering her things together. 'Have you heard about the car?'

'I did. They had to order something for the undercarriage so it will be ready in two weeks.'

'What can you do? Have you been stuck in the flat all this time?'

'No, Nicholas takes me out every afternoon for whatever I need.'

'Very considerate, but he sounded nice when I spoke to him on the phone. How did you meet?'

Dani laughed. 'Now that's a story I have to tell you in person because it's out of this world.'

'Those are the best.'

'Mom, I have to tell you something because I think I'll burst if I don't. I can't sit still, sleep, or eat.'

Carol heard a sound, the one Dani made when ecstatically happy. 'Do I detect a romance in the air?'

'Yes,'

Carol balanced the phone on her shoulder as she started dinner. 'Nicholas?'

Dani exhaled. 'What is this amazing feeling? I feel as if I will die if I don't see him. Am I in love?'

Carol smiled. 'Sounds like it. It's as if your universe becomes tiny, just the two of you. And yet, there is so much room for so many things.'

'Exactly,' Dani said breathlessly. 'And half the time I'm just speechless.'

'I'd like to meet him.' Carol said eagerly.

'Isn't it too soon? I don't want him to think I'm trying to push something.'

'Dani, you are still our child, and no one should get upset about parents wanting to know what kind of man or woman is in their child's life, whether casually or seriously. That is family, we look out for each other. If more kids did it, maybe there wouldn't be so many abuses and disasters around.'

'I will see what I can do, I just don't know when.'

Carol grinned. 'Try next weekend, he promised to bring you if you didn't have a car.'

'Why, Mrs. Creswell, you are sneaky.'

'I have my moments. Dani, you do remember that we are going to your grandmother this Friday. I'll be there around two, I do not want to sit in that city traffic.'

'Okay. Mom, can I ask you something?'

'Dani Marie, now what kind of question is that?'

'Would it be weird for Nicholas to sleep over when he visits?'

Carol became silent.

Dani continued. 'And mom, not in the same bedroom. First, that is so disrespectful to the parents. Second, it would be to me. Third, we are nowhere near there, and fourth, did you or did you not raise me?'

Carol smiled again. 'Sorry, honey, and he's okay with that?'

'He's a man, where do you think his mind is half the time? But we have decided not to. It kind of complicates things as you're trying to learn about each other, because it blinds you and you start basing everything on how it feels in the bedroom, even if everything else is going to hell.'

Carol sniffed. 'I did raise you right.'

'Are you busy with dinner?'

'Yes. And as it happens, Sams is here.'

'Mom, please don't tell him where I am.'

'You underestimate me, Dani Marie, as I have noticed for years that you are rather far from interested.' A silence followed. 'It's all right, honey, you don't have to tell me anything.'

'Who do you think will get to the finals this year?' David asked.

'From the log, Stormers and Sharks, but the Bulls could still cause an upset.' Sams wondered why David persisted in talking rugby when he knew close to nothing about it. Then again, if David chose to discuss soccer, what would he know? Wasn't there something neutral they could discuss? 'How is business, Mr. Creswell?'

'Very good. I know people are talking recession and all sorts of things, but I haven't seen any of it. Our people are safe and that is what I care about.'

Sams knew what kind of business practices David liked, ancient ones. Yet, somehow, Creswell Enterprises made money, heaps of it. If only the man asked for advice, because he was willing to give it freely. But it seemed the thought had never even entered David's mind.

Dinner was excellent because if there was one thing Carol did well, was to cook.

The conversation drifted back and forth between all sorts of topics, annoying Sams because Carol no longer talked about Dani as she had done when they had been in school, no longer revealing much. Yet, he got the distinct impression that she was dying to say something every time she looked at David. If it was about that idiot Nicholas, then by all means, rather keep it to herself. But regardless of how they were behaving right now, he liked being in this house. They were still in love, and Dani was proof of what two contented people could produce. In an odd way, he had always thought of Dani as a mascot of good things. She was a cheerful girl and he was certain that having her in his life would make him happy.

After dinner, he thanked them for their hospitality, and drove home. His mother's car was in the garage, but she had already retired. He did likewise.

'You will never guess,' Carol said as she and David prepared for bed. 'Dani is in love.'

'What?' David stuck his head out of the bathroom. 'With whom? Oh, wait, Nicholas?'

Carol nodded. 'And she is going to bring him home next weekend.'

He looked at her searchingly. 'Do you think…'

'If you are going to ask what I think you are about to, no; because I asked and she corrected me very quickly. Separate rooms; thank you.' She announced proudly.

'You do know that not sleeping together at parents' home doesn't mean they are not doing it elsewhere.'

'I know, but she told me straight. I liked him very much on the phone, so I hope we won't be disappointed.'

'Do you know what he does?'

Carol shrugged her shoulders. 'I know nothing.'

'Now this will be a huge shock to Sams. He has been following her around like a puppy for years.'

'I know, but the choice is hers to make. And we couldn't possibly tell her, *oh, by the way, you have known him all your life and he follows you like a puppy.* And about that, if she stands clear of him there might be something she sees or knows that we don't.'

David nodded. 'As usual you are probably right. Now, this visit tonight, he is looking for something, do you have any ideas?' He asked curiously.

'Maybe her address, because that is what she asked we don't tell him.'

'Noted,' he said, then pulled her to him and looked at the green eyes she had passed onto their child.

'All I want is that she finds what we have.' Carol told him.

David kissed her and whispered against her face. 'Definitely what we have.'

Sams awoke to an empty house Friday morning. He found his mother's note, where she apologised for leaving so early, but that if he waited until Saturday, they could spend time together.

'The story of my life,' he told the ceramic cat that sat in the sunny spot on the kitchen floor, as he opened the fridge, while investigating possibilities for breakfast. Feeling adventurous, he made himself an omelette. He was quite sick of eating box and packet food.

As he cleared the breakfast things, he noticed one of the cupboard doors was leaning. Opening the door, he tested its hinges, loose. Going to the garage, he returned with the toolbox, and spent the morning going through the house tightening, screwing, adjusting, cupboards, taps, switches, and globes. When would his mother have time for any of this?

After taking a shower, he got dressed and went down to Key West for lunch. He grinned when he saw Peter and Mark—talk about coincidences—and invited them to share his table so they could reminisce.

Peter was about to join the family business in property development, and Mark, who had a BA in Management, was now at TUKS for his LLB.

'This is so weird;' Sams announced. 'I saw a picture of the gang yesterday. Do you remember that Grade Eight one where we were all posing before the Halloween party?'

'We were what, fourteen?' Peter recalled.

'Did you keep in touch with the others?' Sams asked.

Peter shook his head. 'But I did hear Leslie is doing well in the entertainment world. Remember she always wanted to produce and direct plays? Has apparently written a few things and they're on somewhere.'

'I ran into Justin a couple of months ago in Pretoria.' Mark announced. 'Unbelievable, but he was still dating Ashley.'

'And I heard they got married last Saturday.' Sams provided. 'Either of you dating?'

Mark grinned. 'I'm floating from flower to flower, and hell, do I have a garden. But he's in a relationship, beautiful girl.' He said as he pointed to Peter.

'Speaking of which,' Peter clicked his fingers. 'How is Dani, the cute one you were always chasing?'

That pretty much summed it up.

'I'm guessing she's still gorgeous. Do you ever see her?' Peter continued.

'I do,' Sams leaned back in the chair with a smug grin. 'Spoke to her last week.'

Mark asked. 'Did she pursue fashion design as she always wanted?'

'Yes,'

'And did you manage to finally catch her, or is she still running like a scared rabbit?' Mark laughed.

Sams glared at him. 'That is not true.'

'Of course it is,' Mark continued. 'And hell alone knows what you did after that last dance.'

Peter pointed to himself and Mark. 'We knew she would never go to the dance with you, because you two had been going downhill for a while, but then, there you were, and no one in the group understood it. As it turns out, the mystery was explained by Liam Smith, you recall, nice guy, who happened to like her and was planning to ask. But when the head boy and captain of the first rugby team orders you to not ask Dani to the dance, who is going to stop that? I guess your persuasion skills were outside school hours, because that bloody nose he sported for a few days must have been compliments of your fist.'

'Heroes with clay feet,' Mark supplied. 'You are lucky we were all eighteen, and just as idiotic as you were, because if it were today, we would not have kept quiet, and you would have been stripped of all your little achievements. That alone was enough to make any girl mad, but you definitely went further, and did something worse because she could not stand the sight of you afterwards.' Mark nodded. 'So, what was your inspiration?'

Sams did not like this conversation, and why did they know so much about everything? 'Who told you all this nonsense?'

'Know what the thing is about school kids? They enjoy spreading rumours, especially when it involves one of their so-called stars.' Peter informed him.

'Dani did not hate me.'

'She tolerated you, but after that blazing row in the school yard, she wished you'd disappear. No one heard what you fought about, but hell, it was interesting because none of us knew Dani had it in her to fight like that. She slapped you, twice.'

He didn't stay long after that, making a mental note to never talk to the two losers again. And he was furious that they seemed to be onto something. Something he himself was wrestling against with every fibre of his being. Annoyed at how everything was against him, he wrote his mother a note, apologising for not staying but that he would return the following weekend.

Friday evening, Nicholas went to his favourite nightclub in Rosebank, as he had nothing else to do while Dani was away at her grandmother's. He ran into friends who were celebrating someone's birthday, drank something, chatted, and decided to skip dancing.

'Is something wrong?' Andrew Lambton asked.

'No.' Nicholas told his friend. Odd, he was doing the same thing he had done for so long but tonight he had no wish to be here. He kept seeing Dani's face.

'Of course there is something wrong.' Andrew announced. 'You have been sitting alone for over an hour, you have not danced, did not notice at least six women eyeing you, and what's worse, you are just not caring for any of it. So, what gives?'

'Six? Do you keep tabs on everything?'

'Always. By the way, Laura is heading this way, so I'll see you later.'

Nicholas made a face but now there was nothing to do but talk to her. She made her way around his left shoulder and he waited for her to greet first.

'Hello Nicholas,' her dark eyes drowned in his good looks.

'Laura,' He nodded and gave her shapely legs a cursory glance.

'May I sit?'

He made a gesture for her to help herself and watched curiously as she sat on the edge of the sofa, then scoot herself along until she was beside him.

'How is work?' He queried without much interest.

'Good. Where have you been?'

A smile spread inside him and he wondered what she would say if he told her that he had been having the best time with the most adorable girl he had ever met, that right now, he was missing her something terrible, that all he wanted to do was gaze at those striking green eyes and taste the kissable mouth. He studied Laura's face, neck, chest, and the short hem of her skirt, looking for hunger to rise... The only hunger he felt was for someone who was absent. Unconsciously, he drew in breath.

She noticed, misinterpreted, and smiled. 'I'm glad I can still move you.'

He looked at her uncomprehendingly. 'What?'

'I see you still react to me. Perhaps we are not as dead as you think we are.'

'Huh, no.' He leaned back on the sofa, making sure to put some distance between them.

She noticed that too. 'There's confusing, I thought...'

'Sorry Laura, but when I told you we were over, even I didn't realise how momentous the occasion was.'

'What are you talking about, Nicholas?'

Laura could very possibly turn out to be his last empty relationship. Many would say that it hadn't been empty at all, for they had fun, went out often, spent a lot of time in clubs such as this, and the sex had been fantastic. He knew a few things about her but now realised that although meaning her well, he was not particularly interested in any of it. With Dani, he wanted to know everything; about her past and her future, where she had been and where she was headed; who she knew, what she had done, and what her dreams and hopes were, emotionally, mentally, and eventually physically. He shifted further away from Laura.

She pointed to his face. 'All of that, and none of it for me. Is she here?'

'No, this is not her kind of place.'

'To each his own,' she moved closer.

Discomfort filled him as her leg rubbed against his. Feeling as if he were cheating on Dani, he grinned broadly.

Laura did not misunderstand this time. 'Wow, lucky woman, it seems there is some good stuff going on between you two. And I congratulate you, Nicholas, as I imagined you're incapable of it. So, may I kiss you goodbye?'

'I'd prefer it if you didn't,' he told her quickly.

She smiled sadly. 'I'm feeling sorry for myself now, wishing this was meant for me.' Then she got to her feet, leaned over anyway, and pressed her lips to his.

He kept his mouth closed, feeling strange that someone other than Dani was touching him. Heck, here it was, that irreversible thing; she had already ruined him for every other woman. 'Goodbye, Laura.' Then he jumped to his feet, went outside, and grabbed his phone.

'Hello,' she greeted with a smile in her voice.

'Hello my sweet,' his heart started pumping harder.

'What are you doing?'

'Nothing right now,' he noticed a woman eyeing him and turned his back. 'Are you enjoying your grandma?'

'I already cried with some story she told me.'

'Was it sad?'

'No, I cried from laughter; she has a nutty sense of humour. I think you'd like her.'

'I'm sure I will.' He glanced at his watch. 'Okay, give me forty minutes to get home, and then I'm calling you again. I miss you.'

Sitting in front of her laptop, she wished she wasn't reading about people's weekends but rather spending time with Nicholas. She understood that people felt the need to share their events, challenges, and experiences, but sometimes... She leaned forward to read a few. Jimmy got drunk on Saturday. Wonder if his boss will believe him next time he phones in sick on a Monday after he's seen the post and the accompanying picture. Maddie tried sushi for the first time. Considering she has a seafood sensitivity, that should go down well. Oh, and DJ Bully spun a record off the turntable, almost slicing three wine glasses in half. She closed the laptop. Computers and internet felt old.

Could she ask Mr. Ridley to move her to another department, should she e-mail her CV right now, or tell Nicholas straight that she didn't want to be in IT? No, she couldn't do any of those things; it would go against everything she had asked him not to do. Usually, one had to be working to feel unhappy, but no, she was right in the middle of workers' regret long before getting to sit in the office. Grabbing the drawing pad, she got lost for a couple of hours.

The phone rang. 'Hello,'

'Hi Dani,'

It took her a few seconds to recognise the voice. 'Julia! Goodness, this is a surprise. How are you?'

'Okay I guess, but so stressed that I had to call you. Am I disturbing you? I'm not sure what you're busy with right now.'

'You are not disturbing me, and I am in the city. As for work… my apparent boss is lying in a hospital bed.'

'Oh yes, that's true. I heard about the accident, and I am sorry. Do you know how he's doing?'

'Apparently getting better, how can I help you?'

'If it wouldn't be too much trouble, could you come over? We have a huge problem and no one knows how to fix it.'

'What kind of a problem?'

'Some smart Alec did heaven knows what to our Facebook page and website. Pictures from events that should have been on are missing, started a blog that no one can explain, and we are being bombarded with stupid comments, reviews, and emails.'

'Oh dear, when would you like me to come in?'

'As soon as possible.'

Dani glanced at the time. If she ran, she could take the next bus. 'I can come now.'

Julia let out a sigh. 'I will adore you forever.'

'I just have to make a phone call, but I am on my way.'

'Thank you.'

'Hello, my sweet.' Nicholas greeted. 'This is a nice surprise.'

She grabbed Coco and her handbag and went quickly next door. 'I just want to let you know that I'm going to college, as they are having some type of emergency. I don't know if you want to pick me up from there later as I have no idea how long I will be...'

'How are you getting there?'

'I'm taking the bus.'

'Sure you don't want me to take you?'

'I'm fine Nicholas, and I'll let you know when I'm finished.'

'Okay.'

She called back three hours later.

'Are you done?' He asked.

'Almost, so I thought I'd call you. But if I'm not standing outside, and that is on the side street, not the front, when you get here, you can come up.'

'Your boyfriend?' Julia asked as Dani sat her phone down.

'You could say that.'

'I'd say more than that.' Julia smiled and noticed Dani's blush. 'Much more than that. So, spill.'

'There is nothing to spill, we are just at the beginning of whatever this is. No, no!' she exclaimed as she pressed a key. 'I'd like to get my hands on the idiot responsible for this.'

'Get in line then.'

Dani became incredibly busy then, so Julia sat in the corner going through a pile of storyboards. Fifteen minutes later, she was startled when Nicholas walked into the media centre and rose immediately, having no idea what he could possibly be doing there. 'Nicholas! This is a surprise.'

He offered a hand. 'Hello, Julia.'

Dani turned her head. 'There you are. I wondered if you would come up.'

He went to Dani and bending down, kissed her lightly then grinned. 'Julia, close your mouth, and yes, we are dating.'

They moved in the same fashion circles, so she knew him, even if not intimately, but it was disconcerting to see him here, waiting for Dani, of all people. She furrowed her brow with concern. She had never been blind to Dani's looks, for the girl had more than most, and while here, she had gone undetected, but now she was out there in the world. The mind-blowing fact was that this particular man should be the first to discover the beautiful innocence, as Dani was not the type of girl he picked for himself. He went for the professional woman, the one who knew her mind, and was as strong-willed as everyone knew he.

She sat a few moments watching the two as they exchanged soft words. There was something different here, this man did not look like the man she had seen before and heard about from some of her friends, and as he reached for Dani's face, she saw it. Nicholas Galfrey was in love. Now, she found it disturbing that what she had told Adam weeks previously had become prophetic, when she had not meant it romantically, but merely that Dani's goodness had a way of getting to people.

He swivelled the chair around to look at her.

'Wow, Nicholas, this is a shock, but a good one.'

He smiled. 'How is your family?'

'John is away.' Her husband was a journalist. 'And the kids are well, excited about the new school year. But we'll see how long that lasts. I heard about Adam. I hope he's getting out soon.'

He was about to announce that he had seen him, but would Dani believe that he had not tried to manipulate something? He took the safe route. 'I hear that he is. The doctor is concerned about his arm, but I believe a full recovery is expected.'

When Nicholas saw Dani do heaven knew what it was she was doing, he realised why Julia had referred her and why Adam was taking her blind. He doubted many IT guys could understand what she was doing.

'Now that you are here,' Julia said suddenly and got to her feet. 'May I pick your brain about something?'

'Sure.' Nicholas followed her.

'What did Julia want?' Dani asked as they drove away.

'She is planning some renovations and new courses and she wanted a bit of a house of fashion advice. They are doing a good job.'

Dani smiled and nodded. 'I always loved it there, even all those endless stairwells.'

'Where did you learn programming?' He asked then added. 'Didn't look like school stuff to me.'

'I spent many hours alone, so I experimented, but Sams taught me.'

'Oh.' He felt annoyed, he wanted that man nowhere near her. 'When was this?'

'His parents divorced when he was fourteen, so we started spending time together because he needed someone to talk to. Many days, he would go home with me. We did our homework and then fooled around on the PC. He used to take extra computer classes so he had already figured out a lot of things, and showed me. As technology evolved, we moved right along with it. The two of us always had the latest, best, fastest whatever came out, including programmes, so we have stuff no one else does. And you should see what my laptop can do.' She looked out the window. 'We inspired each other. Then one day, things changed.'

'What happened?'

'He asked me out. I had never seen him in that light and was happy just being his friend, but he wouldn't accept it. I started distancing myself but he took it as a done deal. I think I would have succeeded if I had persevered, but I made a mistake.'

'And what was that?'

'I went to the Graduation dance with him. I was too busy, didn't have time to look for someone else, and no other boy had asked. I eventually heard that Sams told them off because he wanted to make sure I had no choice. Come into my parlour said the spider to the fly. Stupid fly flew straight into the web. Ever since then, this has been going on.'

'He'll give up now that you have a boyfriend.' He threw her a glance.

She wished his words were true, because heaven knew that she must resolve this thing. But when, and how? She placed a hand on his leg. 'I have one, do I?'

He covered her hand with his and squeezed it. 'Yes you do. So, hungry?'

'Famished,' she admitted.

'Nicholas,' his aunt's voice broke through his daydream. 'Where are you today?'

'Sorry,' he apologised. 'What did you say?'

Samantha studied him with a smile. She had two children, who, for different reasons were absent, but this boy had always been her darling. 'Is there something on your mind? You seem very distracted. Please tell me you have not forgotten that you have to be in Cape Town tomorrow.' She leaned back in her seat.

He made an impatient gesture, as if Cape Town was in another galaxy. 'Can I ask you a question, and it has nothing to do with work.'

'Dear boy, of course you can ask me anything, anytime of day or night.' She had always loved that he confided in her. She was as much a mother to him as his own mother.

'How do you know when you have met the one, that person who will understand you, and put up with your nonsense because they love you?'

This was interesting. She had watched him go through women regularly and he had never looked or sounded like this. 'I am assuming you have met someone.'

He nodded, and only she witnessed the look of joy that appeared on his face. 'And I can't explain what I feel, because I just do.'

Samantha smiled. 'Then you are already close to knowing. So, who is she?'

'Dani. I say her name and my heart leaps. She is the most gorgeous creature, kind, smart, and talented. I feel as if she has invaded my life, yet, she hasn't invaded it enough. Am I making sense?'

'Completely. And I'm guessing it's quite the experience since you've never been serious about anyone before.'

He got to his feet and started pacing in front of her desk. 'I can't bear to be away from her. All I want to do is touch her, to stare into her green eyes. I shake when I think about her.' He showed her the trembling hands. 'My breath catches, everything is so intense I feel as if I am losing myself. Yet, I can't stop; I want more, so much more.'

'Well, then you do have your answer. Does this then also explain where you have been disappearing to every afternoon?' Her blue eyes danced. 'And since you are not being much help now either, you may go see your Dani.'

CHAPTER FIVE

They were at the zoo and Nicholas laughed as he watched her have conversations with the animals. She addressed them by name, often made-up, asked them about their families, the kids, how work was going, why they put up with the unfair treatment, and they usually ended up coming closer to the fence; as if they were answering her.

'I have never seen that,' he said, throwing his arm over her shoulder as they headed for the restaurant.

'Makes people wonder who is crazy, me for doing it, or them for watching.'

As they sat down, he took her hands. 'My sweet, I am sorry I have to leave you alone tomorrow, but I can't get out of this Cape Town thing.'

'Nicholas, why would I expect you to stop doing all the things you have always done and just come sit with me?' She asked. 'Everyday life has to continue, even if you're not here, so I will be fine alone for a day. Maybe even design a few things.'

He was about to suggest that she should go with him then bit his tongue. This trip was about work and that he intended to do, so what time would he have for her? Only the night... He felt his body tighten at the thought but knew that it was an unacceptable suggestion. He was starting to understand something with this relationship. Abstinence was not as hard as he had first imagined, yet by no means easy, and he viewed it as breaking a habit, such as smoking. Now he also wondered, would the lack of physical rewards affect the way he felt as time progressed, perhaps making him tired, or bored?

'What's wrong?' She asked.

His eyes became blank for a second. He was forgetting that she was beginning to discern his expressions quite well. 'Nothing my sweet, I'm just going to miss you.'

She dropped her head to hide a smile, knowing what had gone through his mind. She was flattered and felt the incredible pull to give in, but if she did guilt would never let her forget that she had gone against a decision she had made a long time ago. Her gaze fixed on him now, everything in the right order, as her parents often said. 'I am going to miss you too. What time do you leave in the morning?'

'Eight, so I will call you earlier than seven.'

'Good you told me, I'll set my alarm.'

'What do you want to do tonight?'

'How are you with theatre?'

'Fine, what's there to watch?'

She gave him a title. 'Have you seen it?'

'Can't say I have, but it sounds weird enough. Do you watch stuff like that often?'

'No, but the director went to school with me so I would like to support her.'

'Well then, let's go.'

That evening, he found it hard to say goodnight, because behind it was a goodbye. It was just for a day and night, but it felt excruciatingly long. How could a couple of weeks change a person this way? He was an accomplished man but right now, nothing mattered, except being in her presence. Then to make matters worse, she kissed him.

She pulled his head down and covered his mouth with hers, her hands going to his neck and shoulders so she could hold him tight. Her inexperience was maddening because she aroused him in ways no one else ever had. It spoke of promises, secrets, and glorious rapture. Well, he could not possibly stop being kissed, because he wanted it to go on forever. And when she looked at him like that, it was as if a new world unfolded before him. As if he were an explorer just arrived on a mysterious continent, and she its very deity claiming his complete worship.

Dani grabbed the phone as soon as it started ringing. 'Hello.'

'Hello my sweet.' Nicholas said. 'Did you miss me today?'

'A lot,' she admitted.

'As I imagined, I couldn't fit everything into today, so I have to see the manager at our store tomorrow morning. I miss you so much.' What he said was not half of what he felt, and he felt as if he were caged. All he wanted to do was bust out and run all the way to Johannesburg. *Stop depressing yourself,* he told himself. 'I am in a hotel.'

She burst out laughing. 'Sorry, but you are the one who likes them so much.'

'Now that I am in one, I see it's not them I like. What's Coco doing?'

Dani looked around. 'Lying where you always sit, I think she misses you too.'

'That is cute. What are we doing this weekend?'

Dani wondered how she was to broach the subject. 'I'm not sure, but...'

'You want to go home, don't you?'

'Yes. But...'

'Dani, do you want to go home alone or for me to come with you?'

'I want you to come with me.'

'Done, we will sort it out when I get back.'

Dani took a deep breath. 'Would you consider sleeping over?' She closed her eyes waiting for his reply.

'How would your parents feel about that?'

'They would die if we were to share a room.'

He made a funny sound. 'Dani, what the heck are you talking about, we don't even share rooms at my place or yours. And it's not the room that would bother them.'

'I am just telling you what kind of people they are. They believe in things in the right order.'

'I know Dani, you are their child, and I—' He stopped. Right there he almost told her that he loved her. Did he? 'Dani,' he couldn't hear anything. 'Are you still there?'

'Yes. What were you saying?'

'I said I understand about the right thing to do.' He could barely breathe as his heart pounded. 'What are you doing?'

'I was pacing until you called, but now I'm going to the laptop because I can't think of sleeping.'

'Do you have Skype?'

'I do.'

'Okay then, let me grab my laptop. Why didn't I think of this before? Why didn't you, Miss Internet?'

'You know, Internet has not been quite as exciting since I met you. I used to spend endless hours before, but now...'

'I'm your new toy, huh?' He teased as they spent a few minutes connecting. 'Are you set?'

'Yes. Ah, there you are.' As she saw him lean towards the screen, she did likewise, both kissing the screen.

'Definitely nothing like the original.' He sat looking at her. 'But I miss you.'

'Thank you.'

He laughed. 'Only you could thank someone for missing you.'

'My car will be ready next week.'

'Does that mean I can't come see you after twelve anymore?'

'Nicholas, you are silly. I'm not getting my car to go drive all over the place if I don't have to.' She made herself comfortable on the chair. 'But soon you will have to start working full days again.'

'I know. I just want to enjoy this.' He pointed to her and himself. 'And I am learning how to do things in the right order.'

She yawned. 'I don't know what you are turning into.'

'Someone I actually like.' He grinned at her. 'Did you just yawn?'

'Sorry.'

'Don't apologise, let's get ready for bed. Leave it on, but tilted it to the wall and lower the sound.'

Thirty minutes later, they were looking at each other again.

Dani felt queasy as she saw him bare-chested. He looked good in his drawstring pyjama bottoms.

Nicholas on the other hand, was having trouble breathing. She wore a pair of boy shorts and a body-hugging camisole.

They placed the laptops so they could see each other from where they lay in bed, then after a few minutes of chatter, Nicholas noticed that Dani was drifting. Coco jumped onto the bed and nestled behind her. Sleepily, Dani patted her then turned back to the camera. 'Nicholas,' she whispered and then was fast asleep. He snuggled into bed and just watched her.

'My sweet,' Nicholas hugged and kissed her. 'I missed you.'

'It was rather quiet in Johannesburg as well.' She told him with a twinkle in her eyes.

'Dani,' he told her seriously. 'I wanted to tell you something last night. But I couldn't because I wanted to see your face when I do.'

'Yes, Nicholas,' she encouraged softly.

'I think I'm in love with you.'

She tried to calm the lump in her throat. 'Are you sure Nicholas?'

'Of course I'm not, I don't understand any of this. It's all new, confusing, contradicting, things I never felt before... but it's the only explanation that makes sense. So, what do you say to that, Dani, that I love you?'

'Huh,' she could barely speak. 'I think I may be in love with you too.'

He grabbed her hands. All he wanted to do was to let them roam all over her body, but he wouldn't, because he had already done too much of that in the past. So he kept them both immobile as they kissed. He was giving his heart the chance to experience.

Dani's face rested against his. 'Is it really possible?'

'How we feel?' He pulled her to the sofa, every moment he touched her was a wonder. 'I keep thinking the same thing but who wrote the book on what must happen when? So perhaps we are simply going through the process in fast forward, that what takes other people six months, a year, we know in weeks. Does it frighten you?'

She nodded. 'I don't want to be dreaming,'

'It's all quite real. And don't ask me to explain it, because I can't yet, I just feel overwhelmed and happy. But Dani, do you still want to date other men?' If she said yes, as much as it would hurt, he knew that he would let her go.

She shook her head. 'I want you.'

Her words tended to make his head spin. He saw possibilities and dreams. 'Right...' he said. 'Let's discuss this weekend business now.'

'You're sure it's okay?'

'This may have escaped your mind, but you have to come home with me sometime as well, how do you expect to feel then?'

She had not thought about that. 'Are they very bad?'

'Dragons,'

'Really?' she gulped nervously.

He laughed. 'I'm teasing, they will love you. Okay, tell me how you want to do this.'

'Either we go today and come back tomorrow, or go tomorrow and stay until Sunday. Which would you prefer?'

'Make it today. And sorry for you Dani Marie Creswell, I have just decided that I shall take you to meet the Galfrey dragons for Sunday lunch.'

She felt a flicker of fear. 'Okay.' She told him with a brave face. 'Tell me what is expected of me.'

He giggled at her worried expression. 'Relax Dani, they are quite normal, you'll see. Now, I have to go report in at the office then go pack again. Just give me a time to be back here.'

'Three, so we don't hit traffic, and daddy has time to get home.'

'This is odd, because I have never asked, but where do you live?'

'Bedfordview,'

'Oh.' He had the same reaction as when he saw her car the first time, when he had imagined she drove an old battered Beetle.

'Mom,' Nicholas was surprised to find her sitting behind his desk. 'Are you looking for something?'

'You know,' Catherine glanced at him. 'Three times in your life you kept secrets. The first time, you were seven, the second ten, and then fourteen, and as much as I pressed you to tell me what you were hiding, you would not confess. So I always had to snoop to discover what you were up to.'

He stared at her blankly. 'What are you talking about?'

'Do you remember what you were hiding?' She got to her feet and opened a cupboard.

He scratched his head, why would she imagine he would hide something here?

'At seven, you found a mangy stray cat. You kept that sorry creature hidden for a week until I eventually tracked down the mewing and took it to the vet. He suggested putting it to sleep. I said; *don't you dare break my boy's heart, just give it whatever it needs.* Well, he lived ten years, and made himself an absolute pest leaving his fur on my velvet couches.' She smiled.

'You think I have a cat in my cupboard?' Nicholas' lips twitched.

'At ten, it was worse. Heaven knows how you did it, but one day I was walking at the bottom of the garden when this monstrosity of an animal came out from behind a bush and gave me an anxiety attack. I still have not forgiven you for losing my best straw hat to that horrid thing. Whatever possessed you to bring a goat home? And how did you do it, that is what I always wanted to know? Again the thing needed help. That one lived six years. And strangely, the cat also liked him.'

Nicholas had a perplexed look on his face. Was his mother going insane or senile?

'But at fourteen, I eventually understood what it was all about. You found a street urchin, and you kept him clothed, fed, and hidden a fortnight, until you figured he too needed to go to school. Then with tears in your eyes, you begged me to look after the child. Do you remember George? Of course you do, you couldn't get over the fact that he chose to go back to the streets, and for over a year you tried to convince him to come home.'

'Don't remind me.' Nicholas sat in one of the chairs in front of his desk. 'Still my biggest failure.'

'Oh honey, no, you succeeded. You simply forgot that people are free agents and he chose his own path. But now, back to today. So, what have you found? Because, you are acting precisely as you did then. There is something or someone you have rescued and fallen in love with, and again you are keeping it all to yourself. It probably needs help, so, out with it.'

Nicholas burst into laughter. 'For a moment there I thought you had lost it. No mom, no animals, or street children, but you are half-right.'

'Ah, so something is going on.' She sat opposite him.

'I have met someone.'

She placed a hand on her breast. 'You mean a woman? And she makes you act this way?'

He nodded. 'Yes mom, it seems that I am finally in love.'

She clasped her hands together in a thankful gesture. 'This is what I never understood about your relationships. You are able to love so deeply but none ever satisfied you. This I see ...' she gestured towards him. 'I see the eyes, the smile, and the way you stare vacantly to see her in your mind. I like this very much.'

'Well, then I am glad it meets with your approval. So, if you promise to behave now, I will bring her to lunch on Sunday.'

'Really,' Catherine was excited. How many times had she tried to meet the women in his life, but none lasted, and after a while, she had given up? 'May I know her name?'

'Yes mom, she is not a secret.'

Coco sat in her cage, although, the door was open.

'I'm guessing she knows she's going home.'

'She knows everything.' Dani pulled a case on wheels.

Nicholas did a double take. It was the first time he was seeing her in jeans, and did she look good. Those curves were so perfect… *Stop it,* he told himself. 'Anything I can take to the car?'

'I just have this.' She grabbed her handbag and keys and bent down to close Coco's cage door. 'Are we going to mommy and daddy?'

Coco howled excitedly.

'Cute, but please tell me she is not going to do that in the car.'

He would have taken the shortest route he knew but not Dani, because she did not do normal. She made him drive all the way to Houghton, down 11th, Ivy, up Goodman Terrace, through Cyrildene, and Kensington South, saying something about scenic route.

She directed him until she said, 'here we go, number twenty-five.'

He did not understand why he kept thinking that she might not have some type of means. Because when he looked at the double-storey house, he realised that she was used to good living. And her father was CEO, of Creswell Enterprises no less. But it was that flat she was babysitting; it confused who Dani really was.

Coco started that dreadful howling, obviously aware that she was home. Dani pressed the remote-control to close the gate and scrambled to get her out of the cage.

Nicholas shook his head; he had never seen anything like it. Then, two gorgeous Labradors came running as if they had known him forever and threw themselves at his chest; unprepared, he was knocked off his feet.

'Bad dogs,' Dani reprimanded. 'Say sorry.'

Both dogs sat beside him and put their faces down.

'Well,' David said with a smile. 'Not the welcome I planned,' and helped Nicholas up.

'Thank you, sir.' Nicholas shook his hand and introduced himself.

'Pleased to meet you, I'm David.' He turned to his daughter, hugged her, and kissed the side of her temple. 'Hello my baby.'

'Hi daddy, where is mom?'

'In the kitchen, having a conniption over a soufflé.' He laughed. 'Please don't go in there because she believes all vibrations will collapse the thing. I told her not to try it but she wouldn't listen.'

Nicholas took it all in as they walked through the front door, liking how everything looked comfortable, organic, and lived in. He noticed the reading glasses, magazines tossed to the side, a newspaper on the table, dog toys, and juices.

'Honey,' David called down the passage. 'They are here.'

'I'll be there now.' Carol's voice came back.

Nicholas was startled when he saw the woman. She was as gorgeous as Dani, just older.

Carol kissed her daughter then turned to Nicholas with a smile.

By dinnertime, Nicholas felt at home. He liked both parents, finding them interesting and funny. They laughed and joked in an amazingly open way, but always so correctly. They were a true window into why Dani was the way she was.

After dinner, David asked who wished to go out and who wanted to stay in.

'In,' Dani raised her hand as if she were in a classroom.

'Me too,' Nicholas said because he was tired.

'And you, honey?' David asked.

'Three.'

'Okay, good.'

They sat on the patio with coffee, Dani snuggling alongside Nicholas on a wicker sofa, David and Carol on another, just talking family, which mostly consisted of stories out of Dani's childhood, all four laughing at her little misadventures.

'What do you think?' Carol watched David eagerly when they retired to their room.

'Good man, very presentable, respectful, patient, gentle, and kind. You know what I say about watching how people treat animals, and he always had a ready hand to scratch an ear. But he also has a very expensive car outside, so I am curious as to what he does. He never mentioned his surname, so I have no idea who he might be. You?'

Carol shook her head. 'Don't know either. But as I hoped, I like him. And how they met... so very romantic.'

Dani and Nicholas gazed at each other as they lay in their beds. It was now a given that Skype was to be on regularly.

'Umm,' Nicholas said, as he smelled his pillow. 'It is quite delicious, is it chocolate?'

'Probably. I have told her someone is going to choke when they try to eat one in their sleep, but she doesn't believe me.'

Nicholas laughed. 'Let it not be me. Doesn't Coco sleep with you here?'

'No, I am not as interesting as Karan and Kline.'

'Dani, did you name all your dogs?'

'What can I say; I was already showing signs of where my passion lay.'

He lifted his head. 'Please rephrase that, because your passion lies right here.'

She blushed. 'Fine, where my interest was,'

'That's better.' He snuggled down into bed. 'I am very tired, those people in Cape Town drove me nuts this morning, do you mind if I leave you now?'

'No,' she told him softly. 'Goodnight, Nicholas.'

'Goodnight my sweet,'

And tonight, Dani watched him sleep, wanting to know what he thought about visiting a woman's parents so soon after meeting her. Did he think she was already thinking marriage? She wasn't. Well, that wasn't entirely true. She wasn't thinking about it pertaining to him, but she thought about it because of what it represented.

It was about meeting the one you could lose your temper with and who wouldn't hate you for it; the one you could have a world war with and wouldn't abandon you, the one who would walk through hell for you, with you, even against you, and come out loving you more. That was why girls dreamt of marriage, because somewhere, they had learnt that marriage represented all of that. So who did not want to find that anchor, that safe place, that haven?

But Nicholas came from a different world, one where he had found everything ready and easy and commitments were taken and made as he saw fit. On the few occasions he had mentioned past relationships, she could tell he had barely focused on a woman for any decent period of time. Yet, as different as that world was, she didn't want to negate its influence, because it had created this man she was beginning to love above all else. Likewise, she hoped he didn't expect her to change, perhaps to suit an ideal he imagined a woman should be. He was also as good as a playboy, even if he went to Galfrey's every day to put effort into something there but for all she knew, he was a confirmed one and would remain so. Yet, there was not one thing she wanted to change about him.

Nicholas awoke feeling refreshed, glad they believed in good mattresses in this house, because a bad one could put angels in the worst of moods. Jumping out of bed, he opened the door and peeked outside, all was quiet upstairs, but he could hear Carol's muffled voice downstairs. Then, he heard Dani. She started giggling and Carol joined in. How could the sound of two women laughing make him feel so complete? He heard little tic-tic sounds coming up the stairs and saw Coco. She went straight for the master bedroom.

Within seconds, he heard David's sleepy voice. 'Coco, must you do this every Saturday? Can't a man sleep in? But it's not your fault, it's that woman's, who leaves the door open all the time. Yes, lie there, and let me sleep a while longer too.'

Nicholas smiled and went to the bathroom. Returning, he glanced at the clock then decided to climb back into bed as it sounded like a good lazy day. Speculating how it would unfold, he heard someone knock. 'Come in,'

'Good morning,' Dani greeted as she walked in with a tray.

Nicholas stared at her.

'Every Saturday, daddy gets breakfast in bed, so I thought I'd surprise you.'

'Thank you.' He grinned and wondered where she would sit. She plopped herself beside him on the bed. He didn't know which was the biggest hunger right then; the one that growled in his stomach or the one for her. This was the first time they were anywhere near a bed together and it was making his head buzz.

This was not a good idea, she thought as his arm rubbed against hers and the masculine smell raided her nostrils. She would soon smoulder, so she started talking.

He couldn't focus on what she said. She was too close, that scent of hers invading his senses. His body tingled and he felt as if he were becoming asthmatic. But clearly, he finished eating because she got up, took the tray from him, placed it on the desk, then stood beside the bed and said something again. He grabbed her wrist and pulled her down onto the bed. She fell across it and he swooped on her.

'Nicholas,' she reached up for his face.

He gazed at her, then one hand slid under her top, so he could feel her stomach, it was flat and smooth like velvet. He groaned as he kissed her deeply, letting her know that there was still so much missing. Her breathing quickened and he felt his heart thumping. One hand ran down her side and leg. She was wearing pants but he could imagine how it would feel to touch her skin. He moaned again.

Her hands moved across his chest, loving the way his skin felt, how he reacted when her fingertips stopped somewhere.

He let her go, lay beside her, and turned his head to gaze at her.

Her eyes were intensely green. 'Why did you stop?'

'Because if I don't, I will have you naked before you know it and then nothing will be in the right order again.'

She smiled, plonked a kiss on his chest, another on one shoulder, and then got off the bed. 'So, which one do you want to do?'

'Which what do I want to do?'

'Nicholas, were you listening at all? I told you about the dog show and the flea market.'

'When,'

'During breakfast,'

'Huh... well, that was before I could get my brain to function. Heck Dani, I have never had you on a bed and it made my mind and hands wander.'

'I apologise, and will try not to tempt you again.'

He gave her a crooked smile. 'Very bad choice of words, it's not as if I'm unable to control myself.'

'I know what you mean,' she added. 'Because apparently, men never are when a woman is in the area.'

'Yes, well, losers. Okay, so, which do you prefer?'

'Maybe the flea market,'

'What are your parents planning?'

'They are leaving it up to us.'

They went in David's Range Rover, because David took one look at the Audi and announced. 'If you want a broken bumper or something worse on that one, then go right ahead and drive it to that nightmare of a terrain.'

'No,' Nicholas said quickly. 'I was not planning anything like it.' He grinned at Dani. 'It was quite a sight and I should have kept my head and taken pictures, and put them all over the Internet.'

'Does she still spend all that time on it?' David asked curiously.

'Not as much as I used to.' Dani defended herself.

'Goodness,' Carol interjected. 'There were days when we could not pry her off the computer.'

'And I discovered how to do things no one else knows how to do.'

'That is true, and quite scary; she has programmes and gadgets most people have never heard of.' David added.

Nicholas nodded, recalling the afternoon he had gone to pick her up from College. 'I have seen her in action.'

When they returned four hours later, they had only two things, an umbrella, which was quite suitable for rainy days, and enough dust to start a sandpit covering their clothes and shoes. The decision was unanimous, all went upstairs to wash and change.

Dani dawdled as she searched for a box of coloured pens. When she couldn't find them, she went to the shower. She washed and rinsed her hair, then turning, she saw it. She let out a blood-curdling scream and instinctively plastered herself against the shower wall.

Nicholas was first in her bathroom. He saw the misted glass and heard something like a whimper. Automatically, he reached for the door handle; then stopped. 'What's wrong, Dani?'

'Nicholas,' she was crying now. 'Please take it away.'

'What is it?'

'Snake,'

'Don't move, Dani, but tell me exactly where it is.'

'Huh... by the door, your left corner,'

Nicholas grabbed the bath towel and opened the shower door. Thankfully, the water jet was keeping the reptile cornered. He threw the large towel over it, took hold of Dani by a wrist, yanked her out of the cubicle, closed the door, and wrapped her in another towel.

She trembled violently against him, as two sets of footsteps came rushing.

'What happened?' David took one look at his daughter's face and knew something had terrified her.

'There is a snake in her shower. Does the SPCA deal with this sort of thing or is there a special line?'

'A snake?' Carol cringed. 'Ugh, don't tell me it's one of Ryan's again.'

'Is this a regular occurrence around here?' Nicholas asked.

'Not regular, but our young neighbour has taken up with reptiles and now and then we see him searching the neighbourhood for them.' David announced. 'Let me call him.'

'Are you okay?' Nicholas asked.

Dani nodded but shivered.

He tightened his hold around her; she was definitely in shock.

Thankfully, it turned out to be Cedric, Ryan's brown house-snake, and although not poisonous, also known to bite.

CHAPTER SIX

'You haven't mentioned,' David said halfway through lunch, addressing Nicholas. 'And I don't know if there is a reason, which then I should respect, but I'm still curious. What is your surname?'

Nicholas and Dani exchanged a quick glance.

'He did this to me.' Dani told them. 'Kept it back until I sort of knew him first, doesn't like people judging him based on his name.'

'Oh yes?' Carol was intrigued. 'A man who wants his actions to speak for themselves, I appreciate that.'

'Then I respect that too.' David continued with his meal. 'It's Galfrey.'

Carol's green eyes widened. 'You mean you are Dani's boss?'

'No, and yes,' Nicholas saw how it looked, not good at all. 'My side of business is in the Executive, not in IT, and that is where she's going.'

'But you two do see a little conflict here, right?' David hoped they did see.

'Not at all,' Nicholas replied. 'Dani is being hired by Adam, not me, and she has to prove herself the same way everyone else does. I do not interfere, meddle, or give glowing reports.' He quoted her. 'Besides, what she is being considered for is so far from fashion that I am nowhere near it.'

'It's true,' Dani nodded then turned to him. 'What am I being considered for? Do you know what a Creative Virtual Assistant does?'

'It has to do with social networks, which you are obviously brilliant at.'

'But...' She wanted a job, but she wanted a designing one.

Now, what did he tell her? 'This is merely a starting point. You can move from there, we do it all the time. Do you know the *Simple A* line?'

She nodded. Those dresses were always exquisitely cut, the fabrics carefully chosen, and the finishes fantastic.

'That designer started as a personal assistant to Deborah Potts. We encourage talent, find out what people do, and if they are interested in design, we ask to see their work. The same will happen with you.'

'I haven't even got it yet. Do you know how much longer Mr. Ridley will be in hospital?'

'He's doing well and will be out shortly. Will probably need crutches and a sling, so I'm not too sure how he will manage to be mobile, but I know Adam and he's trying to get back to work as soon as he can.' He saw that assuaged her somewhat.

They got home past mid-afternoon and Nicholas hung back with Dani. 'If it's okay with you and your parents I would like to stay until tomorrow. I'm still tired and don't feel like driving back.'

'You are not upset at daddy's nosiness.'

'Would I be asking to stay if I were? He loves you, it's his right to ask questions.'

'You just had to.' Carol said as she plopped herself on a chair inside. 'Didn't I tell you to leave his name alone?'

'It certainly isn't what I was expecting.' He furrowed his brow.

'Stop that,' Carol pointed to his forehead. 'They'll figure it out without your good intentions.'

'I didn't mean it can't work. They just have to think about it.'

'And they are what, ten?' Carol shook her head and sighed.

'The problem isn't now, it's when things don't go right, fall apart, and become unbearable between a couple who is trying to run away from each other. Do you remember Richard and Bianca Strauss? What a mess that was.'

Carol nodded, recalling it well, and that she had thought about it only the week before, when Sams visited. 'Let's pray that will never be them.'

They barbequed that evening and Nicholas noticed that the dogs enjoyed it as much as the humans did.

'I'm trying to guess what your parents think of me.' Nicholas said later on Skype as he fixed the bedcovers around himself.

'Daddy likes tough customers as they make him work harder, so he definitely likes you. Mom is a pushover for charm, and what are you?' Dani teased.

'I think most women I know would disagree.'

'But your mom and aunt must like you.'

'They love me so it doesn't count, but you will see tomorrow.'

'Is there a dress code for lunch?'

'Dani,' he rolled his eyes. 'Stop imagining weird things, your dress sense is perfect.' *Just as your body is perfect,* he thought. Heavens, when he recalled that image that was now stamped in his brain. Sure, at that moment, there had been nothing sexual about it, because he had been frightened for her, but now that danger was past, he could see the collarbones, perfect breasts, flat stomach, hips...

'I'll see you in a minute,' Dani said as she jumped out of bed. 'Have to tell my mom something before I forget.'

Nicholas also got out of bed and started pacing. It was way too hot.

The bedroom door flung open, Dani flew in, threw her arms around his neck, and smacked his lips. 'Goodnight.' Then she flew out again.

He was going to see an early death, because she was definitely going to kill him.

Nicholas glanced around the room in the morning, liking the feeling of at-ease he got from this family. There was nothing phoney about them. They were who they were, did not apologise for it, and were happy. They were also thankful people, taking nothing for granted, and were not filled with pride over their accomplishments. More and more he understood why Dani was so sensible. She had grown up with strong foundations and he doubted there was much that could deter her from her convictions.

There was however an area where she stood on very shaky ground, where she was never sure, often shy, and yet so very open; their relationship. When he thought about it, and he had not been able to stop since seeing her on the side of the highway, it also felt like the most incredible lie. No one, no, not a one person, male or female, could say that three weeks were enough to change a person's perspective of life, love, or anything else, and if anyone had told him a story like this, he would have said *never*. Yet, here he stood, knee-deep in never.

His feelings were of an intensity he never imagined impossible, and he was beginning to suspect that when sex entered their lives, it would become worse. His mind drifted again to some of the women he had known. He remembered being excited about them and then being content in that place of non-committal. With Dani, everything was different. He hungered for her, and not merely physically. But when he thought that he might have never met her, he felt like crying. Not knowing her would have been the cruellest fate, even if not aware that she existed.

He threw himself onto the bed, same place where he had pinned her down, the image of her naked body filling his mind. Would she always excite him, even when she was sixty? Could they turn this thing into a forever wonder? In a few hours, they would be at the Galfreys, and he was certain that would be the last piece of the puzzle that had befuddled him over these past weeks.

Nicholas took Dani to the flat first, so she could unpack, apparently change again, and leave Coco with Mrs. Brown, while he went home to drop his things. He could sense her anxiety. 'Relax,' he told her softly as he kissed her. 'And I will be back at twelve.'

She watched the roads with interest as he drove to his family home then sat up, realising there was something oddly familiar about the route. When he turned into a tree-lined street, she pointed to a tall white wall in the distance. 'That is the Galfrey house.'

'How do you know that?' He queried.

'Oh my goodness,' she exclaimed. 'If only Anya were here now. Nicholas, you will never believe it.'

'Do I detect an interesting story?'

'Interesting?' Her eyes were wide with excitement. 'I call it spooky.'

He pulled over to the side of the road immediately. 'Do tell.'

'Now?' She kept a close watch on the property and shook her head in disbelief.

'Is it long?'

'Well, okay.' She turned towards him in the car seat. 'It happened right at the beginning of our first year in college, which makes it what... five years ago? Anya and I were still trying to figure out all the routes, so one day we drove up this road when we came off the highway. Anya was driving her Mini and just around the corner,' she pointed behind them. 'One of the tyres popped and we ended up here. We got out of the car, grabbed the jack, and were about to take the spare out, when out of that gate flies a Porsche.'

A strange expression appeared on Nicholas face.

'So this dashing young man driving without a care in the world zooms right past us. Anya says, *idiot, can't you see we would appreciate some help? It's not as if women are really strong.* And she had a point, because she's tiny. I glare at the back of his head and think, *If you don't come back this instant, I swear I'll...* he does a U-turn, and stops right there.' She pointed to a place ahead of them.

'No way, Dani,'

'Oh, there is more. So he saunters over in his crisp white shirt and I think, *does he even know what a jack looks like?* Anya can no longer focus because all she sees is handsome guy.' Dani giggled.

'So what did I say?'

'*Are you girls all right*? Anya looks at you and says, *do you know how to change a tyre?* Then she turns to me and mumbles, *naturally, he is only going to see you.* I say what... why. *Because you have that thing.* I don't know what thing she's referring to but tell her anyway. *Not if I can help it.* And I went to stand there with my arms crossed.' She pointed to a tree. 'So without another word, you take the jack, and do the whole tyre thing in four minutes flat, said whatever to Anya as she thanked you, and then threw me a glance.

'I opened my handbag, took out a few wet wipes and gave them to you. You said *thanks*, I nodded and said *pleasure*. Anya walks over to you, all giggles and crazy. She was nineteen, I was eighteen, really sophisticated. She thanks you again, you say *don't mention it* and I notice you're trying to look at me properly. I turn quickly sideways then walk back to the car. We get in, and drive away. And there you stood watching us until we disappeared and went to get lost further up the suburb. Right after that, my dad bought us a GPS each so we would stop getting lost all over the place.'

'So I was right when I thought I had seen you before.'

She nodded. 'I just couldn't pinpoint the exact event. I thought perhaps one of the fashion shows, but no, it was here, outside your house.'

'Know the funny thing about that story?' He said. 'For weeks afterwards I kept hoping to run into you girls again.'

'You do know that it wouldn't have been the same back then. And it might have been Anya who interested you.'

'How do we know? Maybe some things are just meant to be and no matter how much we run, they will find us.'

She shrugged. 'Perhaps, but that was the little adventure Anya and I had right opposite your house.'

He recalled the episode vaguely, but he did remember that he had been intrigued by the girls, especially the one who stood against the tree trying to make herself invisible with her pretty light brown hair falling over her face and shoulders. It might work on others, but not on him. He had been sorry to have never seen her again, but now, thankfully, here she was.

If there was one thing Dani was proud of, it was that her mother had drilled into her how to treat people, no matter what age or status, so she knew that at least her social graces would not let her down.

She noticed straight away that only the bodies were aged, that the older Galfrey minds were very much alert, funny, and intelligent, and all had her giggling within minutes of being in the house.

Nicholas disappeared for a few minutes, then re-entered with a woman who looked like she might be in her mid-thirties, but who obviously had some physical difficulties.

'This is my cousin Veronica.' Nicholas announced.

Dani greeted her politely and before she knew it, and possibly because Veronica might not meet too many visitors, she had a hanger-on.

They discussed... heaven knew what they discussed because her mind was inundated with information. Jonathan Galfrey was a treat; he had been born in Scotland and still had an accent, so he swapped and changed at will, and confused everyone.

Dani got the feeling that she was a freak occurrence, as both Catherine and Samantha studied her with undisguised interest. Obviously trying to figure out how she was different from all the other women Nicholas had dated and not bothered to bring here.

Veronica eventually left them, as she tired easily and needed rest. Dani also excused herself and asked where the bathroom was. Either one or all explained where it was and she was soon lost. They had said downstairs and up, so she had gone for up.

The house made her think of English magazines; beautiful, warm, sumptuous. She walked down one passage, then another, and as she turned yet another corner, she heard a thump and a moan. She thought it sounded like Veronica and following it, knocked on the door and walked in. Sure enough, there lay Veronica prostrate on the floor, struggling to turn to her side, so she could get herself upright again. Dani ran to her immediately.

'Dani,' Veronica said and then repeated it three times.

'You have a very good memory.'

Suddenly, Samantha stood in the doorway.

Dani could tell she was less than pleased, perhaps even about to tell her that she should not be so eager to help without asking, or concern herself in what was none of her business.

'What happened?' Samantha asked.

'I heard a sound and thought she might have fallen...' Dani said as she helped Veronica to sit on the sofa and gazed at Samantha with hurt in her eyes. 'I apologise if you didn't want me to touch her.'

Dear lord, Samantha thought. *She is like an open book. Look at those puppy eyes.* 'No, you did well. It's just that some people have no idea how to handle her.'

'Dani,' Veronica repeated again.

'I see you have impressed her already. It usually takes a lot.' Samantha smiled.

'Thank you Veronica.' Dani said and smoothed the dark hair.

Veronica reached for the hand on her hair with some difficulty. 'Dani is friend.'

Dani sat beside her. 'Is she supposed to be doing something I'm interfering with? Please tell me if I'm doing something wrong. I don't want to upset anyone.'

'No, you are great.' Samantha said and sat on a wingback chair nearby. 'And now I understand why Nicholas is crazy about you. You have the softest heart.'

Dani smiled shyly.

Ten minutes later, Nicholas appeared. 'Did you get lost?' He queried.

'Lost?' Dani asked uncomprehendingly.

'You went in search of a bathroom and never returned.'

'Oh, yes, I got sidetracked.' She got up then. 'I'll be back.'

When they were alone, Samantha glanced at her nephew. 'Where did you find that wonder of a child?'

'Would you believe on the side of a road?' He saw his aunt's face and grinned. 'I'll tell you the story another day.'

'Dani, my friend,' Veronica said.

'I'm sure she is.' Nicholas told her. 'I will see you downstairs.'

'Nicholas,' Catherine called from the study when he came into her line of vision.

He walked in and stood before her, as she sat in the Queen Anne chair.

'You have no idea how happy you made me today.'

'How is that?'

'Because I am guessing Dani is unlike anyone else you dated before. There is such a contented look on your face that if she can keep it there I already love her too.'

He sat down and leaned towards her. 'Be good to her, and you will discover on your own how wonderful she is.' Then he kissed her cheek and whispered. 'And if you really behave, I may even be tempted to give you grandchildren.'

Catherine's eyes burnt brighter, a broader smile spreading over her face.

Veronica refused to be in her room while Dani was in the house, Samantha had taken a shine to her, Catherine smiled a mysterious smile, and Jonathan thought that Nicholas was just like him, knowing how to pick a good thing when he saw it.

Sams sat in his car opposite the block of flats at what he imagined was a safe distance—lest Dani recognise him or his car—when they arrived Sunday evening. He watched with fervent interest, wondering if that usurper would spend the night. The entire weekend had been a nightmare, and he was more than upset that Nicholas was becoming a real threat. One he had never considered.

He had almost not returned home, as he had promised his mother the previous weekend, then changed his mind. The first thing he did Friday afternoon, which was his habit every time he arrived in Bedfordview, was to drive past the Creswell residence. As he did, he could not help but notice the glaring white Audi R8 in the driveway, and he knew at once whose it was. Now, what kind of man lent a car like that to a woman, unless he knew and trusted her? But worse, perhaps the owner was here as well.

He stared at the first floor windows. David and Carol's room faced the back garden so he couldn't see those lights, but this side showed two bedrooms' lights on. One was Dani's and the other, one of the guest rooms.

His hands cramped on the steering wheel, and he felt the hair on his neck and arms stand on end. He waited until the lights went out, and oddly, the guest switched his off first. Had he snuck into Dani's room? He drove home enraged.

Then, it got worse. He had been at Bedford Centre's Piazza Saturday afternoon when he suddenly saw them come up the escalator. He sat riveted as he watched them go into one of the restaurants across the courtyard, feeling a rushing of blood to his temples every time Nicholas gazed at Dani. When he drove past the house in the evening, the car was still there.

He did some guesswork on Sunday, hung around, and managed to follow them here, finally discovering where she stayed. He should have suspected it; this was after all Anya's place. Seeing Nicholas leave soon after, he tried to follow, but lost him on the highway. Uncertain if they were to see each other again, or if the visit was over for the weekend, he had returned a couple of hours later, so here he sat.

His head hurt, his heart ran a rhythm his coach would find dangerous, and his hands felt clammy and clenched often as he tried to guess at the relationship. One thing gave him confidence; it seemed they had not shared a bed at her parents' home. But that did not mean they were not about to share one here, because the minute he clamped eyes on Nicholas at the restaurant, he knew that was a man of the world, one with a lot of experience, no doubt, and a mile long trail of conquests. Would Dani succumb? She was an illiterate in love, and stood no chance against that man's skill. His mouth felt dry as he imagined Nicholas touching her.

Sams visualised Dani naked and groaned as his body responded. That was the wonder; even a memory did things to him. It always had, even at sixteen. He remembered those times; how excited he became seeing her at school, sharing classes, breaks... He had tried so hard to make her see that they belonged together.

He struggled to understand. She had such a wonderfully open and giving heart, so why couldn't she care for him? But he already knew why. He blew it when he made that incredible mistake after their school dance. He shook himself mentally as he saw Nicholas return to his car and leave. His spirits lifted, this looked promising.

The visit to the house had been successful, Dani was simply a worrywart, and he loved her for it. Yet, she was a happy person. Just as he had always been, except for never feeling satisfaction in his previous entanglements. He sat in his office wondering about the future, but kept seeing his past. He should have conducted some relationships more seriously, avoided others altogether, and been more discerning in general.

A few had pushed, trying to force him into a commitment, but he never budged. Now, he was between two places. The first told him that this was an incredible opportunity. That the odds of randomly meeting someone like Dani were of cosmic proportions and there was only one direction for a relationship like this. On the other side, what if as soon as he satiated his physical cravings, he realised this would not last? He knew he wanted her now, but what if he stopped wanting her.

'Nicholas,' Catherine's voice filtered into his brain. 'Good heavens, Nicholas, I have never seen you this lost.'

'I apologise, but I can't help it, and just wander all the time. Know what I really want to know? Does it stay like this forever?'

'Nicholas, if you think marriage is easy then someone lied to you, and I hope it was not me.'

'You mean what I see is not what is going on?'

'Goodness no,' Catherine sat opposite him. 'The honeymoon wears off and then you see you married a person, not an idea, not the feeling, but a real person who is going to drive you nuts. People never realise that the person you date is not the person you marry.'

'Have you ever been sorry?'

'There were times I felt like packing bags, but, here I am. You remember why you are there, that you made promises, and meant to keep them. But mostly, you remember what brought you together, why you fell in love. So when those times come, leaving must never be the first option. You think alternatives, you talk, and you fight.

'Fight until you feel as if you could kill the other person, and then realise that you cannot because you love them too much. Besides,' she said with a grin. 'Blood on the carpets is so messy. So, after you have thrown your tantrum, the other one has exasperated you beyond endurance, and you feel as if you could not possibly live under the same roof, something happens and one of you breaks, or both. Do you know what happens then? The making up makes you fall in love all over again. You cry, you apologise, you worry, and you do things for each other.'

'Why are you telling me this?'

'Answers are never as straightforward as you imagine. And a simple yes or no isn't always applicable. Know this too, nothing is easy or free. Do you ever know beforehand if it will work? No. The wonder of life is that it's filled with hope, and after that comes hard work. Don't think about what you will get, because you do anyway, think of what you will give.'

'Do you like Dani?'

'I do. And apart from her gorgeous looks, she is level-headed, charming, and very sweet.'

'How does that moment happen, that moment when you just know?'

'Nicholas, you knew the moment you met her, you are just over-thinking things and making yourself scared now. Take a chance, leap into the unknown and she will catch you. Dani will never disappoint you, but hell, you are going to have some fights with that one, and bloodless they will not be. Stick to each other, and that making up will be like heaven all over again.'

He liked the fact that he had always been able to talk to his family. None glossed over, covered up, or pretended. His father and aunt were the same, so if he asked them, he would probably be told the same story three times.

He realised and understood his family's position; everything rested and depended on him, but thankfully, none would ever press him in any direction. He just hoped that he would soon be able to think clearly again, because right now, he had the fuzziest head this side of the Jukskei River. He looked up, going to say some last thing to his mother, but she was no longer there.

The lines had been clearly drawn, it was never to be Sams and Dani, but Nicholas and Dani. Now, it all depended on how Nicholas took his chance and what he did with it.

CHAPTER SEVEN

She was glad she had a foot in the door, but did it have to be in the IT department? Her mind did cartwheels as she drove to her first day of work, but not all were celebratory ones, as she wondered how she could get herself out of a department she had not even joined yet. But when the building came into view, she stopped thinking about such things. It was a cylindrical blue glass marvel. She felt both excited and apprehensive.

Ground floor had reception, showrooms, and a gorgeous store where their Haute Couture shone proudly. She was not sure what departments were where because she had never bothered to ask but she counted another four floors above. Glancing past reception and wide sliding doors, she saw a tranquil courtyard in the centre of the building, the glass roof flooding sunlight in, as if the structure wore a giant hat.

'Hello Simone,' she greeted. 'I'm Dani Creswell.'

Cute blonde prim and proper Simone came running around her workstation, threw her arms around Dani, and gave her a squeeze. 'Thank you for my flowers, it was very thoughtful.' She pointed to the blooms. 'Everyone comments on how beautiful they are and asks where I got them.'

'I'm glad you like them. And I apologise for that day.'

Simone made a gesture with a hand. 'It is gone. So, you're starting today?'

'Mr. Ridley said I should come meet the gang.'

'Do you know where to go?'

There was no board or sign anywhere, how was she supposed to know anything? 'No,'

Simone looked around and beckoned to another young woman. 'Abby, can you stand here while I take Dani to IT?'

Abby made a face but went to stand behind the counter.

'I really want to do this,' Simone said. 'IT is full of guys so I want to see their faces. Of course there is Margot, but she is in her office most of the time.'

They went up two floors, and Dani liked the way one could look into the courtyard from anywhere in the building. Simone stopped outside one of the moon-shaped offices, knocked, and opened the door. 'I have your new recruit here. Can I introduce her to the boys?'

Margot gazed from Simone to Dani. 'You just like to push their buttons, don't you?' She came from around her desk and shook Dani's hand. 'Margot Becker. I wondered when Adam was going to have circulation restored to his brain because we have been waiting for you impatiently.'

'I didn't know he hurt his head as well.' Simone said.

Dani opened her mouth, then glancing at Margot, saw her shake her head.

'Okay, go give the boys a heart attack.' Margot shooed them. 'And I'll be out shortly to show you your place.'

They walked around a curved wall and then there it was. Large desks everywhere, computers on every surface, a room full of men.

Simone had told her that the other side of this floor, past the lifts was HR and administration. Basement was the parking area. Under them, on the first floor, was financial, legal, and restaurant/cafeteria. Above, were the three designing departments. And the top floor had the executive suites and two boardrooms that were the envy of many a larger corporation. It was from there that Samantha, Catherine, and Nicholas reigned supreme.

'Boys,' Simone called.

Work came to a standstill, as all looked their way.

'I have a present for you.' Simone continued.

Dani groaned under her breath. *I had to find a circus ringmaster.*

'Your new colleague, Dani,' Simone announced theatrically.

Dani plastered smile number one on her face and waved. 'Hi guys.' Thankfully, Margot appeared and Simone left them.

At eleven, her phone rang. Seeing the number, she smiled. 'Hello,'

'How are you enjoying your first day?' Nicholas asked.

'Interesting so far,'

'Have any of those men done any work since you walked in, or do I need to threaten them with something?'

She glanced up and saw a few watching her, then, she studied Margot Becker's dress code. *Stick to something similar*, she told herself. 'They will get over it.'

'Do you want to come up for lunch?'

'Is that okay?'

'Do you forget whose company this is?'

'No,' she told him shyly. 'But people might say something.'

'It is not as if we are going to keep us a secret, we'll just not be blatant from the word go. Besides, my mom is here, and she wants to see you.'

'Oh, okay. When should I come, and where do I go?'

'At twelve, come to the top floor and turn right. Go through the double doors.'

When she ended the call, all pretended they had not been listening. She continued her work for another hour and then told them, 'See you later.'

She was barely out of earshot around the curved wall when she heard gasps, whistles, and moans. She shook her head and grinned, men.

'Dani,' Catherine greeted cheerfully and offered her face to be kissed. 'How did you find the room full of boys?'

'Okay, I guess. I did my work and they did theirs.'

'No they didn't,' Catherine laughed. 'They couldn't stop wondering why you are there and when they can ask you out.'

'That is not going to be a happy day for someone.'

'And don't tell Nicholas,' Catherine whispered. 'He will be tempted to punch them.'

'I hope not. I heard you wanted to see me?'

'Yes,' Catherine said and touched Dani's hair. 'I studied metallurgy many years ago, and I have been thinking about starting a jewellery line.'

'That is very nice, but I don't get—'

'The connection?' Catherine finished. 'I have also always liked natural lines and was looking for something inspirational. I looked around the garden, then at some birds, but when I saw you the other day I started thinking. You are soft and feminine, so I would like to use you.'

'I don't know what to say.'

'Then say yes.' Catherine tilted her face. 'You have such gentle contours, I'm getting wonderful ideas.'

'Thank you, I'm flattered.' She had never heard of jewellery designers who did that. Then again, how many jewellery designers did she know?

She realised quickly that two of the guys were interested; best follow Catherine's advice and say nothing to Nicholas because he'd probably threaten to fire them and land himself in all sorts of trouble. She wondered if she should practice a little speech... What if it took them weeks to approach her? Instead, every time Nicholas called, she made sure they got the drift there was someone in her life.

Adam Ridley arrived days later, and as Nicholas had said, with crutches and a sling. How the man managed to move she did not know, but she ran around trying to make his life easier. Not because she was trying to score points, as the guys insinuated, but because she could not watch people struggle. They called her teacher's pet and she ignored them completely. It was all in fun and she liked it.

She eyed the things on her desk, wondering who had brought the sweet offerings. It was Valentine's Day, and naturally, the world went a little crazy. But for her, this was what it was about, chocolate.

She glanced towards Margot, a beautiful woman with a direct gaze that said; *I know things*. That woman was knowledgeable in every manual in the building and Dani truly believed that it was impossible for her to make a mistake. They had started talking on friendly terms, and she was beginning to think that Margot liked her.

A form of friendship was also developing with the guys, and she felt a little sorry for the two who had a crush on her, as her scheme had worked and everyone already knew that she was off-limits.

Simone had somehow made herself her friend, and she didn't mind. Now Simone was an aberration; extremely efficient at her workstation, but shame, both she and Margot realised that she was silly and hare-brained concerning just about everything else. One had to be careful when telling jokes around her; sarcasm and irony were languages from another planet.

Dani perused the cards, squeezed the stuffed bears, smelled the flowers, and leered at the chocolates. She glanced towards Daniel, who was watching Tom stripping something. She wondered what part of the pile was his. Mr. Ridley had made him her first student, and she appreciated that he was very smart. He already had a bunch of accolades in heaven knew what part of IT, so he understood what she explained, he just thought it was girly.

She opened one chocolate heart and put it in her mouth. 'Thank you,' she said aloud so all could hear her. 'Very nice, and you can all come share.' She pointed to the corner of her desk where she pushed everything.

They threw her a glance and grinned, liking it that she hadn't expected anything from them. She also never told them that they swore badly, but once did mention that she thought it a pity that people picked only one word to describe all modes of catastrophe. She grabbed a thesaurus, opened it on a page, and read them a list of words that meant careful. They stared at her then continued with their work, but within a week, there were some creative words flying around the office every time something went wrong.

Her phone rang; she glanced at it and smiled as she answered. 'Hello,'

'Happy Valentine's Day my sweet,' Nicholas told her.

'Thank you, to you too.'

'Do you really believe in this day?' He asked curiously.

'I like the chocolates but otherwise it's just a day.'

'That's what I thought, so, I did get you chocolates. If you come up for lunch, we can have some.'

She laughed. 'Did you get them for me or for you?'

'Both, and they look very nice. I wanted to send them down then thought the guys in the office would feel bad.'

'What kind of chocolates are we talking about?'

'Gorgeous ones, but you can see them just now. I love you.'

'I love you too.' She looked up and saw the guys watching her. 'What?' She grabbed another heart.

So at twelve she left the office, went upstairs, and disappeared down the executive suites.

'Dani,' Samantha beckoned as she saw her. 'Have you seen the jewellery Catherine is working on?'

'No. Apart from the pages she scribbled the other evening when we came to dinner, I haven't seen anything.'

'It's quite unusual.' Samantha smiled. 'Dani, I know that you like Veronica, so may I ask a favour?'

'Of course, anything,' Dani said eagerly.

'If only the world existed of people like you and Veronica. What I need to ask. Would it be possible for you to take her to physiotherapy a few weeks from now?'

'I would love to. Just give me all the details and I will be there.'

'I usually do, but the Cape Town store is going through something and I need to be there that Friday. Catherine or Jonathan do occasionally, but as it happens, they also have something on that day.'

'You don't have to explain, just ask me. I would love to spend time with Veronica anyway.'

'You are the only person who says that and I believe means it.' Samantha told her seriously. 'Are you on your way to Nicholas?'

Dani nodded. 'He said chocolates.'

'Then go, enjoy, and bring me some.'

'I will,' Dani promised and left the office.

The door opened immediately, as if he had been waiting for her, and pulling her into his arms, kissed her thoroughly.

'Oh, thank you, it's beautiful,' Dani exclaimed when she saw the room. He had obviously asked someone to set it out for lunch and she was glad whoever did it had not hung red hearts, streamers, or balloons, as she was not keen on any of those. Then she saw the chocolates. The most exquisitely designed bonbons rested on velvet in a carved wooden box, and she knew exactly what they tasted like because she had had some once before when her father had given her mother just such a box. He was right; she should not take it downstairs.

'There you are,' Bruce, the head graphic designer said as she walked back in. 'Come look at this.'

She stood behind him and stared at the screen. 'What must I see?'

'What kind of designer are you?'

'Fashion,'

'Good,' he did something and a floating naked figure appeared on the screen. 'I need to dress her, but, there is a theme. So how do I cover her in fire without being cliché and having flames all over the place?'

She looked thoughtful for a second. 'When do you need it?'

'As soon as possible, but you have a couple of weeks.'

'Done,' she told him and went to her computer.

She had been working for about an hour when something caught her eye on the screen. It flickered for a second but she knew it had been there. She glanced around, wondering if anyone had seen it or was doing it, but all seemed normal. She went to walk past Daniel. He was busy removing infections, Tom was still stripping things, Jack was downloading something, and Bruce was busy with a backdrop.

Nicholas took her to dinner and dancing at ELLA's. The band was playing love songs and when they started on Take That's Rule the World, she glued herself to his body. He automatically held her tighter, suddenly paying attention to the lyrics. 'Wow, good love song.' He said as it ended.

'It's from Stardust,'

'Is that a film?'

She nodded, pleased he liked it. It was just one of those things. Something didn't have to be the best anything to touch one's heart and she just got that song.

'I have never seen it.'

'Anya has it, we can watch it sometime. I got you something as well.' She announced as they sat in their red velvet booth.

'More chocolates,'

'No. Since I was not around to give you something on your birthday...' She opened her bag and took a gift that said, ball; it looked like a giant sweet.

He unwrapped it and stared. It was a steel sphere with markings on encircling rings, somehow reminiscent of hieroglyphics, and it looked like it could open. He was already fascinated. 'What is it?'

'It's a puzzle. You have to move the whole thing to get to a secret inside.'

Did she know he really liked gadgets? 'Does the secret come with it or does someone put it inside?' He asked curiously.

'You have to open it to find out.'

His eyes shone. 'I really like it. But how did you know what to choose?'

'Well,' she began and her eyes twinkled. 'You do know what a jack looks like, you can draw, you are good with numbers, and very smart. You like cars, and I have been in your office and seen the stuff you have on your desk and shelves. Put them all together and you would be interested in something like this.'

They watched her with interest when she arrived with the portfolio folder under one arm. She had been working on Bruce's fiery dress and an idea was forming.

'Hey Dani,' Jack called. 'Happy birthday,'

She opened her mouth in shock. 'Oh gosh, I forgot.'

'How do you forget your own birthday?' Daniel teased.

'Does that mean we are not getting cake?' Tom asked.

'Are you supposed to?'

'We are men, of course we want cake.'

'Okay, I'll get you some, but where?'

'Where what,' Margot asked.

'I forgot it's my birthday, so no cake; and I don't know where to get.'

'There is a confectionery nearby, it's called Cakes & Bakes. You can order online and they will deliver.'

Dani went to her computer to find the place. She might have blinked but she knew that she had seen it again. She tried a quick track but the snoop was having none of it.

Her phone rang. 'Hello,'

The guys stared at her, already knowing from the way she sounded that her *boyfriend* was calling.

'Happy birthday, sweetheart!'

She laughed. 'I forgot about it and thought my working friends were going to kick me out, so I have ordered cake, and all is well with the world again.'

'Good, but I've decided this. We will leave two hours early today and we can go to your parents, and to mine later.'

'Oh, thank you. But what about—'

'I've spoken to Adam already, it's settled.'

'I'll see you at the flat then.'

Adam arrived and smiled. 'Happy birthday, Dani,'

The guys pretended they were working for three seconds then all looked at her again.

'What?' She asked.

'Can't we meet this guy?' Daniel begged. 'He must be a cool dude if he's got you.'

'He is.' She told them.

'A cool dude?' Adam grinned and pointed with a finger. 'That is something.'

Daniel turned to Adam. 'Do you know the dude?'

'Okay, back to work,' Adam told them, rolled his eyes, and shook his head.

Margot came to Dani. 'Simone says there is something for you at reception.'

'Must be the cake,' Dani grabbed her purse and went downstairs.

Simone pointed to a square carton box. 'It has no from address.'

Dani stared at her for a second then realised what she meant. 'Oh,' she said as she studied the stamps. 'It's from my friend in London.'

'The one who designs for Gurggle?'

'The same.'

Simone handed her a pair of scissors. 'Please open it now.'

Dani laughed, opened the box quickly and lifting the tissue paper, stared. 'Oh my,' Anya had promised that if one of her designs was used in any Gurggle line she would send one. Simone went ballistic and Dani ran upstairs, afraid the crazy woman would steal her dress.

'Wow,' Margot nodded appreciatively when she saw it. 'That is gorgeous.' She looked at the label. 'Double wow.'

'My best friend designed it.'

'Oh yes?' Margot was impressed. 'Like you Dani, not just a pretty face?'

'I suppose.' She took out the note Anya had enclosed and returned to her chair. She had barely sat down when her phone rang again. Recognising the number, she made a face. 'Hello,'

'Happy Birthday, Dani.'

'Thank you, Sams,'

'Are you having a party tonight?'

'No, just celebrating quietly.'

He did not like the sound of that. 'With or without parents?'

She hated his digging, as she was often tempted to lie. 'I am having a belated lunch with my parents.'

'That is nice, can I see you then, I have a gift for you.'

She closed her eyes. 'Thank you Sams but no, I'm going with...' she wondered if he had already snooped enough to know; if not, he was certainly going to now. 'I'm seeing someone, I'm going with him.'

'Ah,' he said without much emotion. 'Then say hi to your parents.'

'I will.' What else was there to say?

They had one of the best late lunches she could remember. Then again, she was hungry, as she had only had a slice of cake at work. She showed them Anya's dress and could see Nicholas inspecting it appreciatively. And, not only did she get a new watch from dad, delicious perfume and stunning jacket from mom. But to top her happy day off, she already had so far thirty-nine messages from Sams. Things like, *he's just hot smoke, he'll never love you as I do, who is he anyway? This is very unfair.* And of course, she would bet anything, he was already digging. Wanting to know who Nicholas was, what he had, accomplishments, schools he had gone to, ad nauseam...

Nicholas also bought a gift.

She stared at the diamond pendant, 'it's so pretty, like my earrings.' She realised. 'Where did you find it?'

'I colluded with parents, so they pointed me to the right store.' He told her. 'May I?'

She turned her back to him immediately, sweeping hair out of the way, while trying hard to stop giving Sams space in her mind, even as her phone buzzed another time. She was now seriously considering changing her phone number.

Nicholas placed the pendant around her neck then brushed his lips on her shoulder. Was there any part of her body that did not turn him on?

She turned around and hugged him. 'Thank you.'

She would probably be just as pleased with a pet rock, he thought.

'Dani,' Carol said when she saw her grab Coco's cage as they were about to leave. 'Do you really want to take her back? Now that you are working the poor darling is always between flats.'

'Huh,' Dani gazed at the little dog metres away playing with Karan. 'You're right, it's not fair, she's more with Mrs. Brown than with me. She should stay with her best friends and have fun all day.'

The Galfreys treated her like a princess and it warmed her heart that they liked her so much. And by now she had turned that darn phone off because she just couldn't take Sams' *good wishes* any longer.

'Come,' Catherine called later and took her to the back of the house where she had a studio. Opening a drawing pad, she asked Dani to tell her what she thought.

Dani gasped enthralled. 'They are wonderful.' She said as she followed the lines of the bracelets.

'Thanks to you,' Catherine pointed to something that resembled a flattish M. 'Do you know where that is?'

She studied the curves and tried to think where something like that was on her body. She looked at one arm, squeezed a hand, and glanced over her shoulder. 'Where is it?'

'It's the line from your shoulder to your wrist. And that one,'

Dani saw a bent T. 'Tell me.'

'Right here,' Catherine placed a hand on her shoulder blade. 'Odd, Nicholas is better at guessing these.'

'What metals are you using?'

'Silver, rhodium, titanium, and palladium, and for contrast I'll use gold.'

'I am thrilled that you see all of that on me,'

Catherine took a box from a drawer. 'Tell me what you think.'

She opened it carefully. It was one of the bracelets; a polished silver cuff with inlaid blue-green stones. 'It is stunning.'

'The first one, and it's yours.'

Her eyes sparkled and danced. 'Thank you so much.'

'I must thank you, because whatever you're doing with Nicholas is making him happy and I have never liked him more, even through his ditzy moments.' Catherine told her seriously.

Dani dropped her head shyly. 'I'm glad it pleases you.'

'It does, but that's quite irrelevant. I am more interested in how you treat each other. Love, respect, and trust one another and you will be fine. Okay, we can go back.'

'There you are,' Samantha said as they entered the sitting room. 'I have heard that you are quite the designer, so I am giving you a gift to show me.' She presented a beautifully wrapped parcel.

'Oh my goodness,' Dani's eyes opened wide as she saw the printed logo on the gift paper. It was from a most fantastic fabric shop in Paris.

'I have had it for a while but never knew what to do with it. You might.'

'Thank you,' Dani held the parcel tightly to her chest and kissed Samantha.

'Dani's birthday,' Veronica said.

'Yes,' Dani nodded. 'When is yours?'

'July,'

'That is a very cold month, so we'll celebrate with marshmallows and cocoa. Did you know that I have a little dog called Coco?'

Veronica started laughing. Everyone stared at them.

Dani made a helpless gesture. 'Did I do something wrong?'

'No, it's just that we haven't heard Veronica laugh in two years.' Samantha told her.

'Oh, then I hope she will laugh again.'

'With you around, I'm sure she will. So, is Veronica's therapy still all right with you?'

'Of course,'

'That reminds me,' Samantha dug in her pocket and took out a remote control. 'So you can come and go as you please.'

CHAPTER EIGHT

She wondered what Daniel meant when he pointed to the screen and said 'ugh.' She pressed a key and couldn't understand it either.

'Actually,' he said suddenly. 'I think I have an idea.'

She was glad he caught on fast, because she wanted to get out of here. Her phone rang. She glanced at the number. What now? She put the phone on silent, got up and went to be busy elsewhere. When she returned there were fifteen missed calls. She shook her head. What was she supposed to do about this? The darn thing started vibrating.

'Hello,' she said curtly.

'Hello, Dani,' Sams greeted. 'How are you?'

'Fine,'

'How is work?'

She disliked it intensely that he took the time to inform himself about her life and that he visited Carol way too often to fish. She was still roiling from his intense pestering on her birthday and she was sorry she couldn't tell her mother not to talk to him. 'I am busy all the time. How is yours?'

'Going well. Listen, Dani, I am actually calling because of work.'

That was a bit different. 'Oh yes?' She was slightly curious.

'I have a work dinner this Friday, sort of a fancy one. So would you be willing to take pity on a dateless friend and go with him?' He had told Robert that he would not, under any circumstances attend that boring do at Harris International but by hell, he would go if he could pry Dani away from Nicholas, even if just for a few hours.

Her heart dropped, why had she imagined that this would be an actual impersonal call? 'Sams, I told you I'm dating.'

'I know, and I'm only asking as a friend.'

'Can I call you back?' This was a waste of time, because the answer was an outright no.

'Sorry to spring it on you at such short notice, as you need to think dresses, shoes, and hairdos. But you have always been great with that stuff and it wouldn't take you that long to throw something amazing together. What time should I come fetch you?'

His arrogance annoyed her infinitely. And his assumption that all he had to do was pick up a phone and command, showed yet again how much disregard he had for her. 'Sams, I don't think—'

'And by doing a friend a favour, maybe we can finally resolve *our problem*.'

She could feel herself shrivelling. Of course he knew how to coerce her, had ever since that stupid dance. 'I'll call you.'

If she told Nicholas, he would say no, not because he wanted to control her life, but because he knew how unsafe she felt with Sams. So why was she even considering it? What if she didn't tell Nicholas, pretended she went somewhere with Simone, did a favour for someone who had once been a friend, and then the whole thing was finished? Was she mental?

'Okay,' Nicholas said as he stared at her plate that evening. 'You have been marching vegetables around long enough, what's up?'

'Can a person be too good?'

She had a knack for asking strange things. 'Dani, what is bothering you? You are jumpy.'

'Sams called.'

'Do I have to beat this guy up before he stops? What did he want?'

'He asked for a favour.'

He watched her. 'Either you didn't like it or I'm not going to like it.'

'How do you just read what's in the air?'

'It is not in the air,' Nicholas reached for her hand. 'It's on your face.'

'I love that you can read me like that.' She dropped her gaze.

'So do I my sweet.' He kissed the tips of her fingers. 'So, back to Sams, what is the favour?'

'There is a thing happening at his work and he asked me to go with him.'

Nicholas let go of her hand and leaned back. What the hell? *She is crazy! I can see she doesn't want to go, yet she is considering it, and I can't stop her.* If ever in his life there was a moment when he wanted to be married, it was right then, because no wife should go gallivanting with another man, for any reason, anywhere, anytime, ever. He shook his head. 'You shouldn't go, but it's not what I think that counts. So, you decide and let me know if we have a date on Friday or if you are unavailable.'

'Nicholas,' she stared at her plate.

'You know the first question you asked? The answer is yes. A person can be too good, and other people just walk all over them.'

She felt like crying. He was not telling her no, she knew she should say no. What was this power Sams had over her? She wasted her time asking because she knew it well, hence why she had never been able to free herself of him, and for that very reason, she had to go, no matter what it looked like to Nicholas.

He took her home soon after, as both lost their appetite. He wanted her to tell him that she wouldn't go, but that wasn't happening. Yet, she was utterly miserable. He felt confused, disappointed, and hurt.

Dani didn't put Skype on that evening, not because she didn't want to see Nicholas—because in fact, she needed him more than ever—but because she didn't want him to see her crying herself to sleep. How could she do this? This was not only shabby behaviour but a betrayal.

At work, she sat silently until twelve that afternoon.

Bruce had obviously had enough by then because he wheeled himself over next to her. 'Dani,' he called. 'Are you okay?'

She nodded without looking up.

'Dani, look at me.'

She did, with tears in her eyes.

'Crap,' he said. 'Sorry, but I can't stand seeing girls cry. Can I help?'

She shook her head and grabbed some tissues to wipe her eyes.

'Dani, I am not trying to get into your pants; I have a girlfriend, whom I love very much. I just want to be your friend. So if I can help, please let me. The other guys too, even if we think you are teacher's pet.' He said jokingly.

The faintest of smiles crossed her lips, but her eyes still refilled.

'We like you a lot and this is not right.' He gestured. 'Is your boyfriend hurting you?'

Dani shook her head. 'No, I'm the one hurting him.' She dropped her head on the desk.

Bruce placed a hand on her back and patted her kindly. 'Go fix it.'

She lifted her head and grabbed more tissues. 'I can't.'

'You mean you've broken up?'

She shook her head. 'I wish I didn't have to do something because I don't want to, but I have no choice.'

'Is he trying to force you into things you are not ready for?'

She shook her head again. 'It's not about that.'

'Have you eaten today?'

'I can't when I'm upset.'

'I suggest you go force something down anyway because you are paper white, then, go get some air, and think carefully about this.'

Grabbing another handful of tissues, she went to the ladies' room to wash her face, then down to the courtyard, not yet ready to eat anything. Sitting on a garden bench, she dropped her head, feeling the misery this thing was bringing her. But how she felt was irrelevant, she cared how Nicholas felt. He was unhappy, or perhaps, raging mad. All the same, she had to fix this, because she had left it far too long already, five years too long.

Nicholas was angry. Not at Dani but at what was making her do something she didn't want to do. It was all over her face, he could feel it, and yet she was not budging from her insane decision. He had hardly been able to concentrate, so he took a walk down to the security room. He asked the man on duty to check some of the cameras but when they got to IT the unfolding scene captivated him. 'Can you make me a copy of this?' He asked.

'Yes sir.'

'Will there be sound?'

'Yes.'

'Does it take very long, or can I get it now?'

'You can have it now, sir.'

On his way back, he glanced towards the courtyard and his heart dropped two floors as he saw her sitting dejectedly, alone, miserable. In his office, he put the CD into the computer. He played it twice.

'What the hell,' he said aloud. No, he did not dislike Sams, he was beginning to abhor him. Realising he had not called her the whole day, he grabbed his car keys, and left.

'Hello my sweet,' he showed her the beautiful flowers he had gone to find, as he stood outside her door.

'Nicholas,' her voice faltered.

He put his arms around her and kissed her gently. 'Dani, I don't care what you do, what I do care about is your wellbeing. So let's not let this stupid thing come between us.'

'Thank you.'

'Have you eaten today?'

'Not really,' she admitted.

'I'm sorry I upset you like that.'

This was her fault, yet, here he stood, apologising for something he had not done. Now, more than ever she needed to do this thing. 'I can make us dinner.'

'I have a better idea, I'll cook for you.'

'Can you?' She asked.

'Quite a few things,' he closed the door behind them, pulled her to the kitchen, and immediately went through the cupboards and fridge. 'Good, you have all the basics.'

'Sure you want to?'

'Yes, and you go do whatever you wish.'

There was only one thing she wanted to do, sleep, because then she didn't have to think. When she opened her eyes, it was past ten o'clock. Sliding from the bed, she went to the sitting room and saw the dining table set. She smiled but she wanted to cry.

Nicholas was on his laptop, glanced up, and rose to his feet immediately. 'Feel better?'

She nodded. 'Did you eat?'

'I was waiting for you.'

They sat at the table silently with that thing between them and neither liked it, but they were not about to mention it because neither wanted to upset the other one.

Nicholas did not stay long after the non-dinner. He desperately wanted to know what this was about, but unless she trusted him, what could he do but wait? But perhaps it was not about trust, because he knew that she did, and that, was one of the scariest experiences he had ever had. When he walked away from her, she never doubted where he was going, or what he would do, as if it had never occurred to her that he might cheat. The amazing thing was that she was right.

After a quick shower, he climbed into bed and turned to look at the pillow beside his. How he wished she were lying here, so he could hold her in his arms, and tell her that everything would be all right.

She had been careful with the dress, making certain there was not a visible inch of skin. If she had to dance, he was not going to touch anything but her hands. She did her hair in a slick ponytail, did not overdo the makeup, and wore no jewellery. She thought she looked plain, but that was because she was used to looking at herself.

When Nicholas arrived to take her to the venue—as she clearly wanted Sams nowhere near her place and didn't want to drive later on her own—and saw her, all he wanted to do was punch Sams' lights out. She looked wonderful in the long-sleeved black gown, and the hair tied back only served to show off the perfect bone structure. Why had he thought that she wasn't sophisticated or classy? She was everything.

He drove her to that fancy hotel, and knowing that she was in one with another man, drove him nuts, as he did not trust that whatever former friend. He climbed out of the car, held her close to his body before kissing her, and saw that look. The one that told him she was so very uncertain how to do this, whatever this was then watched her until she disappeared inside. He stood there wondering what he should do. Did he follow her to see how everything went, hang around, or go home? But if she saw him... he had no choice but to keep quiet and do nothing, for the moment.

'Wow,' Sams said as she reached him and gave her a quick hug. 'You look amazing.'

'Thank you,' *okay,* she told herself, *no more insecure little girl, this ends tonight.*

There was dinner, conversation, and dancing, and she tried to figure out when to bring up the topic. She picked a moment during a dance number he thought was romantic and she detested. 'I need some air.'

They went outside and walked for about three minutes before she broke the silence. 'Sams, we need to talk.'

'I know. Look,' he began as if he were about to start some business negotiation. 'I don't mind if you date other people for a while, we must just draw the line somewhere. Give me a date, and I won't pester you until then.'

Cold showers had nothing on this feeling. 'I don't want to date other people, I only want—'

'Good,' He gave her a pat on the cheek. 'That makes this so much easier.'

What the hell did he think she was? 'Sams, I want to be with Nicholas.'

'I think our communication is not working.' He made a gesture with his hands.

'Yours is not working.' Her temper was flaring fast. 'Mine is working fine and I am telling you I don't want to be with you.'

'Isn't this Graduation all over again?'

'And you didn't learn anything then either.'

'Ah, memories,' he looked up, as if reminiscing. 'Not for you, though.'

Every time she thought about that day anxiety filled her, as she suspected some serious misdeeds. The story he had inveigled sounded feasible, but no one knew him like she did, and contrary to what everyone believed, he was not a nice person, with any type of principles, and there was no better liar.

'Dani, did you ever remember anything from that night?'

'You know very well I don't, and being you, I know it's because of some unspeakable thing you did, but instead of trying to fix it, you make it worse by torturing me.'

'Only because you refuse to accept that we belong together.'

'But I don't want to be with you.' She felt like throttling him.

'Now; because you are all taken with a man who is pampering you. I can pamper you, and probably so much better than he does, if that's what you want.'

'Sams, this is not reality, Nicholas is my reality.'

'You have it all wrong. I have known you longer, loved you longer, I need you, he doesn't. Any woman will satisfy him, not me. There is only you for me.'

How could she get through to him if he refused to accept facts? 'Then this is where we stand. I no longer care if I remember or not, what I do care about is what you did afterwards. How could you undress me and take those pictures while I was unconscious?' Heavens, she had been near madness that day at school when he placed his phone in front of her and she saw pictures of her bare chest. Heat travelled up her face now. How did she get him to delete that garbage from his phone?

Taking the phone out, he pressed two buttons and showed her the screen.

It was worse than she had imagined. There were more, and these were of parts of her body no one had ever seen, in a gadget that could be borrowed, stolen, and manipulated. If only her face hadn't been so visible and recognisable in so many of them... Her ears started ringing and she shook her head. 'Why, Sams?'

'You're the freak-show, who thinks people go around doing good and right. I'm not like you, I do what I want.'

'Oh, I know about that, because no one wraps concoctions in believable lies quite like you do. But we were both sick afterwards so that has muddled me somewhat.'

'It's called laxatives.'

'What?' She wasn't following what he meant now. 'Is it at all possible that you tell the truth just once in your life?'

'Have you never heard of Roofies, Purple, Forget Pill, Black Hole, or Jet?'

She did not like the sound of any of those things, but she recognised the name Roofies. She tried to access her mind; knowing she had heard of it before.

'People call them date-rape drugs.'

Against her volition, she started hyperventilating, feeling so light-headed, she had to sit down and put her head between her legs. 'Please tell me you didn't.' She grabbed her chest. 'Sams, did you rape me?' Looking for a way to deal with something she believed bad, something so much worse had just unravelled itself.

She had hoped that the pictures were the extent of his warped brain that day, which was bad enough. Her aim was to get them deleted from his phone and wherever else he had stored them, because this was Sams. He made copies of everything, knew programming like few, and was a genius at infiltrating and damaging things. She dropped her head again; she was going to be sick, and was. Tears welled in her eyes, 'I implore you.'

'What exactly does one do with truth?' He asked coldly.

Tears slid down as she grappled with the possibility that someone had robbed her of her dignity and choice. 'I don't care what you do with those pictures anymore, send them to my parents, or Nicholas, I just don't care. But please tell me.'

'This purity nonsense you had all your life is crap and what the hell is it worth? And this little outing just told me what I wanted to know,' he smirked. 'You have stuck to your good girl decision otherwise you would already know the truth, wouldn't you? Now, it's all up the air. Oh, by the way, thanks for the evening.'

When Nicholas picked her up, he knew instantly that she was unhappy. Not just unhappy, there was a deep sadness that had not existed before. He did not know what to do and wished she would just let it go as well.

'Water,' she said suddenly. 'Take me somewhere where there is lots of water.'

Nicholas closed his eyes for a second, trying to imagine what could possibly have taken place to make her feel this way. So he drove in silence to the only large body of water he recalled that time of night, the James and Ethel Gray Park.

Taking her hand, they walked to the water's edge. She stood there a minute, staring at its darkness then sat on the grass. He sank beside her.

'Nicholas, you know what you said the other day,'

'I say so many things, but what are you referring to?'

'About walking all over good people. Why do they do it?'

Nicholas took a moment to answer. 'Maybe because good people look as if they can't fight anything. But I know that is not true, their strength is just different. My sweet, what did Sams do to you?'

'Sams is a very mean and self-centred young man. He has put unrealistic expectations in his head and refuses to accept that they will never materialise. I think his father's absence damaged him more than I previously realised. We used to talk as kids, but now I think he needs counselling.'

'Do you think he's dangerous?' Nicholas asked concerned.

'I don't know, because he behaves quite normal most of the time. It's just certain personal things that he doesn't deal well with, and that's what fools people.' She started rubbing her arms.

'Are you cold?' He reached for her.

She let him pull her into his embrace, sitting between his legs as his arms enfolded her, her face resting against his. Right now, it was the safest place in the world.

'Dani, I don't care what you've done before,' he began softly. 'What I do care about is that you are in my life now. So if I can help, please let me.'

'Maybe, but I will let you know.' She snuggled closer to him.

This sounded encouraging, and her voice was slowly changing, as if finding strength and confidence in his very embrace. He rubbed her arms and she tilted her head back against his shoulder.

'Nicholas,'

He had not heard that voice in a little while. 'Yes,'

'May I kiss you?'

He smiled in the dark. 'My lips are yours, do as you will.'

She half turned and covered his mouth with hers. Except for once before, he always kissed her and she adored the way he did, because he made her feel part of him. Now, she wanted to make him part of her. She bit his bottom lip ever so gently, making him open his mouth, and then invaded him. How she loved his reactions to her touch.

She was doing that thing he had experienced only once before. No one had ever kissed him like this, and he knew some masters. But this was not taught anywhere; it was Dani's innocence and inexperience. He felt as if he were about to pass out and moaned, his eyes struggling to stay open as she was taking him some place incredible. He was quite certain he would never kiss another woman again, because he wanted this forever.

Her hands cupped his face and she dropped tiny kisses around his mouth, lightly tugging at the lips here and there. 'Thank you, Nicholas,' she whispered against his face.

He opened his eyes and gazed into hers in the moonlight. 'I love you.'

'I hope you like it,' she said as she dropped her folder on Bruce's desk.

Bruce looked at the page and saw she had labelled the entire design. He said nothing until he read all she had written. 'Looks great, I'll call you when I have a sample.' Then placing the page alongside the keyboard, he sat in front of his computer.

At her desk, she took a hard-drive from a bag. She had loaded a few interesting programmes and today she wanted to see if she could catch the snoop, who was starting to irritate her. The sneak invasion felt a little too familiar, so she needed to make certain before exposing him for the creep he was and teach him that not everything was his playground or wanton pleasure. It took three hours before he appeared. It was fleeting, but she knew he was there and she wondered what it was he was looking for or wanted to prove. The search began immediately, and she hoped she was fast. Annoyingly, he was faster, and then gone.

It was mid-afternoon when Bruce called her. 'Ready? Remember, it will be quite rough, with much polishing needed, but you'll get the general idea.' He played the clip.

Even if rough, she could see it would be amazing.

'You sure have good ideas.' Bruce told her with a happy grin. 'Hey guys, do you want to see it?' And he played it again.

'Wow, that is clever.' Daniel told her proudly.

'What is it for?' Dani asked curiously.

'It's the backdrop loop for the next fashion show.'

'Is it going upstairs for approval?'

Bruce nodded. 'We'll see what they think and if they like it at Monday's meeting.'

'Then please don't tell them I had anything to do with it.'

Friday, Dani took Veronica to therapy and enjoyed chatting with the other patients. She watched what the staff did to Veronica, keeping a close eye on how they touched her. If there was one thing she disliked, it was tough hands on helpless bodies. After therapy, she wondered what they should do and when Veronica pointed at a shopping centre, Dani pulled over, took her to a coffee shop and the two enjoyed waffles. Then, Veronica pointed to a clothing store. In there, she took a liking to a pair of shoes. Dani looked at them judiciously; those things did not look comfortable, especially if they were to be on Veronica's feet.

'I don't think we should get them, they don't look nice.'

'Other shoes,' Veronica suggested.

'Okay, but not in this store, let me show you where.'

Veronica followed her willingly.

By the end of the day, she did not feel well, and lay curled up on the bed as she waited for Nicholas. They were supposed to go out to dinner; she did not see that happening.

'You are so pale,' Nicholas said as he kissed her. 'What's wrong?'

'Veronica and I had waffles, so maybe...'

'I'll call the house and check.' He spoke to his mother for about two minutes. 'No, she's fine.'

'Good, but I'm not,' she went to throw up.

He watched her from the door, then grabbed a towel, wet it, and waited for her to finish. After wiping her ashen face tenderly, he picked her up into his arms and took her to the bed.

'I'm cold,'

Covering her with the throw, he sat on the bed's edge and placed a hand on her face; hot. Grabbing the discarded wet towel, he wiped her forehead. She got up and went to throw up again.

How many times could someone throw up on an empty stomach? Because she had emptied it hours ago, yet she was still throwing up. He made her tea, and that calmed her down for a while. Eventually, both were exhausted and he climbed into bed with her. She started shivering and he held her tight in his arms so she would stop.

Not too long ago, he had spent weekends trolling clubs, enjoying them greatly, and often searching for that thrilling woman. He had found her, for here she was, but not where he had expected. It was the oddest thing; she was as sick as a dog but he could not think of a better place to be.

She fell into a fitful sleep, her face towards his. His hand went to her hair, smoothed it back then touched her cheek. Even in her sleep, she reacted to his touch, immediately drawing closer.

'My love,' he whispered.

'My lo-ve,' she repeated.

Should he call one of their parents, a doctor, take her to hospital, or simply wait? He knew nothing about things of this nature so how did he know what was acceptable or not? His gaze fell on her laptop. Jumping out of bed, he turned it on and looked up everything he could find on vomiting, nausea, food poisoning, and things he was sure he didn't have to be looking at, and discovered that symptoms ran between two and three days.

It was four in the morning and she seemed to have settled down, so he climbed back into bed, wrapped his arms about her, and fell asleep. He woke slowly, and felt the wondrous joy of having her in his arms in the morning. She didn't feel as hot, so the fever was breaking.

She turned slowly and her eyes fluttered open. 'Nicholas,'

'Hello my sweet, how do you feel?'

'Very sore, my head hurts, my eyes burn, and my throat...' she rasped

'It sounds like a menu,' he told her with a smile. 'What do you need to do?'

'I hate feeling dirty.'

'Bath?'

'What if I drown?' Laughter forced her to brace herself. 'I'll shower, just help me up.'

'I don't think you're strong enough.'

'Take me to the bathroom, my head just needs to settle.'

How did she think she could do anything?

'Give me a few minutes alone and I'll see.'

He walked out, closed the door, and wondered what she was doing because he could not hear any bathroom sounds; then, he heard the shower running. He hoped she knew what she was doing, waited twenty minutes then knocked. 'Are you done?' There was no response. 'Dani,' he knocked again. Nothing. Sorry, he had to go in.

His first reaction was to laugh but then realised it was not funny at all. She was standing in the shower in her clothes, obviously been unable to remove them. He turned the water off, grabbed a towel, started drying her, and realised what a ridiculous thing he was doing. After peeling her clothes off, he wrapped her in a bath sheet, lifted her into his arms, and took her to the bedroom.

She couldn't lie in bed with wet hair when she was already so sick, so he grabbed the hairdryer to dry it then helped her into her nightclothes. How could a person become so weak in a matter of hours? He put her to bed and went to make her something she wouldn't vomit. Apparently, she was to stay away from solids. He settled on weak tea again.

She drank slowly, then turned on her side and fell asleep. He needed to go get her some things because he could not play with this anymore. Grabbing a piece of paper, he wrote quickly. Clear juices, sports drinks for electrolytes; dilute them with water, no coffee or anything with too much sugar. Go to the pharmacy...

He went to knock on Mrs. Brown's door, asked her to keep an eye on Dani, and left his number in case she needed to call him. Never did he think that someone could do as much in two hours. He thanked Mrs. Brown profusely on his return and asked if Dani had done anything.

'She became worried and restless when she realised you weren't here, but very little throwing up. I think it's a good sign.' she told him.

'Okay, and thank you so much again.'

It was pretty much a repeat of the previous day, but now, he made her drink just about all the liquids he had bought and the medication the pharmacist had given him. Thankfully, she only had nausea and vomiting, because her body would not have been able to deal with any other punishment.

Saturday evening, he noticed her breathing changed. She sighed and fell into a continuous sleep, did not move, was restless, or sweated. He closed his eyes and drifted into a peaceful sleep.

He could feel he was being watched. Opening his eyes, he found himself under considerable scrutiny. Her beautiful green gaze looked surprised, curious, and quite alert. 'My sweet, you look so much better.'

'I am,' she said in a hoarse voice. 'Was I a very bad patient?'

'I loved looking after you. Have you been up yet?'

'No, I don't know if I'll be light-headed.'

'Probably, you haven't eaten since Friday.'

'I'm sorry about the weekend.'

'What,' he grinned. 'Why wouldn't I want to spend an entire weekend in bed with you?'

A blush coloured her paleness, she tried to laugh and grabbed her stomach. 'Stop it.'

Getting out of bed, he helped her up. 'How do you feel?'

She leaned against him. 'Not great, but I will be able to walk.'

'Is there anything specific you feel like eating?'

'No, just tea.'

They spent the best part of the day in and on the bed; he had brought his laptop so he sat working as she took regular naps. She didn't eat much, just nibbling at things during the day, but she didn't throw them up either so that was comforting. By six o'clock, he could see she was on her way to recovery, and together, they changed the bed as she mumbled about infections and quarantine.

'I think I should stay one more night, just in case.'

'You can,' she told him shyly but really liked the idea.

So did he. The weekend had been a revelation but now that she was conscious and alert, he had no doubt that he was to learn something new again.

'Will you watch a movie with me?' She asked.

'Of course, what do you want?' Going to Anya's TV cabinet, he discovered an eclectic collection.

'Pick something you haven't seen, just not too much gore or I might puke again.'

He smiled. 'Not comedy either, you will hurt yourself. How about this?'

'Stardust,' she went into the bedroom and returned with the fleecy throw. When he sat down, she snuggled against him, covered herself, and said play.

Thirty minutes later, she had lost the fight against slumber, and when that song started, he just gazed at her as the lyrics sank into his heart. Never in a million years would he have imagined himself a romantic. When done, he returned the DVD to the box, switched the TV off, and wondered if he should wake her or simply carry her to bed. Gently, he flicked hair away from her eyes.

She stirred. 'Nicholas,' she called sleepily. 'I need to wash.'

He helped her to her feet. 'Don't be too long otherwise I'll worry. But I have some catching up to do anyway.' He sat at the dining table in front of his laptop, but he could not work, check, or analyse anything. Strange, why hadn't he taken her to his place yet? He knew why, and suddenly, he didn't like it as much either. It had too many memories of other women, and it felt wrong to throw Dani into the same mix. No, he actually didn't like it at all.

When she came out in her cute mid-calf length pyjama pants and loose camisole, he got all hot. She did not have to wear teddies, silks, or slits to turn him on, which he had always got from his sophisticated girlfriends. The money some of those women must have spent on nightclothes. 'You mustn't go to work tomorrow.' He told her.

'My boss might not understand. He'll think I spent the weekend living the good life and now I'm too boozed up to focus on work.'

'What boss are you talking about, Adam or the one upstairs?'

She gave him a lopsided smile. 'I don't know, but I'm much better so I think I'll be okay.'

'Let's wait for the morning, we'll decide then.'

She went to climb into bed, because the idea of waiting for him and getting into bed together was doing peculiar things to her senses. She lay there between the clean sheets looking at nothing, but feeling exhausted. She wondered how many people would believe that Nicholas Galfrey had spent an entire weekend holed up in a flat with a woman, who also happened to be his girlfriend, without sex being involved.

When he appeared in his drawstring pants, his chest made her feel mushy, so she looked away. She imagined it was the equal reaction to what men felt when they saw a good pair of female legs. He disappeared to the sitting room and she could hear he was checking the gate and door, switching lights off, and making sure taps didn't drip. Sliding a little further down the pillow, she was glad Coco was comfortable at home.

'Everything is right.' Nicholas announced as he came into the room and went to his side of the bed. 'Dani, now that you're conscious I can sleep on the couch. You tell me what is acceptable. You know I want to, but I will never force you. And as hellish as it feels, I like the feeling of control I get from restraint. I can't quite explain it, but there it is.'

She loved the fact that he was so honest. 'Get in, Nicholas.'

It was something between a grin and a sigh, and the realisation that she was being a little reckless because she trusted him more than she should. He climbed in, turned to her immediately, and could see she wasn't completely well yet. 'You must sleep,' he caressed her face.

She closed her eyes, loving his touch. 'Goodnight, Nicholas.' No, she couldn't open them again, because if she did...

He woke in the middle of the night, put the soft light on, and gazed at her peaceful face. He wanted to wake her, but she needed rest. He wanted to touch her, but knew he could not. She turned her back on him and pressed herself against his body. He bit his bottom lip and enfolded her into his arms.

She did not go to work on Monday. Nicholas called Adam himself and told him she had been as sick as a dog. She shook her head as she imagined what Adam made of that on the other side.

During the day, she received a bunch of text messages, the guys telling her they missed her but did not dare phone because they didn't want to make loud noises while she slept. She smiled, liking the camaraderie they had built already. Even Simone and Margot sent messages. Perhaps a memo had gone around the building announcing her diseased status.

CHAPTER NINE

She had created a routine; visiting specific sites, making the standard social media pit-stops, and followed a charming fashion blog where she often commented and engaged with other followers. She also made it a point to spend more time on it every Saturday morning, and hoped she had set out the near-perfect bait for the infuriating spy, so when her laptop bleeped, she was hardly surprised. She didn't try to track him down, because she had no doubt his security system was up and running, was of superior quality, and was more than ready to thwart her feeble attempts. That had been her mistake before; he knew when she started the chase, and clearly got his kicks from frustrating her. So today, cool was the order of the day and she wondered if he had any inkling about what she was doing. At twelve o'clock, she activated the implanted tracking device, let it run until the bar turned red, and listened to the whirring sound coming from the hard-drive as the programme did what it was designed to do.

Her phone rang five minutes later.

'What the bloody hell are you playing at?'

'Hello to you too. Did you think I was stupid? You must be careful who you teach stuff to.' Of course it had been him, because who else went out of his way to prove how annoyingly good he was?

Sams was hopping mad. 'Remove that thing immediately.'

'Or what, you spread my pictures all over the Internet? You made the mistake, not me. And now, you can't really blackmail me anymore, can you? Because my dear Sams, I wonder what the police would make of what I got off your cute machine.'

'Okay, fine, I won't release them.'

'Stop pretending, I know you are not going to get rid of them, because they obviously mean something to you. I just want you to put them somewhere where no one else can get to them, and that, is not on your phone.'

'Crap, I never thought you would be able to do that.'

'Do what?'

'That track and lock. I did teach you well. Imagine what the two of us could do together.'

'No thanks, hacking is not really my thing, but you gave me no choice. And, get off Galfrey's system too. It's a criminal offense.'

'Oooh,' he laughed out loud. 'I enjoyed teasing you there, and now I do get your paranoia. Being in a high profile relationship, these pictures should not find their way to the media. I wonder what Nicholas Galfrey or his family would make of them.'

'Go right ahead and see how much I like you then.'

'Are you really choosing him?'

'Sams,' she said patiently. 'Relationships work two ways, not just what one person wants. That is a dangerous place to be in because it's selfish. It's like expecting a flower to grow underground, it's just not possible.'

'Will you take that thing off?'

'And I am never seeing my pictures as wallpaper, or whatever it is people do with that stuff.'

'No, you won't see them.'

'Thank you, Sams,'

'You do know that I love you.'

She hated it when he stirred pity in her heart. 'Maybe you do, but I don't love you so it can't work.' She exhaled deeply, feeling almost dizzy that she had accomplished this incredible feat, because no one knew better than her what an adversary Sams was.

When they were teenagers, she had watched in awe as he just got into places, and not only in South Africa, knowing that if NASA sent a computer to Orion, he would be able to make contact with it. No, people had no idea what kind of brilliance was in Sams' head, and since he was brilliant, he had chosen not to pursue IT. Because that would have exposed him to the world and people would have known his potential. This way, he stayed hidden to do as he pleased. Who would suspect a B Comm. or MBA graduate of being a lethal weapon?

'Dani, this may come as a surprise, but I only consider the battle lost, not the war.'

A shiver ran down her spine. 'What do you mean?'

'Look, I am not going to release the pictures. They are mine and I don't feel comfortable having other men ogling over them. So I will wait for you to come to your senses.'

'I must come to my senses?' She was going to lose it.

'I'm sort of patient when it comes to your little fixations.'

She felt like screaming. 'No, you're putting your life on hold, wasting time on things that will never happen. There are so many wonderful women out there.'

'It's a matter of opinion, isn't it?'

'Sams, I can still tell people about your clandestine activities.'

'You know what, I have something over you, and you have something over me, so that should keep us away from each other for a while. By the way, you'll never be as good as me because you just did the one thing I tried to drill into you, never become distracted. So, I already removed your fancy little thing. And since you decided to start this sparring contest, you have provoked me, so the motto from now on is *may the best mind win*.' He disconnected.

Anger was something she felt regularly when having anything to do with him. So now, they did have a dilemma of a different sort and neither would benefit or lose by harming the other. She went into the files. He lied, he had not only removed what she had pirated, but also a few other things from her laptop. Thankfully, he hadn't accessed the hard-drive. Score one for him, even if she hadn't completely lost either. She kicked her desk. She needed to rethink this.

'Mr. Galfrey, Andrew Lambton is on line two,' his secretary announced.

Nicholas wondered what his friend wanted, as he had not seen him in a while. 'Put him through.'

'Nicholas, are you still alive?'

'Yes Andrew, and how are you?'

'Wondering what the hell happened to you. Where have you been, man?'

'Same place, working,'

'I know where you are during the day, I mean all the weekends. No one has seen you for weeks. And now, there is a rumour.'

'What rumour is that?' Nicholas asked curiously.

'That you have met someone. But I denied it, because if you had, why would you be absent from all the lists and parties? You haven't been sick?'

'No.' Nicholas leaned back in his chair, enjoying his friend's confusion. 'Were you concerned?'

'I didn't know if I should be, and that's why I'm calling. Have you met someone?'

A smile spread on Nicholas' lips. 'Yes, I have.'

'So what the hell... when are you showing her off?'

'Not this one.'

'Why not,'

'Because she's special,'

'Nicholas, they are all special.'

'No, you don't understand. I'm in love with this girl.'

'Did you just say love and girl in the same sentence? And when you say girl...'

'I mean she is younger than all the dates I've had in the past five years.'

'How old is she?'

'Twenty-three,'

Andrew guffawed at the other end. 'Is this a student?'

'No, she's working, right here at Galfrey's as a matter of fact,' and then just to sit his friend in a spin, he added. 'In the IT department,'

'You have got to be kidding me, a geeky nerdy girl?'

'Dani geeky or nerdy, now there's a thought.' He laughed, as he recalled something he had said to Margot.

'You have never dated anyone in your employ, are you sure it's wise? You know what hell can come from this.'

'Come have lunch with me then. You can meet her and tell me what hell I'm about to embark upon.' Nicholas said and grinned to himself.

'Hello,' Dani answered her phone at eleven.

The guys looked up; it was like clockwork.

'Hello my sweet, you're sure it's okay to have lunch with my friend?'

'Of course,'

'And my mom wants to share, as does Aunt Sam. So it is a full and busy table today.'

'That will be nice.' She disconnected then studied the guys, as they pretended to be busy with nothing. 'What?'

'There is a mystery here,' Daniel said. 'You disappear somewhere every day at the same time. Sure you are not a fairy princess?'

Dani laughed. 'That is definitely a new one.'

No one hid anything, it was just that she disappeared into the executive suites and not many people went up if they had no reason to be there, at least not the normal staff, because she did run into the heads of departments often enough. As she walked out of the lift, Samantha seemed to be waiting for her.

'Dani,' Samantha began. 'What did you do with Veronica that she does not want me to take her to therapy anymore?'

'Oh dear, are you very upset?'

'Only if you are going to make me listen to her tantrums,'

'I can take her every Friday?' Dani beamed. 'That will be great. It's a date for the two of us.'

'Really child, if only the world had more of you.' Samantha waved her hand. 'You know, Nicholas always imagined himself quite the playboy, but of course he never measured himself against the one he has in his office today. So you go in there and show Andrew what he should be looking for, not chasing after all those floozies he does so well.'

'Okay,' Dani said with amusement.

Stepping out of Samantha's office, she saw Nicholas standing with a man who looked around the same age. Both turned at her footfall and seeing the ecstatic smile she loved so much on Nicholas' face, she smiled back, forgetting there was a strange man in the vicinity.

Andrew's mouth fell open, then, he tried to pull himself together. 'Holy cow, what kind of women do you employ around here nowadays? I need to have a closer look.'

'Look all you want, but not at this one. And whatever raced through your mind, erase it immediately.' Nicholas took the remaining steps between them, put his arm around her, and dropped a kiss on her lips. 'Andrew, Dani.'

'IT, huh? I am very pleased to meet you,' Andrew shook her hand then turned to his friend. 'No wonder you can't bear to be parted from her.'

'Mom,' Nicholas called as she appeared at the end of the passage. 'Lunch,'

Dani noticed that Andrew cast her many glances during lunch and Nicholas seemed unperturbed. Either, he trusted his friend, trusted her, or was just sure of himself. She could also tell Andrew had already figured out this relationship was different because here she sat, sharing time with family members. Samantha and Catherine left, and she too returned to work.

'Old man,' Andrew told him. 'If there was a woman in Johannesburg for whom you would want to change, it's obviously her. But just as a matter of interest, how serious is this?'

'As serious as you can imagine, or maybe I should explain it because I think there are words you don't know, such as commitment.'

Andrew made a face. 'All those women out there, they are going to be devastated. I can already see it; they will call for a day of mourning.'

'Oh please,' Nicholas laughed. 'Besides, they have you.'

'I saw Laura the other day. She's the one who told me you had met someone.'

'How is she doing?' Nicholas asked but wasn't really interested.

'Pining for you,'

'I'm sorry about that.'

Andrew studied his friend's face. 'I'd say you probably are; but apart from that there is not one woman out there for whom you give a hoot about. And here I thought I would never see the day when you would be bitten by this love bug. How does it feel?'

'I wish it on all my friends.'

'Yup, that is my cue to leave.'

The fashion show drew closer, and everyone, from top to bottom floor, was on edge. Dani knew how the designers felt, the rush that came from getting those garments ready and onto the runway. That was all they lived for now, so although she could not participate, she was thrilled to hear that the executive had liked her idea for the show's backdrop, and that meant one less thing to worry about.

It was an important date on the Galfrey's calendar and she wanted to make Nicholas proud, but as excited as she was about the event, she also felt jittery imagining the clicking cameras aimed at everything that moved.

As the last week dawned, all sorts of problems reared their heads; not least of which was that she had to take Veronica to therapy on Friday. She could not let Samantha down, but definitely never Veronica, who didn't understand breaks in her routine. She was smart, possessed an excellent memory, and loved telling everyone at home about their escapades. She giggled like a schoolgirl when she felt they had been a little *naughty*, was so very happy, and that made the rest of the family happy too.

Nicholas planned to arrive with Dani, as he wanted to make their relationship official and end all rumours, but both Catherine and Samantha said no.

'Unfortunately, there is a price to pay when you're in the public eye.' Samantha said.

'This is all PR nonsense anyway.' Catherine added.

'Besides, Dani would make you late for your own debut, as she'll be with Veronica first, then go home to get ready, and then face the traffic.' Samantha pointed out.

'And as we discussed,' Catherine continued. 'This year, our silver anniversary, we want people to accustom themselves seeing you at the helm. Therefore, you have to stand there alone and open proceedings, not have a gorgeous girl by your side fuelling only keyboards and cameras, and where she came from. As lovely as she is, and not to blame for inane behaviour, she will detract from the seriousness of the business. Afterwards, Sam and I will continue, and you find your Dani and enjoy the show.'

Nicholas felt exasperated. Why he had to do this no one could explain, because whose business was his life but his? But apparently, a demented unwritten rule existed that said successful people had to put themselves in front of the world as if they owed it something. What happened after that... he hoped Dani drew on those strong foundations she had been brought up with because she was going to be grilled by the media zealots.

He had taken some time to choose his words, and it appeared as if they had gone down well, and thankfully the PR gang looked happy. So after doing his bit and handing over to Catherine and Samantha, he went past the IT section and stood around chatting for a while. They stared at him, as if trying to guess what problem he wanted to dig up. But when he asked decent questions and listened with interest at the responses, they relaxed.

He went into the designated room and wondered what Dani had chosen to wear because she had a knack for creative surprises. He waited fifteen minutes. Should he call? No, she was hardly late.

Dani never rushed with Veronica, had limitless patience, and indulged her easily. People stared because they made an odd pair, but it never bothered her. What did they want, to hide anything that did not look how they expected it to look?

She was glad she was going to be slightly late, because taking Veronica to treatment had been the perfect reason for Nicholas to stop feeling guilty. She appreciated it that he wanted her up front and centre, just as he did every day, but the PR team was right, and it was bound to turn into a circus regardless of everyone's intentions. She shivered for a second, perhaps some liked all that attention, she'd be happy without it.

She stared when she arrived at the parking lot gate, there was an endless stream of humanity as far as the eye could see, thank goodness she had a VIP pass and there was a designated parking spot for her, otherwise, she would never get into that building in time.

Oh my, where did she find that? He could swear his eyes were glazing over. She looked stunning in the strapless knee-length high-waist light blue dress, delicately rushed at the breast area, a broad black ribbon tying into a bow to the side. Her feet seemed to float, until he realised the bottoms were transparent, and only the black satin ribbons were visible. She had the earrings and pendant on, and her hair was in that slicked ponytail he found so alluring. He reached out for her immediately. 'You look gorgeous.'

'Thank you,' she smiled. 'How is everything going so far?'

'Except for the occasional, *oh gosh, I forgot...* fill in the blank yourself, it seems to be going well.' He glanced at his watch. 'Let's waste a couple more minutes. Give mom and Aunt Sam time to actually sit down.'

'I have no problem with that.' She half-leaned against him. 'I'm so excited I need to get my breathing rhythm back.'

'Breathing rhythm, huh?' Cupping her face, he kissed her. 'This is worse,' he whispered against her mouth. 'Think you are ready for the relentless cameras?'

'I don't think anyone ever is. You just have to focus on who you are, be polite but ignore them as well. Anyway, let's leave that for later. How are the guys?'

'I went to check on them earlier.' He grinned. 'They looked a little concerned that I stopped there, but then they were okay.'

Her phone rang. 'Hello,'

'Dani, where are you?'

'Daniel?'

'Are you anywhere in this building?'

'Yes,'

'Do you know where the IT section is?'

Nicholas could hear the urgent tone in the male voice. Without a word, he took her hand, and they started the long walk.

'What is happening, Daniel,'

'You know that thing that can happen but you never want it to? It's happening now. Everything was fine this afternoon, we ran it dozens of times, now... And it happened when I went onto Facebook to start posting pictures.'

As they rushed, people started to notice. Most had never seen Dani, so they had no clue who she was, but many a Galfrey employee was stopping dead in his tracks. Arriving in IT, the guys went into a stupor as they first stared at her and then realised why Nicholas was there again.

'Show me,' Dani said and pulled up a chair.

'Do you understand that?' Daniel pointed as stripes flickered across the screens.

'Are we connected to the Centre's system or are we on our own?'

'We're on our own.'

'Good, where is their closest line?'

'Right there,' Bruce pointed.

'Dennis, please go to my car and get my hard-drive. I parked...' She gave quick directions and dug for her keys. 'Bruce, your backdrop and loops, is everything still running?'

'Still unaffected, but when Daniel touched Facebook, they went down, one by one.' He pointed to the four screens.

'Why today of all days?' She asked of no one in particular. 'But why not, megalomaniacs like to shine at the most inopportune times. I need a PC here.' She pointed to where the Centre's connection was. 'Does anyone have a laptop?'

'Mine is that side.' Nicholas told her. 'Be right back.'

'Wow, Dani,' Bruce told her as he rolled up a cable. 'You don't do small stuff. And you look so good together, congratulations.'

'Thanks.' She started pacing then went to Daniel, who was switching things off.

'He's the cool dude, huh?' Daniel grinned.

'Maybe you don't know him like that, but he is. Now explain how it started.'

'A strange icon appeared on the screen and for a second I had no clue what it was. Then it flashed again and I would swear it started taunting me. So I went into the programme.'

Dani made a face.

'Shouldn't have, huh? I know programming back to front, but that was creepy.'

'It was a trap and you had no way of knowing it.' She walked back to Bruce, Tom and Simone, who was the designated landline operator for the evening, keeping track of general queries and complaints.

Simone pointed to one of the dead computers. 'What now?'

'Don't worry yet, we'll fix it. Are you coming back tomorrow to watch the show?'

'Of course, Abby is on duty then.'

'Where is Mr. Ridley?' Dani asked.

'He was searching for Mr. Galfrey, but obviously, we found him first.' Tom piped in. 'And there they come.'

'They nearly thought I was breaking into your car.' Dennis doubled over as he placed the hard-drive in her hands.

'I didn't tell you to run, but thank you.'

'So,' Adam asked. 'What is going on?'

'It seems we have an uninvited guest.' She sat down, as Nicholas had already opened the laptop. 'Do you have any secrets in here?'

'Such as what? But no, nothing, just work.'

She plugged her hard-drive into his laptop and that into the Centre's system. Since their little duel a few weeks ago, she had reformatted it and loaded a couple more goodies she hoped would feel like torpedoes. She started her tracking.

Daniel stood behind her and watched. 'Crap, Dani, where the hell did you get that? Is it even legal in South Africa?'

'What?' Nicholas asked concerned.

'She is using...' Daniel did a funny turn-around and pushed his hands through his hair. 'She is working on a CIA/FBI/NATO programme. We are all going to be arrested.'

'It's not a CIA/FBI/NATO programme, I bought it myself, and I have a licence for it.'

'You have a licence for that? Our Defence Force and Police don't even have that.'

All Nicholas knew was that she was beyond remarkable. His mind wandered. If she had learnt from Sams, then what did he know? Didn't a student always know less than a master? Sure, there was a point, where a student could surpass the master but that took time and he didn't think Dani had reached it yet.

'Found him,' she said.

He placed his hands on her shoulders and squeezed reassuringly.

She typed some gibberish in the black screen then commanded. "GET OFF."

They waited twenty seconds for the reply. "WHY?"

"You are ruining something that does not concern you."

"Make me."

"I can, but I am asking first." She continued.

"You have no functioning hardware, where are you doing this from? Oh, I see it. Smart."

"It's a victory for you, because I am begging." As she said that, she opened another window.

"I know you're doing something; ah, very smart."

"And I'll keep doing it."

"What do you want?"

She typed furiously. "Surrender."

"Hell no, but I'll restore your computers."

Dani motioned to Daniel. "Will they be completely functional?"

"In a couple of minutes. What do I get?"

"I should report you, but all we want is for the show to continue unhindered."

"Fine, but what do I get?"

"NOTHING,"

"So, it's deal time. I want a mention in tomorrow's papers."

"How am I supposed to that?"

"I don't care, just do it. And stop trying to infiltrate me! And just because of your arrogance, because you will never be better than me, I want both Saturday and Sunday newspapers to carry the story."

"And what story is that?"

"How Galfrey's system is pathetic because they were hacked within minutes."

"Are you RSVPeeing your name to us?"

"Funny. I don't care about the wording, just get it right; blah, blah, blah."

Daniel waved from one of the computers, showing the thumbs-up.

"Okay, they are coming on again, get off." Dani wrote.

"Wait, this is an interesting place."

"I am warning you now, get off this computer."

"No, this is really fascinating."

"Get off or I'm sending you the worst Trojan you can imagine."

"You wouldn't dare."

"Says who?"

"I say, because you're a girl. Besides, I can see you; very pretty in that blue dress."

They all started looking around, but there were thousands of people everywhere, how would they find one?

"I want you off here." She typed.

"Going, but don't forget, I will check tomorrow. If it's not there, you may refund all tickets for the next show so long."

She shut down immediately. 'I hope you don't have anything you didn't want people to see, because he has just been through everything.'

'It's only work,' Nicholas helped her up. 'Thank you my sweet.'

'Yes, thank you.' Daniel said. 'Next week, we're going to talk about the things you know. And these illegal activities—'

'Throw me a party instead.'

'Where in heavens name did you learn how to do that?' Adam asked.

'I just picked up stuff that other kids didn't.' She dismissed, a frown spreading across her face. Knowing and proving were two different things, and no one could cover tracks as well as Sams, for she had no doubt, that this had been his little handiwork again. He was relentless, without an ounce of ethics, and pretty much a sore loser.

CHAPTER TEN

They tried to sneak past as many people as they could without looking at them, and hoped to arrive at their seats without a flashbulb going off in their faces. They managed it to an extent.

'You take instructions well,' Catherine smiled. 'You look radiant.'

Samantha nodded recognition, and grabbed one of the chiffon hems. 'Excellent work.'

'Thank you.'

'You made your dress?' Nicholas asked in her ear.

She nodded happily.

'We need to get you out of IT.' He said, meaning it sincerely.

'Look,' Samantha took her hand. 'Bruce outdid himself this year. Such beautiful work.'

The screens had dropped to play the theme and logo between the different lines, and she couldn't wait to see how Bruce had put everything together, because after the executive approved it, she had told him she only wanted to see it again at the show. The naked figure spun towards them, as if it were a satellite, sparkles like fireworks shooting in every direction. As it approached, the dress began to assemble itself in layers, the colour changing from white to blue, the hottest flame. The figure stopped spinning and advanced slowly, the eyes reflecting the intense blue flames.

Dani sat spellbound.

Nicholas pointed to the screens. 'That was your idea, wasn't it?'

'How do you know?'

She would probably have trouble recalling which had come first, the video or the dress, but anyone in design could see they were connected. This was a conundrum. He had just told her that she should get out of IT, now this, not to mention what she had done earlier to save the show. He turned to gaze at her. She was sweet, desirable, smart, and so blooming talented he was having trouble deciding where she should be, but in his life was definitely number one. Without thinking, he leaned over and kissed her.

Just about every flashbulb exploded.

'Heaven help us,' Catherine moaned. 'Nicholas, in view of what we have just witnessed, do you want to be here for the insanity that is surely to befall us after the show?'

He leaned forward in his seat. 'Are you sure?'

'Tell me you want to stick around until two in the morning answering questions.'

'No I don't.'

'Then before the next segment begins, find your way out, run, and go prepare for tomorrow, because they will be back in a larger swarm.'

'When you put it like that how can I not want to stay?' He cast his gaze around the room and he would swear he could only see camera lenses. 'Right, let us prepare for the retreat.'

'We can't, you have to speak to one reporter.' Dani told him.

'What... why?'

'Have you forgotten? There has to be a mention in the papers. We cannot risk problems tomorrow.'

'You have a point there.' Trust her to keep her head about stuff like this. He looked around again, trying to find someone suitable, then, he saw Julia. 'I'll be right back.' As he rose, cameras clicked.

Julia had been watching from across the runway and thinking that she had never seen a more gorgeous couple. Suddenly, she realised Nicholas was walking towards her. He stopped in front of her, and went down to his haunches.

'Hi Julia, enjoying the show?'

'Which one? You poor kids.' She shook her head. 'But the Galfrey collection is fantastic. As for the angel you have over there, how is she handling the circus?'

'Actually, quite well, she is no star-struck, celebrity, I-wanna-be-famous anything.'

'Never was. Can I help you with something?'

'Is John here?'

'No, why do you ask?'

'Because we want to get out of here, but we need one reporter to help. You know how it works; whoever gets the scoop kicks all the others in the teeth.'

She laughed. 'I'm glad that even in love you can still think straight.'

'Oh no, not me, angel over there's idea.' He grinned.

'I love that girl.'

'Me too. So, who can I get involved in this before the show ends?'

Julia looked quickly around then focused on someone. 'This is a rookie at John's paper and they thought they were doing her a favour by sending her here.' Julia waved at the girl.

'She's good?'

'She was our student for a year and then moved to journalism. Brilliant writer, they are just not seeing her potential.' Julia smiled at the girl. 'Pabi, I have a surprise, do you know who this is?'

'Mr. Galfrey,' the twenty-two-year-old Pabi offered her hand immediately. 'What an honour to meet you.' She threw a look across at Dani. 'Your girlfriend is beautiful and so very stylish, I'll wager she's the best dressed woman tonight, and there are some amazing clothes here.'

Nicholas nodded and smiled. 'I want to give one interview, and you are it.'

Pabi almost burst into tears.

'You can do that later. Right now, tell your crew to pick a place, and my girlfriend and I will be there.'

'I don't have a crew, they sent me alone.'

'Fine, let them regret it. Do you know where our IT section is?'

'Yes.'

'Go there.'

They gave Pabi the interview of her life, let the girl click her digital camera in joy as her eyes danced at the sight of Dani's dress, and then mentioned that as with everything of public interest, someone had already infiltrated their system and the team had a few headaches as they scrambled to get it up and running again.

'Why did you think of coming here?' Dani asked, as they stopped at the Botanical Gardens. 'Is it even open?'

'Not after certain times, unless you book it. And I did. It was for after the show, but well... here we are.' He led her down the path.

'Oh, wow, I didn't realise it was so pretty at night, even if it is winter.'

Going around the trimmed but dry hedges, they arrived at the gazebo where they had shared their first kiss. The scent of jasmine permeated the air.

'What are we celebrating?' Dani saw the small table, candles, and flowers.

He smiled, pulled a chair out, and invited her to sit. 'I am trying to be romantic.'

'You are amazing.'

'May you always think so,' he sat across from her.

A waiter appeared with two bowls.

She smiled as she saw the contents. 'Vanilla ice cream with cashew nuts, I love it.'

'Taste it, it's very good.'

She took a spoonful. 'Ooh yes; where did you get it?'

'That is my secret, so, every time you want ice cream you have to ask me.'

They savoured every delicious mouthful.

'I'm glad we left that press mess behind, though I am dying to see the show.'

'Tomorrow, and as mom said, we will be better prepared. Would you like to dance?'

'Really? This place is full of surprises. What kind of music do they have here?' She noticed a speaker on one of the columns.

'Well, only one song tonight.' He got to his feet, took her hand, and nodded somewhere into the darkness.

'Aww, you are romantic.' She said as the song began. The one that articulated so well how she hoped a man would feel about her; and Nicholas understood it. She couldn't help it, so tears started flowing as she pressed herself against his chest. She looked up, thinking she was going to see gazebo, but instead, stars were there because they had somehow danced their way under the sky. She didn't know how it happened but suddenly, both were on their knees, and he kissed her in a way that just finished her.

'You know that you shouldn't trust me, yet you do. You know what I was before, but you don't care. You should be suspicious of everything I do, but you aren't. It is truly as the song says, you saved my soul, and now you can't leave me. I love you endlessly and cannot imagine the rest of my life without you. So my question is this, Dani, would you do me the honour of becoming my wife?'

Her eyes refilled as she nodded and stuttered. 'Wh-at? Oh gosh... I don't know why you picked me, but I am so happy you did. And yes, I want to be your wife.'

'You make me ecstatically happy.' He lifted himself up then helped her. 'I almost forgot.' He stuck his hand in his pocket and pulled out the ring.

She stared, was he insane? 'You could have lost it.'

'No, I had my pinkie in it all the time.' He took her hand and slid it onto her finger.

'I see you like this type of diamond.' She smiled.

'I asked them to make it when I bought that one.' He touched the pendant.

'It's stunning, thank you. But...'

'Oh Dani,' he traced a line down her jaw and smiled. 'What is it you want to know?'

'Huh... well, don't you think it's too soon? That we don't know each other well enough yet?'

He laughed. 'I know all I need to know. You are amazing, wonderful, caring, kind. You have a huge heart for all the important things and I love everything about you.'

'You are right, amidst it all you are a romantic.'

'At least where you are concerned. Want to know when I knew for sure?'

'Yes.' She nodded eagerly.

'When you were so sick and let me stay over. It was...' He took a deep breath. 'I just knew I never wanted you out of my sight. I want to look after you, care for you, to give you everything you will ever need.'

She smiled. 'That is sweet, but you do realise that I'm not really a needy person, right?'

'I know, which somehow makes me want you so much more.'

'Thank you Nicholas, it was beautiful.'

'I'm glad I pleased you. Now, I think we can go thank the good people here who were kind enough to see to a foolish man's idea. And henceforth you are going to use this day against me, aren't you?'

'Only if you forget something important,'

He grinned.

'About tomorrow,' she lifted her left hand. 'It's going to be insane enough as it is, let's leave this for another day.'

'It's all up to you. Would you like me to propose again on Sunday after family lunch?'

He must have enjoyed himself. 'Why not,'

Pulling her into an embrace, he kissed her then let his face rest against hers. 'I want to do everything over and over with you.'

'Nicholas, did you intend to be at the show at all?'

'Of course, but the first day is always for mom and Aunt Sam to shine so I wasn't planning to stick around too long, even if I had to do the opening. And it would have been a normal show if this celebrity insanity was not so prevalent nowadays. Because now they know you are amazingly stylish and they will make your torn jean days hell.'

For someone who had practiced bachelorhood to perfection, shouldn't he be scared, nervous, feel like running, or something equally wild and depressing? Instead, he felt nothing but peace. Recalling how she had plastered herself to him when the music started, he couldn't wait to dance to it again at their wedding. She would look beautiful in white. Would she design her own dress? He glanced at the time… Didn't he have sleeping pills in this place? He was too wound up.

Dani gazed at the discarded dress on the chair, glad she had looked good; she would hate for the future head of Galfrey's being ragged over his girlfriend's dress sense. Stretching her arm out, she studied the ring then reaching for her phone, typed a message, impatient to wait until morning.

Her phone rang.

'Did I wake you?' She asked.

'No. This is so fantastic.' Anya's voice sounded quite clear. 'Am I the first to know?'

'Yes, even before mom.'

'I won't tell.' Anya laughed happily in London. 'I'm guessing you have no plans yet.'

'None whatsoever. Oh Anya, it was perfect, I felt as if I were in a movie.'

'How, when, where?'

Dani laughed and explained.

'That press/media nightmare, but it's the kicker, you also need them.'

'Do you like the place better now?'

'Maybe we do live in a fishbowl in South Africa, but it's one we understand. Here, so many people have already made it so far that they don't care about the little guy. Everything is about beating the best thing that came out last week. Nothing satisfies people anymore. And it's the same with relationships.'

'No men?'

'What are you talking about; I could sleep with a different guy if I wanted to every hour of every day.'

'Do you want to?'

'These famous world places are starting to frighten me. Everything is so casual, so flippant, so gross actually, that I don't want to get mixed up in anything.'

'Well, at least you will have passed the halfway mark one of these days. You do know that I expect you to be my maid of honour, right?'

Anya giggled. 'I hoped, but wasn't sure if you have made some other good friends.'

'There are two for the long term. Margot is interesting, she imagines herself this machine, and I believe it.' Dani laughed. 'And then there is Simone. You can't say anything sarcastic, she simply doesn't get it.'

'I'd like to meet them. Dani, you are making me homesick.'

'I'm sorry. So, if they offer you a permanent position, do you know what you will do?'

'Not yet.'

'You must do what makes you happy.'

'I know. Get to sleep now; you have another show. Are you announcing the engagement then?'

'Are you kidding? It's enough craziness for one weekend.'

'Agreed, and I hate not being there with you.'

'I know, but I want you to design and make my dress, so you will have to come.'

'What about all those stunning Galfrey creations?'

'Oh, they are all very nice, but I still want you to do it.'

'Dani, get your rest, we'll discuss this again.'

'Yes, but start thinking so long. You know me, even my designing style.'

'Okay, and now, congratulations, I love you lots, I miss you lots, and goodnight.' Anya disconnected.

They left early, planning to sneak through the back entrance and beat the media frenzy; it did not work out that way. For reasons that no one understood, this had become a national event.

Carol pressed her nose against the thick glass to look at the entrance. She gasped; it looked like a movie premiere, cameras firmly aimed at one spot. She shook her head, having no idea why the world behaved so oddly.

'I don't know when I signed up for weird, but we will go out, give them fifteen minutes and then get on with it; I'm not giving them the chance to trick Dani.' Nicholas announced as he tried to peer out from a different angle, so they didn't see him.

Carol smiled. 'Don't be fooled, that child of mine has more sense than many people double her age.'

He smiled back. 'I do know.'

There they stood answering questions that had nothing to do with the business they had come for and Nicholas held her hand throughout the invasion of privacy. They asked stupid things, funny things, irrelevant things, and personal things. He answered generally, disclosed one or two *secrets*, and steered clear of the personal stuff. Then, they wanted to question Dani, one particular reporter goading as he suggested Nicholas was chauvinistic for not letting her speak.

Dani squeezed Nicholas' hand this time, knowing that he would rather throw a heavy shoe at the head of said annoying man. He told them they had five minutes.

They asked three questions about fashion then gunned straight for Nicholas' previous relationships. She had not been around then, or knew the names of any of those women, so what was it they expected her to say?

'Okay,' Nicholas said irritated. 'That's a wrap.'

'Just one last question, to Dani,' begged annoying journo.

'Better be a sensible one.' Nicholas warned.

'What is the sex like?'

Dani glared at the man as if he were an escaped mental patient; which he clearly was because who asked questions like that? Was this what the lives of successful people amounted to? 'That, is none of your business.'

Life returned to normal, almost, as now, they had to contend with snoops trying to catch them at all sorts of places. Why they should have become so interesting, neither understood, but there it was.

Nicholas started making regular trips down to the IT department not only to visit Dani but also to chat to the guys.

Now, Margot realised why he had been curious about Dani's pre-employment days. She knew well what he had been like before, so she was often amazed at how dramatically he had changed since January.

Simone lived for drama and romance, this little story was right up her alley. 'Guys, I'm seeing someone.' She announced as the three sat down to share a meal.

'Oh yes?' Margot wondered if it was someone in the building.

'What is knight in shining armour's name?' Dani asked.

Simone regarded her for a second. 'Sam. And,' she told them excitedly. 'He's a rugby player. My mom is so impressed, but my dad...' she squeaked.

Dani felt a strange sensation in the pit of her stomach. *Stop being paranoid,* she admonished herself. *There must be a few men in rugby whose name is Sam.*

'What does he look like?' Margot queried.

'Tall, dark hair, big muscles.' Simone tried to curl a bicep. 'He can pick me right off the floor when I hold onto his arm. He calls me his dumb bell.'

Margot made a sound, Dani started coughing then Margot did likewise. The two had a fit for about a minute.

'Are you dating, or just seeing each other occasionally?' Dani queried as she tried to breathe.

'I don't know.'

'Where did you meet? Did you find him at a rugby match?' Margot asked.

'No, I met him at the fashion show. He stared at me, sort of followed me around for a bit, smiled, then asked for my number. Told me straight he wouldn't call that night, as I would be too tired and he didn't want to keep me up. But that he would call Saturday and if I wanted we could meet somewhere public. When he did, we started chatting, forgetting about the time and it got too late to go anywhere. So he returned to the show to see me again.'

'He sounds okay.' Margot nodded. 'Have you been out with him yet?'

'To the movies, and dinner,' Simone clapped her hands as if she were a seal.

'Do you live alone, with a friend, or still with your parents?' Dani's protective nature rose to the fore.

'Is it very bad if I live on my parents' property? I'm not in the house anymore, I'm in the flat they built last year. My dad is not crazy about women living alone, and likes keeping an eye on me. He says it's okay to share with friends but that alone is risky.'

'It's good that he cares.' Margot told her.

'Do you have pictures?' Dani asked.

'Not yet, maybe soon.'

'When you say rugby player, do you mean amateur level or professional?' Margot was curious.

'Eagles Rugby Club, so I think he's fairly professional.'

Both Dani and Margot nodded.

'Okay gals,' Margot announced. 'I'm riveted, but there is such a thing as work. Dani.'

When they were in the lift, Margot couldn't help herself. Obviously, her mind was still stuck on it. 'Dumb Belle. Does she even get it?'

'Are you two drunk?' Bruce asked as they arrived in hysterics.

Two days later, Margot squealed when she saw the ring then covered her mouth in embarrassment. 'Sorry, but this is exciting,' She squeezed Dani so tight that air was wrung out of her lungs.

As soon as the guys saw it and congratulated her, they wanted to have a party.

'Must everything be a party?' Dani asked with a smile.

'Will cool dude accept e-mails and messages? If we all phone, he won't work today, and we will paralyze either his phone or Galfrey's lines.'

'I'm sure messages are fine.' She told them then turned to Margot. 'I'm going down to Simone. She will die if she hears it from someone else.'

'Dani,' Simone was glad to see her. 'There is something wrong with that computer.' She pointed.

'I'll have a quick look.'

'I can tell you now, that thing is a mess. I think it's some kind of virus so I put it offline already.'

'Good thinking, Simone, thank you. We don't want to send a thing out there from our side. But before I sit down, I want to show you this.' Dani lifted her hand.

Simone screamed, bringing one of the security guards scurrying. 'Sorry, sorry,' she waved a hand. 'I'm just excited.'

'So, I'm engaged.' Dani went to sit by the computer.

'You are going to be the most beautiful bride ever. Have you set the date, picked the dress, anything?'

'We'll sit down soon and see what both of our ideas are. I want this to be our wedding, not my wedding.'

'I actually understand what you're saying. Huh oh, it's bad, isn't it?'

'Quite,' Dani agreed. 'And you're right; it's a nasty virus.' After switching the PC off again, she disconnected all cables.

'What's this?' Daniel asked as the security guard set the tower down on the desk.

'You will never guess what's on it.' Dani told him.

'Something I'd like to see, or something I should run from?'

'Definitely more run away from.'

'Sounds exciting, whose is it?'

'Reception's,'

Daniel took the cables and connected the machine. 'Okay, what do we have here. Holy crap,' he blurted as rows and rows of binary coding ran across the screen. 'Matrix much.'

Dani pointed. 'What I want to know is how it got in.'

'Good question. We have serious security on our system, so this—'

'Is planted,'

'Who would do that? Okay, quite a few people touch it, and probably more than a few flashes go in.' Daniel made a gesture, already lost in his world.

It took him four days to get the memory wiped clean. Millions of numbers multiplied non-stop making it look as if it would never end. Now, he sat loading programmes, drives, formatting, and hoping it all worked again. And he was dying to know who had brought that rubbish into the building.

If Nicholas imagined Dani with a long and ready list of what she had always dreamt about her wedding, he was wrong. She had nothing and refused to do anything without him.

'It's our wedding, not mine.'

'I thought that women liked to take over at this time.'

'Many do, not me. You don't want to be surprised on your own wedding day, especially with things you dislike. You want to know that everything is right, that you helped choose colours, flowers, tablecloths.'

'Yet again, you surprise me.'

'I'm supposed to be preparing for our marriage, not my wedding. That day is merely a celebration; marriage is the important part.'

He studied her for a second. He had seen the very thing she was talking about. Pomp and ceremony for a couple of hours, and then everything fell apart because something did not live up to that one event. How was it possible that he fell in love with her every day? 'Agreed, we'll do it together. And now, there is also something I want you to help me with.' He pulled out a file. 'I'm getting rid of my place and we are finding a new home.'

'Why?' She was surprised. 'I thought you liked it. Though, it is funny, I've never seen it.'

'Precisely, and you are not going to either.' He realised she didn't understand. 'Dani, that place has seen more women than it should have and I'm never taking you there to have a memory of you standing in it. I want a clean place for us, where our memories will be made.'

'Nicholas,' she said with the softest look on her face. 'You have no idea what you have just said. And speaking marriage, would you consider going to pre-marital counselling with me?'

He gazed at her again, thinking there would never be a day when he would not be surprised by something she did. 'I'm guessing you've set your heart on doing this.'

'I know nothing, and the last thing I want to do is start irritating you on our first day of married life.'

'Neither do I,' he admitted and recalled thinking this a few days after meeting her, if not the very first. No, he did not know anyone like her.

CHAPTER ELEVEN

They stood hugging and crying in the middle of OR Tambo Airport.

'I'm so glad to be here.' Anya said. 'Will they think I'm mad if I kiss the ground?'

Dani laughed. 'Probably,'

'Things are a little crazy nowadays.' Anya pointed towards customs. 'They thought I was smuggling the dress in, didn't want to believe I made it. Good I had lots of pictures, and a tonne of pins still attached.'

As soon as they got home, Anya opened the suitcase and draped the dress on the bed.

Dani clasped her hands to her mouth. 'I told you, you would know. But you must rest now; we are going to have a really busy time.'

'Are you off work?'

Dani nodded. 'And Nicholas will take the last week as well.'

'I'm glad you made him participate. I dislike weddings where the groom looks lost. So, what are we doing tonight?'

'Having dinner with the best man, Nicholas wants the two of you to build some kind of rapport.'

'How is this Andrew?'

'Let me start by telling you to tread softly.'

'Warning duly noted. Okay, after my nap, I want to see you in that dress.'

Nicholas came to pick them up, and as soon as he heard her laugh, he knew that he liked Anya. She was sharp with her comments, and quite the smart Alec, but above all, she was exquisitely stylish. Petite, with flowing dark hair, he realised she too had not changed much. At the restaurant, he enjoyed watching the two as they caught up; it was more like watching sisters. Then Andrew arrived.

Anya had obviously missed home because she looked for everything on the menu that made her feel African, including a hugely decadent dessert drizzled with Marula syrup.

'I'm glad you are not driving.' Andrew said suddenly.

'I would have been careful if I were. It's just that I missed everything.'

'How do you find London?'

'Usually with a map, but now people do have GPS.'

Dani knew Anya was trying to annoy Andrew; playing the spaz of their college days. She had always done it if she didn't like someone. Apparently, Andrew was not exactly her cup of tea.

Nicholas hid a grin and thought, *well, my boy, you deal with a smart woman pretending to be daft.*

Later in the evening, after much back and forth silly banter, Andrew looked frustrated. Getting to his feet, he was saying goodnight when he noticed irritating woman eyeing him. 'Can I help you?' He asked rudely.

Anya glanced at her watch. 'Where are you on your way to?'

'To a club, not in London though.'

'If you promise now, in front of witnesses, no funny business and to take me home safely, I'll come with you.'

He almost swallowed his tongue. 'Fine, I promise.'

'Goodnight Nicholas; and I'll see you later.' Anya pecked Dani's cheek.

'What on earth?' Nicholas asked as soon as the two were gone.

'That's Anya for you.'

'It's fascinating to watch such opposites build the most beautiful friendships. The two of you are like night and day.'

Dani had already climbed into bed when Anya arrived, and was neither giggly nor drunk. Not that she was the type either; she merely pretended to be worse than she really was. Disappearing into the bathroom, she returned twenty minutes later in her pyjamas.

'Where did you go?'

Anya settled into bed next to Dani. 'Some La-di-dah club. He's quite the good dancer. What is it about bad men that makes women insane?'

'You like him.' Dani sighed. 'Please be careful, he will tear your heart out without even trying.'

'Oh, I know, but know what I also figured out? If Nicholas could change, there is hope, so I am going to be me without being crazy. Besides, I'm going back in two weeks, I am not in the mood for pining for any man on this side of the world.'

The marquee was set, the chairs were out, flowers nodded gently in the warm breeze, and an army of stewards marched to the orders of the co-ordinator. They had elected for a garden wedding, and what better place than the magnificent Galfrey backyard? It had won many prizes, and both had felt it would have been a travesty to disregard it during such an auspicious occasion.

The street outside had been commandeered for parking, with another army of guards seeing that no alarms went off, lights were left on, and that curious eyes and bodies stayed off the area.

Family from afar chatted, women looked magnificent, the men dashing, and an air of anticipation permeated the air.

Nicholas paced. There was no reason to be nervous, but he was. He couldn't wait to see her, having no doubt that Anya had created some remarkable thing, which had Dani gushing with happiness. But like all things, time arrived, and he stood at the altar with Andrew, and Leon, who had flown in from Canada.

'You look fantastic,' Leon told him. 'I can see nerves, but not the type that want to make you run away. I have never seen you more sure of yourself.'

'Maybe I've misjudged this thing.' Andrew said.

'Maybe we both have.' Leon agreed.

Andrew straightened Nicholas' tie. 'I see musicians moving, so that means your lovely girl is about to come walking up this path.'

If Anya had ever worried that she would never be recognised as a designer, she had wasted her time. Her eye for bodylines was astounding, making a dress look like a second skin on the wearer. There was no froth, huge hoops, or insane sleeves anywhere.

Nicholas swallowed his breath a couple of times; it was as if he were witnessing Dani change from girl to woman right before his eyes.

They struggled through the vows, sending everyone into their tissues, exchanged rings, and Nicholas grinned. He had never worn anything on his fingers so the feeling was quite novel.

After posing, hugging, and kissing, they eventually moved to sit down, but finally, the part he had been waiting for arrived. Taking her hand, he twirled her towards the dance floor, their song began, and her eyes sparkled. Now, he could not wait to see her face when the surprise he and the co-ordinator had concocted, was sprung on her. He held her tight, lovingly, confidently. Then suddenly, the top of the marquee fell open and stars twinkled. He spun her around, as she laughed her pleasure.

They had chosen a boutique guesthouse in Sandton and when they walked into the room, the first thing they did was lean against the wall, sigh, look at each other, and smile.

'How tired are you?' Nicholas asked.

'I'm okay, just need to wash.'

'You go first; do you want anything to eat, drink, chocolates?'

'No thank you. I've had enough of everything.'

'Surely not everything,' he said suggestively.

Her heart pounded her ribs as she blushed and waved him away.

'But while you wash I want you to think about this.' He kissed her slowly, deliberately, lighting the fire.

He sat on the sofa, basking in the searing heat of that kiss. She didn't take long, and he glanced at the delicate white gown, wondering what she had chosen to wear beneath, wanting to go to her immediately, instead, he disappeared into the bathroom.

Coming out in his drawstring pyjama bottoms, he stopped. There she stood in her virginal lace. He went to stand behind her, just out of reach. 'I love you.'

She turned around. 'I pray I am everything you dreamed of, that I will make you happy in every way.'

A tender smile spread on his lips. 'I should be saying those things to you.' He placed a hand on her chin, rubbing gently, then kissed her, making them melt into each other.

Sliding the thin straps off her shoulders, his mouth dropped to her neck, beginning a line of kisses across her chest, experiencing the bliss of having her flesh in his mouth as he spread the flames. He guided her to the bed and gently laid them both down. Propping himself sideways, he fixed the hair away from her face. Could he do this right?

Green pools burnt and begged, her body desiring the satisfaction only he could provide, and obliging, he let the whole of him touch her. Her eyes stretched wide then shut, her hands flayed, grabbed the sheet, and a throaty sound escaped her. Seeing tears, he whispered as he held her tightly to him, 'don't move.' Instead, she tilted backwards, took three sharp breaths, and tears came again. He knew what panic looked like, and this was definitely it. Falling alongside her, he wrapped his arms around her as she sobbed.

He had taken the time to look into the subject, as she had never had sex and he had never been with inexperienced girls, and discovered that there were extremes, from painful with bleeding, to nothing at all, and from minutes to days of recovery. The last thing he wanted was to traumatise her and give her a bad memory.

When hearing of Sams' intentions and likelihood that he had carried out his devious plan after the Graduation dance, sadness filled her, and it had nothing to do with a piece of skin, but that it represented her choice. Considering the possibility that she might have lost it through a contemptible act, committed by someone she had once called friend, was beyond reprehensible.

She had visited her doctor to discuss contraception and been tempted to put her mind at rest, then realised she was becoming morbidly preoccupied. The doctor asked if she had been sexually active, but looking at her and seeing the blush, answered himself that no, therefore, no physical examination today, here are your pills, and go make your husband a happy man, but do come see me when you get back from honeymoon. So acknowledging that she was not to blame for whatever had taken place six years previously, she decided to accept whatever truth revealed itself on her wedding day.

Three things happened simultaneously. First, the startling pain. Second, the realisation that Sams had not robbed her, and third, how sensitive Nicholas was to her needs.

He lay there physically bereft, but his heart so full that he wanted to cry as well, and somehow, through tears and hiccupping, they managed to drift into slumber. Then as if by accord, both stirred.

'I'm sorry,' She told him tearfully, unable to look at him.

He dropped a kiss on her shoulder then turned her slowly. 'Sweetheart, I want you to have a beautiful memory, not one where only I enjoyed myself. And it will be wonderful when you are ready.'

She placed a hand on his face as tears slid down. 'Thank you.'

His heart constricted, and the lungs weren't doing much better either, as he could barely breathe.

'I need a hot bath,' she announced.

He offered her a hand so she could sit up. 'Share it with me.'

'If you want,'

'Of course I want to lie in a tub with you.'

She sat on the bed's edge, having no clue how she was supposed to be feeling. True, that had been an unexpected moment of incredible pain, but she would soon be well and then they would have a normal life. What concerned her was the question doing laps in her mind; how true was everything Sams had told her? But the reality that those pictures existed still spoke of ugly misdeeds and intentions, even if he had not carried out a rape. And those who imagined that only physical contact was an invasion and humiliation did not understand the feeling of damage and destruction in losing the power to self-determine.

She glanced up and saw Nicholas regarding her. Of course he didn't understand what she was going through, he was nothing like Sams, having never forced himself on any woman. These were the surprises of life. Here stood a man who many thought was simply immoral and yet he had never hurt anyone, at least, not on purpose. Sams on the other hand... he had been everything to everyone, so perfect and talented, such an achiever. What a joke. She grabbed at an extra sheet on the bed.

Nicholas knew how this scene would play out, making her feel worse if he did nothing. He strode to the sofa, brought the gown over, and handed it to her. Throwing it on quickly, she rose from the bed, revealing blood smears on the sheet. 'Are you all right?'

'I will be.'

He hugged her. 'I never realised it could look like that. How did you know?'

'That is why we have mothers,' she told him with a faint smile. 'They teach us stuff, in the right order. I didn't know about it either, she told me I should, especially as hotels are so keen on white sheets.'

'Thank goodness she did, it would be most embarrassing explaining to the people here how we destroyed their good linen.'

She lay against his chest, feeling the relief the hot water brought her body. Just because she had never had sex, did not make her ignorant, so his act of sacrifice spoke volumes of what he felt and what kind of man he was. 'We are going to look like prunes.'

'I still love you.' He whispered in her ear.

She half-turned to look at him and he flipped her over, holding her prisoner between his legs. He took her mouth, and knew that her body understood what it wanted, but pain and anxiety would make it completely unyielding, so he merely pulled her back into his arms and held her tight until she was ready to get out.

They flew to Paris.

He chose not to tell her where they were going, as he knew France had been her favourite when she had visited her family the previous year. He booked at the Concorde La Fayette, where they had a grand view of most of Paris and the Eiffel Tower, but both had already seen most of the usual sights, so they stuck to walking the narrow streets, visiting tiny shops, buying baguettes from street vendors, and drinking coffee at corner cafés.

He knew women thrived on the before, the preparation, the wooing and romance, so he made certain he gave her the hugest foreplay run he could. He held her hand, walked with his arm over her shoulder, around her waist, stopped often to kiss or simply look into her eyes, and at night, he held her in his arms close to his body. Something was happening to them, a bonding neither imagined existed, and all without actual lovemaking.

Coming from the bathroom, he saw her standing at the window, gazing at the Eiffel Tower in the distance. He went to stand behind her, just as he had done the previous four nights.

'Nicholas,' she whispered.

'Yes my sweet.'

She turned, placed her arms around his neck, and tears shone in her eyes. 'Thank you for loving me so much that you could wait.'

'I would die for you.'

She smiled. 'That's nice, but rather kiss me.'

He did, his tongue invading her mouth, making them both moan.

'Nicholas, make love to me.'

'Are you sure?'

She nodded.

He picked her up into his arms and took her to the bed, where they finally touched and tasted every inch of skin, where passion and desire were the same.

'Dani,' he murmured, feeling the oncoming delirious rush. Their mouths meeting again as he held her, teaching hers how to move.

There were no more words, only sounds. Her body was out of control, writhing in ecstasy. A smile crossed her face.

The French were right in calling it little death, because that was how he felt as they became one. Then they lay in each other's arms, savouring the feeling of their skins against each other. A few minutes later, he asked. 'I saw you smile, care to tell me what you were thinking about?'

She turned in his arms and smiled again. 'This is the picture I saw the first day we met. Before you suggested going to the Gardens.'

'Ah yes, that incredible day. I saw you and something happened, not least of which was my body going haywire. But you were so shocked, so I had to slow everything down.'

'Do you regret it?'

'No my sweet,' he caressed her face. 'These months of romancing you have been the best of my life, except for making love to you now.'

Nicholas adored watching Dani learn, and he would never be able to explain what it felt like to be the one to teach his own wife. To know that no other man felt what he felt because she had never touched anyone like that. He also knew that he was becoming addicted to her and every moment they held each other, he looked into her eyes and told her so much more than his body ever could. It was truly a journey beyond comparison.

Dani loved everything about Nicholas, his patience, kindness, gentleness, but above all, his lovemaking. For her, he was the perfect man, and not only physically, although that was foremost because she felt a type of crazy. She loved touching him without fear or embarrassment, to show him what she wanted and liked.

When they arrived home, they realised that some parent had been there because the place was dusted, clean, food in the fridge, flowers in bowls, chocolates, and their bed was made.

After their bath, they stood drying each other, finding the experience extremely sensual. Loving kissing, they started immediately then while never letting go of her mouth, he picked her into his arms, and took her to their bed, wanting to imprint this homecoming into his heart.

Life and work became a glorious extension of everything they loved, and both were glad they worked in the same building, because many times, Nicholas would suddenly call her up, and it usually ended in a good session of kissing and lovemaking. Other times, he went down to IT and stole her away. They often went through the emergency stairs, kissing all the way up to his office. Everyone knew, and smiled a knowing smile for both had the wrong scents on. Nicholas was often enveloped in a jasmine haze and Dani carried the smell of leather and moss.

One Friday, they went to check on Anya's flat. They cleaned, threw out old things from the fridge, and sorted the kitchen cupboards. It was past eleven when they finished.

'We should stay, I'm tired.' Nicholas said.

She nodded. 'You can go shower first, I need to pack my sewing machine.'

When they were getting ready for bed, Nicholas took her in his arms. 'Of all the beds, this one drove me craziest. To stand here with you now is like an aphrodisiac.'

'Why?' She asked curiously.

'Because this was the first place and time I chose to not sleep with someone. Then, you were sick and I was in it, falling so in love with you that I felt I was going mad. And you let me sleep with you that Sunday night and I desperately wanted you, but knew I couldn't touch you.'

'You can tonight.'

'I know,' he kissed her slowly, undressed her, and lay her down on the bed. 'How I want you, need you, love you.'

CHAPTER TWELVE

Excitement reigned supreme over the upcoming Galfrey's Social Ball, especially where the guys were concerned. If they didn't think computers, they thought about parties, cars, or girls, and this particular one was all the more special because Galfrey's was celebrating its silver anniversary. This was also the time when most met their colleagues' partners, or co-workers from other departments, and as Dani understood it, quite a few romances tended to sprout this time of year.

Dani dearly wanted to meet Mr. Becker, Margot's husband, properly. She had seen him at the wedding, a dashing forty-year old, but been unable to draw conclusions. What type of man fell in love with a faultless woman, because to Dani, Margot was an Amazon.

Her thoughts wandered to Simone, not liking the little suspicion that lurked at the back of her mind. She had quite forgotten the issue with the excitement of the wedding, honeymoon, and moving into a new place, so when she couldn't push the thought from her mind any further, she typed Sams name into the search bar. She jumped, as if electrocuted. He had joined the Eagles Rugby Club and been in Australia on tour. No wonder she had not heard much from him lately. As if he had been waiting for this very moment, there it was.

"So, you have returned", the message appeared.

"What do you want?" She typed back.

"Don't you feel stupid when you keep asking the same question?"

"Leave me alone, I'm married."

"About that… now that you don't have previous impediment, I expect a taste."

She looked around, certain she understood the text, but not believing she was reading it. "What do you mean?"

"Back to stupid, are we? You never gave me a proper chance, so I expect one now. That is all I ask. No one will know, not even your husband."

"Are you completely mad?"

"I will be if I don't have you."

"NO!"

"I'll delete your stuff from everything."

"NO."

"Perhaps I should ask your husband."

She started hyperventilating.

Daniel turned in his chair. 'Are you okay?'

She got off the page immediately, shook her head, and grabbed her chest.

'Sit down, I'll get you water.' He ran to the water cooler.

Margot stopped beside her. Daniel had probably called her.

'Here,' he placed the glass in her hand.

'What happened?' Margot asked with concern.

Dani couldn't talk, something telling her this was a very dangerous thing in the making. She drank some water, stood to her feet, and felt like passing out. She sat again and put her head between her legs.

'Must we call Nicholas?' Daniel asked.

Bruce came towards them. 'What's up guys?'

'Dani is not feeling well.'

'Maybe she's pregnant.'

The look she gave them could have shrivelled a willow tree in three seconds flat. 'I can't breathe.' She felt as if she were choking. Two and two added to four and she knew that she had it right that Sams was Simone's Sam. How, when, why? She knew some of those answers, but they still did not make any sense.

'Do you have asthma?' Margot asked.

Dani shook her head and thought she was losing her sight; she couldn't focus on anything.

'I'm calling Nicholas,' Daniel was determined.

Dani's hand stopped him. If Nicholas saw her, he would want to know what had brought this on. 'I'm better,' she managed to say, got to her feet, and leaning over the desk, took deep breaths.

'Is she allergic to something, did a bee sting her, or what was she doing?' Bruce asked concerned.

'She was sitting by her computer, and then this.'

'She is breathing better.' Margot said.

'But looks terrible. I think she should go home.' Bruce told them.

'She can't drive like this.'

That morning, she had driven herself because Nicholas had gone somewhere else first.

'Dani, are there bus routes at your new address?' Margot queried.

Dani nodded.

'Then, let me take you home and I'll return with the bus. If I get stuck, one of you is coming to pick me up.'

'Fine, go.' Bruce shooed them both away.

Dani couldn't speak on the way home. She felt confused, and a strange kind of fear.

Margot took her to the door then about to leave, she stopped. 'Dani, what you just went through is called an anxiety attack. Something caused it and if I have to guess, you have never had one before.'

Dani put one finger up, recalling the Harris International do, as she and Margot entered and closed the door. 'Once before, over the same thing.'

'I'm here if you want to talk. Especially if it is something you feel you can't share with Nicholas, or your mom.'

Dani sat down dejectedly then looked up with tears in her eyes. 'How do I explain that I know something terrible is about to happen?'

Margot went to sit beside her. 'You mean something like a premonition?'

'Not exactly, it's about someone I know.'

'Do you want to tell me about it?'

'I must tell someone because I feel as if I'm losing my mind.'

Margot patted her hand. 'Then we can start now, and we'll sit every day and talk about it. It's not healthy if it makes you feel like this.'

'Are you a doctor as well?'

Margot smiled. 'I studied psychology for five years, was all set to become some fantastic analyst, then changed my mind and went climbing mountains.'

Dani was curious. 'What kind of mountains?'

'Let's just say there aren't many left in the world I haven't been to.'

'Kilimanjaro, Everest?'

Margot nodded.

'I was right, you are an Amazon.'

Margot laughed then looked at her watch. 'When is the last bus here?'

'Really late, can I make us tea?' Dani went to the kitchen.

Margot followed her and glanced around. 'It's a beautiful place.'

'Thank you. We had to make many decisions because Nicholas wanted everything.'

Margot nodded. 'I love that about you, stuff doesn't get to you. You improvise and compromise. Which is why, this attack concerns me. You are not one to be moved, so this is something scary to you.'

Dani sat on the kitchen stool. 'It has been following me since High School and I don't know how to get rid of it. Nicholas knows a tiny bit, and has already felt its ugliness. I felt terrible that day, he was so hurt, and I couldn't tell him why or what I was doing.'

'You said it's a person.'

Dani closed her eyes. 'Someone I wish did not exist in my life.'

'Take it slow and start at the beginning, and we will stop when it becomes too much. You won't feel better at first, but you will eventually.'

They spent two hours raking over High School shenanigans and then decided to leave it there.

'I should return to work.' Dani suggested.

'Rather not, stay and rest.' Margot hugged her. 'And tomorrow we will find time to continue.'

Until the Galfrey's Social, they discussed Sams. Dani hid nothing, telling Margot about the naked pictures, and that he had intended raping her after the dance. How he went to her mother to get news, often hacked into the system at work, badgered her about sleeping with him, and that he erroneously believed she would leave Nicholas for him.

'I know what we have here.' Margot announced.

'I don't and it frightens me.'

'We have ourselves a stalker. I have to meet him and see how he relates to Simone, because it sounds like he's getting himself into the inner circle to be near you.'

'I hate causing other people misery, and what is Simone going to feel if he's just using her?'

'See, right there,' Margot said. 'That is part of this anxiety you have been experiencing, you think you are somehow to blame for something. Listen to what I say and believe it. It is not your fault.'

Not only Galfrey's workforce but also a multitude of fashion people, large press and media contingent was at the Sandton Convention Centre. It was a grand charity fundraising event and everybody tried to get tickets. Fashion labels donated gowns from their lines, which auctioned quickly, and by the end of the evening, there was always a small fortune.

Galfrey's appointed a committee that found worthy causes, and the money was spent on doors, windows, bedding, books, children's clothes, and whatever else was necessary. In seven years, twenty places had been brought to functioning independently.

Dani met Mr. Terence Becker, a man who absolutely adored his wife. He was into medical science at the Internations Research Centre, had a bunch of PhD's, and been part of numerous world expeditions, including Antarctica, which was how they had met on the Agulhas scientific ship. Seemingly, Margot had done more than mountaineering; she had also been part of quite a few expeditions herself, as resident counsellor. Margot looked stunning in an evening gown of green silk, and Dani noticed that her husband's eyes sparkled when his hands touched her in any way.

Bruce introduced his girlfriend proudly; Daisy was her name, but any connection to farmland ended there. A tall athletic girl, who oozed self-confidence in her spiked short peroxide hair, she was a personal trainer at a well-known

Sandton gym. In red chiffon, she cut quite a picture as she floated lightly on her feet. Dani wondered if she was wearing her trainers.

Dani's gown was a gift from Nicholas. He had asked Rene Asher to dress his wife. In cream, it sat as well as her wedding gown had, showing off the figure without revealing unnecessary skin. Thankfully, Margot was standing beside her when Simone appeared because when she turned and saw Sams, not even Nicholas' presence could calm the trepidation in her breast.

Realising that indeed it was the vile male, Margot stuck her arm through Dani's, and prodded her so she would stand up straight, while keeping her eyes squarely on Sams. His sexual reaction to Dani was almost instantaneous.

Margot felt her own throat go dry. This did not bode well, as no man wanted to let go of a woman who had that kind of power over him. Now, how did one tell Simone that these two knew each other or present this mess to Nicholas? She knew what he was aware of, which was not much, and he was way too smart to believe Sams' presence coincidental. Dash it all, how did they not antagonise the creep, because she already didn't like him.

So she did the only thing she could think of. Before introductions, she grabbed Simone and Sams, squealed unintelligibly, and dashed them across the hall, leaving her husband with Nicholas and Dani.

'Wow, the rugby hunk.' Margot hoped she sounded like a manic fan.

Simone beamed. 'And this is Margot. You look so pretty. Is that your husband?' She pointed to someone.

Margot turned and gave her husband an enigmatic smile. 'Darling, I got so excited at Simone's gorgeous date that I wanted to introduce him to...' she turned quickly. 'Daniel, the rugby fanatic.'

'That's Tom, and he's right over there. Nice to meet you man.' Daniel shook Sams' hand.

'Tom,' Margot called. 'Meet Sam, an Eagles' player. Okay, mingle.' She made a gesture. 'Sorry darling, but I had to.'

'I saw that,' Terence encircled her waist and took her to the dance floor. 'I also noticed young bride about to faint into her husband's arms. What is going on?'

'Oh, it's a dreadful story and I'm trying to help her retrieve something. Dani and Sams went to school together. She saw him as friend, he saw her as more, and clashing ideas have led to some nasty consequences. So he has stuff he shouldn't have, and we need to get it back.'

'What kind of stuff?'

'I don't know if I'd be breaking her confidence since I'm not counselling her professionally, but...' she whispered into his ear.

'Please be careful, he looks quite capable of hurting her, or you.'

She nodded.

At the other end, Nicholas was wondering what had just happened. Margot might have moved quickly, but something was amiss. He glanced at Dani; she looked as if she had been dipped in ice. 'Are you all right, my sweet?'

'I have a headache.' That was not far off the truth. She had been getting those lately, because she could not stop obsessing.

'Would fresh air help?'

Automatically, she searched for Sams, and found him on the dance floor with Simone, using subterfuge on her oblivious friend. She couldn't continue looking at him. 'Please.'

Nicholas decided to leave the delving for later, but that Margot was embroiled in whatever this was, was pricking his interest.

It wasn't like walking in a garden, but it would do. She breathed in deeply, letting air refill her lungs. 'It's a lovely evening.'

'Yes,' he said and watched some colour return to her face. 'We also have a wonderful Christmas ball before we close at the end of the year. You know how mom and Aunt Sam love evening gowns.'

She shivered involuntarily at the mention of the name. 'Nicholas,'

'Yes my love.'

'Hold me.'

He did, so she would feel safe. Casting his mind back, he tried to pinpoint the moment when she had gone into nervous overdrive. It was when Simone and her date arrived and he doubted Simone was the one making her as jumpy as a kangaroo. He never heard what the man's name was, as Margot had whisked him off with lightning speed. The question burnt his tongue, but instead of asking, he lifted her face and kissed her. Interesting, they were being spied upon. He prolonged the kiss to give peeping tom something to ponder. 'Feel better?'

She managed to smile. 'Yes.'

Margot appeared as if by magic. 'Hello you two, time for dinner. Dani, a trip to the ladies' first?'

Dani turned to Nicholas. 'I'll meet you inside.'

Nicholas watched them go, not liking what he did not know.

'Are you okay?' Margot asked as soon as they were out of earshot.

'No, I'm so angry.'

'Would you like to speak to him one more time?'

'Would it help?'

'I've seen it work before. You badger so long that they simply give up.'

'And how would we accomplishing this?'

Margot looked pensive for a moment. 'I'll get him to dance with me then bring him outside, you just follow.'

'And maybe he'll also tell me what he hopes to gain from misleading poor Simone.'

'That will be interesting. Let's go in and when I see the opportune moment, give me about five minutes.'

'Thank you Margot.'

'What are friends for?' Margot gave her a reassuring hug.

It would have been simpler if Margot was at their table but obviously, there had been other considerations. They shared with Catherine and Jonathan, Samantha, Adam Ridley and his wife, Deborah Potts and her partner, Rene Asher and a model he had invited, and Louis Wilson with his girlfriend. Margot sat a table across and every now and then, she made hand gestures.

Nicholas had caught a few, and wondered what they meant. He also noticed that while Margot spoke to Terence, the man had a concerned furrow across his brow, and intentionally or otherwise, his gaze fixed on Dani. Then he added something but Margot shook her head vehemently, saying not yet.

Nicholas understood this much. Dani was spooked over something or someone and Margot was involved, trying to do something about it. She was roping Terence in and he made a suggestion, which she did not like, and it might have something to do with Simone's date, who, Nicholas believed had been spying on them earlier.

Where is Simone? He located her quickly, and her date. He was handsome in a rugged way, probably in his mid-twenties. If he were smaller, he could easily do modelling work, but he looked like a professional sportsman, perhaps bodybuilding, boxing, or rugby...

What had Dani said about rugby? Ah yes, Sams was a rugby player. He startled himself. Could that be Sams? That would certainly explain Dani's mood. If so, what was he doing here? How did he know Simone? What was Margot's concern? What was Terence suggesting that she disliked so much? Now that he had something confusing racing in his head, he felt so much better.

What's this? Nicholas watched with interest as Margot made a beeline for Simone's date, and obviously asked him to dance because they were on the floor. As he turned to look at Dani, he realised she was no longer beside him.

'Where is Dani?'

'She went to the ladies with my wife.' Adam Ridley said.

Nicholas relaxed.

'I'm going to be a while, so don't wait.' Dani told Gail Ridley and locked herself in a stall. Waiting a few seconds, she slipped out again.

'Thank you for bringing me outside,' Margot said. 'It's quite oppressing in there.'

'Think nothing of it.' Sams told her.

Noticing the flash of cream, Margot announced. 'But I feel better so let me return to my husband.'

'I'll walk you back.'

'No,' Margot placed a hand on his chest. 'I'm quite all right,' she turned from him and walked away.

'Sams,' Dani called before he disappeared inside as well.

He grinned. 'This is a nice surprise. And you saved me time, as I came especially to see you to talk.'

'Don't get any ideas; I'm here for one reason only.'

'Marriage agrees with you, you are looking lovely.'

'Thank you, but...'

'Let me guess, you are about to ask me to delete the pictures again.'

'Yes Sams, that is what I want.'

'You know I don't give anything away for free, so what is your offer?'

She was already upset. 'What is this payment thing? Why do you think the entire world owes you something?'

'If you don't take, no one gives.'

'How did you become like this?'

'I look at life realistically.'

'It's true it can throw us strange things, but it's not all bad.'

'Says Miss Perfect life,'

'Sams, what are you doing with Simone?'

'Are you jealous?'

She chose to ignore the question. 'Do you care anything at all for her?'

'You know I only care for you, but I will continue seeing her. She's not ugly, is quite sweet, and she might actually give me something.'

'Such as what,'

'You are married now.' He lifted his hand to her face. 'Sex makes you glow, I want some of that.'

She gulped, uncertain if he meant sex in general or with her. 'Sams,'

'That is the wonderful thing after the first hurdle; you can do it with as many people as you wish without it showing anywhere.'

'It shows in your soul.'

'Ah yes, your quaint moral concerns. Know what I think? If you were with me I would probably believe it too, because then, I wouldn't need anyone else either, would I?'

'You are never going to get rid of those pictures, are you?'

'I will trade them for something worthwhile, but so far, I have heard nothing.'

'Okay,' she straightened her back and lifted her head proudly. 'Keep them.'

'Just like that, you simply walk away without certainty of my intentions, if I'll share them with anyone else.'

'You promised a few times that you would delete them, it did not happen. You said you wouldn't release them because you like them, now you are backtracking. What I do know is that you lie. Goodbye Sams.'

'Wait,' he grabbed her wrist.

She looked at his hand on her flesh, disliking the contact.

'What do you really want, the pictures, or that I leave Simone alone?'

'Will you do both, or either?'

'Under these circumstances no.' He said and began rubbing her hand with his thumb.

Angrily, she yanked her wrist free, turned, but only managed to crash into him. Her clutch purse cluttered to the ground, falling open, and spilled its contents. As she went down to pick her things so did he.

'Would you ever give up your husband?' He asked as he grabbed the nearest things and dropped them into the purse.

'How do you mean?' She gathered the remaining contents.

'What would be the reason to leave your husband? If he cheated on you, if you didn't get along, if he abused you, if you stopped loving each other, if his life were in danger, to save him... there is a really long list.'

'I will not leave my husband.'

'Never say never Dani, you never know,'

'Goodbye Sams,' she stood to her feet and returned to the ladies' room.

Walking out again, she found Nicholas leaning against the wall.

He noticed the flushed cheeks. 'Are you all right?'

She placed a hand on her temple. 'It's just these headaches.'

'Do you want to go home?'

Absolutely not, she wanted to stay and annoy the living daylights out of Sams. 'I want to dance.'

He grinned. 'I can do that.' Taking her by the hand, he led her to the dance floor.

During one of their rests, Nicholas managed to follow Simone's date to the men's room. He washed his hands slowly then asked casually. 'Enjoying the evening?'

'Yes, thanks.'

'I saw you arrive with Simone but there was no time for introductions. Sorry, wet hands, but I'm Nicholas Galfrey.'

'Sam Strauss,' Sams made a gesture in acknowledgement and a muscle tensed in his jaw.

'What do you do?' Nicholas asked redundantly. Oh yes, he definitely recalled seeing those eyes on Dani's drawing pad once, and they had been awfully angry in that representation.

'I'm at Harris International, and play rugby for the Eagles.'

Nicholas nodded. 'How do you know Simone?'

'I met her at the fashion show.'

'I wouldn't have imagined that rugby players were interested in fashion.'

'Most aren't. But it was something to do.'

'Sams,' Nicholas made sure he heard it right. 'I'm not going to pretend I have never heard of you, and as it happens, they were not glowing reports. So here is a caution, stay away from my wife.'

A vein lifted in Sams' neck. 'How chivalrous, but what is it you think you know about me?'

'Yes, not much,' Nicholas agreed.

'I know Dani very well, and the good girl in her does not babble about anything.'

Nicholas took a step closer. 'Isn't that fortunate for you? But on the flip side of that, I can tell that you are not a good guy.'

'This is merely a fishing expedition.' Sams said disdainfully.

'It was, but I have already caught what I was looking for, so I will bet anything that your arrogance will ultimately bring you down.'

'Are you challenging me?'

'Call it what you will, but know this. If Dani ever cries because of you, you will regret it.' Seeing someone come into the rest rooms, Nicholas nodded at Sams and left him standing in his own fury.

'Where were you?' Dani asked when he stopped beside her.

He gave her a gorgeous smile. 'Would you care to dance again?'

'Yes,' she placed her hand in his and snuggled against his chest.

CHAPTER THIRTEEN

'How do we tell her?' Dani asked with concern.

Margot sighed. 'I'll try, but please help as we go along, and let's hope she understands. But goodness, I hate it too.'

'What if he lied just to rile me up? What if he is sincere, that their meeting was coincidental, that he really likes her?'

'All that could be true, but then he should not like you as much as he seems to. Has he been online?'

'The whole morning, posting silly pictures and comments all over the place, tweeting incomprehensible nonsense. He is doing something, but I'm not sure what yet.'

'Ugh. But now, let us wait for Simone, and simply break her heart.'

They sat stiffly at the table, neither wanting to be there.

'Hi guys,' Simone greeted happily. 'How was that party?'

'Fantastic.' Margot gritted out. 'What did you do after you left?'

'Sam took me home and we sat on the sofa for a while,' she cleared her throat. 'We don't have to talk about that.'

Dani exchanged a concerned look with Margot, willing her to keep on the questioning.

'Simone,' Margot continued. 'You know that we are friends, right?'

'Of course,' Simone nodded.

'Did you sleep with Sam?'

'Guys...' Simone was embarrassed.

'I apologise for being blunt,' Margot said. 'But there is a reason why I ask. I'm guessing you've had sex before so you know what is supposed to happen. Was everything normal with Sam? What I mean is, is he attentive, does he cares for you, is he kind?'

Simone recalled. 'We started kissing, touching, then went to the bedroom and undressed each other. But before it happened,' she looked up. 'There was something strange. He takes his phone everywhere, so he looks at it often. Creepy.'

Margot made a face. 'He looks at his phone while he's trying to have sex?'

'He did put it away before the important part. Then he grabbed a condom, but as he was putting it on, he just came. That's three times in a row, but if you like someone it shouldn't matter, right?'

Dani grimaced.

'And do you like Sam so much that you could live without fulfilling sex?'

'I don't know yet, but it's not always like that, is it?'

Margot gave Dani a cursory glance, an idea suddenly coming to her. 'Tell me, Simone, have you ever seen him take pills?'

'He doesn't take pills, only supplements, he has to bulk up.'

Margot was starting to get a clear picture of what was going on with Sams. Chasing the physique necessary to make it in the competitive world of rugby he had probably started on steroids, possibly still in his teens, the cumulative effect devastating his body as well as its natural functions. Sure, he had reactions, but he could not maintain them, or take them to fulfilment, and the inability to perform normally had him on a wild goose chase. Dani had always been there, he liked her, perhaps even loved her, in his own twisted way, and his body responded appropriately. He needed her to keep functioning. It was girls with eating disorders and boys with body malfunctions.

'Simone, we need to tell you something about Sam. He is actually called Sams and he went to school with Dani.'

'Really?'

'And the bad thing about that is that he is seeing you because he is trying to get to her.'

'You guys lie.'

'We are friends, Simone, and we like you a lot, so why would we do that?'

'But you lie.' Simone became louder and got to her feet.

'Sweetie, please sit, and let us show you.'

Dani pushed the schoolbook in front of Simone and opened to a page. 'We have known each other for a long time.'

Simone paged through, seeing picture after picture of a young Sams, here and there Dani, and then the dance photo. Her eyes filled with tears. 'Why wouldn't someone just like me?'

Margot placed a hand on her hair. 'Oh sweetie, you are a wonderful girl, and you will meet someone who likes you for real.'

'Like where and who,'

'How about in the IT department? All those guys are great and a few don't have girlfriends.' Margot told her kindly, and if she was right, it was either Tom or Jack who had an eye on her, but been stopped cold by Sams.

'So,' Simone sniffed. 'What must I do now?'

'To sort some things out, you should break up with him.'

'Not yet,' Dani said suddenly.

'I thought we agreed that this has to end,' Margot was confused.

'Simone,' Dani continued. 'Would you be willing to help me?'

'You are my friend, Dani, I want to, but you want me to do something to Sam.'

Dani sighed deeply. 'You are right, it's not fair.'

'What did he do anyway?' Simone asked.

'After the dance, Sams took naked pictures of Dani. They are on his phone.'

Simone had a blank expression on her face. 'Are you guys serious?'

Margot nodded. 'Sorry Simone.'

'Then what are you asking of me?'

'Never mind, I opened my mouth before considering consequences.' Dani told her. 'Firstly, it's a waste of time. Delete them, don't delete them, he has them somewhere else. And if you managed it, he might get upset. So I say, scrap this idea, it's just not worth it.'

Simone placed her hand on Dani's arm and smiled. 'I do like him and I hoped we could have gone somewhere with this relationship, but you were my friend first.'

'I'm kicking myself for suggesting it.' Dani said as she and Margot walked away a few minutes later.

'You know what the wonderful thing is about people like Simone? People don't suspect them right away. They have this strange *I couldn't possibly have done it* air about them.' Margot stared at Dani for a moment. 'Are you feeling okay? You look pale.'

'I'm just lethargic, and my mouth feels funny. I think it's the bad taste from this mess.'

So, they thought life was about to become grand? Then let them fall into the lull of stupidity.

As always, she had looked stunning, and his body could not do otherwise but react. He wanted her, needed her, but as he imagined Nicholas touching every pore of that wonderland, he felt an ire he could barely contain. Not even on the rugby field had he experienced such rage, which quickly cemented into firm resolve as Nicholas dared to confront him.

As expected, she was back on her high moral horse, but he had known her too long; she was predictable, and he knew how to use it, against her, to get her. He grabbed his phone and scrolled into the file. Every time he couldn't focus, he needed to look at the one thing that soothed him. 'Where the hell...' He looked properly again, back and forth; it had to be here, but he couldn't find it anywhere. Now who—

Simone!

So much for him imagining her an idiot. Now, this meant what? Did she find them on her own, or had Dani instigated the deed? But would Dani take such a risk? He confronted Simone, thinking she would start crying and tell him Dani had made her do it.

No, Simone said, looking quite confused, why would Dani tell her such a thing? And why would Dani even know about those pictures? She had merely wanted to look at the ones he had snapped at the ball and found that naked woman... It had made her see red. If they were dating, why did he need porn? She had deleted the file without looking at the rest because they were of another woman and she was jealous and upset. If he wanted, he could take some of her and then look at those.

Sams stared at her. Was she pulling the biggest sock over his head or was she serious? Right now, he could not hate his life more.

'Guys,' Simone told them excitedly as they sat down to lunch. 'I did it.'

Margot leaned towards her. 'What have you done?'

'I invited him over, cooked dinner and then when he was in the bathroom, I erased them.'

'Has he realised it yet?' Margot asked with a worried expression.

Simone nodded. 'He knows I did it.'

Dani's hand flew before her mouth. 'Was he angry?'

'We had a blazing row.' Simone announced proudly. 'He threw a fit. Why did I touch his private stuff, blah, blah, blah? So I told him very innocently that I was looking for the ball pictures and found that naked woman. I said I was so upset that I just deleted the file in the heat of the moment.'

'Thank you Simone, but it was a waste of time.' Dani said.

'Wow,' Margot said impressed. 'So, no break up?'

'Why should I?' Simone asked matter-of-fact. 'And this way, I can keep an eye on him.'

'Smart move, sweetie, but please be careful. And if he looks threatening in any way, just end it.' Margot waited until Simone was out of sight. 'How are you feeling today?'

'Am I looking pale again?'

'Yes. Do you feel sick?'

'I'm not sure. Sometimes I feel as if I can't breathe properly, so I get tired.'

'Maybe you should go to a doctor.'

'That's the funny thing, it's not all the time or every day.'

Dani and Margot glanced at each other as the lift went further up instead of stopping at their floor. When it arrived at the top floor, Nicholas stood there waiting for it.

'Nicholas,' Dani smiled as he stepped into the lift and pulled her to him. 'Where are you on your way to?'

'IT, I need to see Daniel about some strange happenings on our systems. It seems someone has been bringing interesting diseases into the building.'

'Reception had one a while back,' Dani announced. 'Where is this one?'

'In Wilson's department, they already lost a bunch of designs.'

'Completely gone or did they have backups?'

'They do have the hard copies, but Daniel and Jack are trying to figure out why it's happening, because it infected quite a few PC's before they managed to switch the others off.'

Arriving on their floor, they walked into the disaster zone.

'Dani,' Daniel beckoned as soon as he saw her. 'Remember previous chaos? This one is so much better.'

'How serious is it?' Nicholas pointed to the screen as numbers ran in all directions.

'Very serious. I have been trying to find its source online,' Daniel shook his head. 'Nowhere, which means it was specifically fabricated.'

'You mean someone made it especially for us?' Nicholas asked.

Daniel shrugged. 'Looks like it.'

Dani went to her computer and sat there staring at the screen. So, he was back to practicing his malevolent ire. She wished she could simply accuse him and that would lead to his arrest, because this was criminal. But knowing and proving were two very different beasts, and no one could simply catch Sams. But worse, she had no doubt poor Simone had brought her infected flash in, because that was his style, he always had back-up plans that often incriminated others. She opened a programme on the side, typed a message, then closed it and went on with other work. Nothing happened for the rest of the day.

Nicholas was developing a dislike for opening his laptop and PC, because every time he did, something happened. Someone was playing with his files, reports, and documents. For a week now, this craziness had been going on and he wondered if it was connected to the other problems they were having. It was exasperating to find and lose files on a daily basis.

He rose to his feet suddenly; needing air. He stopped as he glanced from the top floor down into the courtyard. Dani and Margot were there, deep in conversation. Returning to the PC, he had a message.

"Now that you know I can do anything, I've decided what I want from you." He read.

It seemed an explanation might be closer than he thought. "I can't wait to hear it." He typed.

"I don't think it's a big price to pay but we are all different."

"What do you want?"

"I want to sleep with your wife."

Nicholas stared incredulously. Who was this psycho? "Are you completely nuts, or do you believe that I am?"

"Do you know what I will do if you refuse?"

"I don't care; the answer is still no."

"I'll strip you of everything you hold dear."

"I'm sorry if you saw her picture somewhere and developed a *bond*. The thing is, it's not real." This could easily be some unstable creep. "I don't know in which world you live but in mine, husbands do not *lend* their wives to other men."

"This is news to me. Did you not share just about everything with your friends before, including women?"

"Get off my computer."

"I have money, and I have bought Galfrey shares. I can bring your company to its knees."

"Perhaps, but you will not have my wife."

"Go to today's trading and watch as your stock tumbles."

"Wipe me clean." Nicholas typed as he opened the page. He watched the drop and grabbed the phone on his desk.

'Yes, Mr. Galfrey,' his secretary asked.

'Get me Murray in financial.'

'I don't have to Mr. Galfrey, he's standing right here.'

'Send him in.'

It was the worst half hour. Phones rang all over the building, people came and went from and to offices, and Murray looked as if he were about to have a coronary.

Then, everything returned to how it had been thirty minutes earlier. None of them understood it. Murray called stockbrokers to check. Everything was normal on the floor.

"What the hell?" Nicholas typed furiously.

"That was a mock trade, a game. Deny me and the real thing will happen."

"Come see me face to face, you coward. It's easy to sit behind a desk and make threats, isn't it? And this conversation is over." He switched the PC off.

Dani realised something was happening; all the guys were staring at Bruce's screen. Some expletives and interesting words flew around and she wondered what they were looking at. Some of the phones started ringing.

'Yes, we're watching.', 'Can you believe it?', 'How am I supposed to know?'

As she was about to get up and look, the message appeared. She gave her standard greeting. "What do you want?"

"Are you also watching the financials?"

"What financials?"

"Isn't everyone glued to their PC's? Are you even aware of what's happening to your husband's company?"

A shiver ran down her spine. "What are you doing?"

"I'm bringing him to his knees."

She wanted to cry. "I beg you, please don't hurt him."

"Only if you do what I ask."

Her mouth went dry, her lips drier, she closed her eyes, her hand shook, and now she really felt sick. "Please... not that."

"Yes that. So you see you are the only one who can save the company."

"But what are you doing?"

"I've bought shares, lots of them, so now I can manipulate the market as I see fit."

Tears filled her eyes. "Don't do this to Nicholas..."

"Well, then we know what you must do."

"You can't do this."

"Why not,"

"Because it's wrong," but she knew pleading had no effect whatsoever; he enjoyed toying with people.

"You know; this is the most fun I have had in a long time."

She got off the PC, grabbed her phone, and dialled the number. But he refused to answer. No, no one could torture like Sams.

"So," the message came up on the screen. "Did you enjoy that little game earlier?"

"You're back! Isn't there a place you're supposed to be? Maybe an insane asylum." Nicholas asked sarcastically.

"A sense of humour too, ha, ha. Have you thought about my request?"

"If it's the same one, it's the same answer."

"Aren't you concerned about your people? If you lose the company, they will lose their jobs. I don't think they will appreciate that you had a chance to save them and chose not to."

How did a person reason with this? "Hear me well when I tell you that I will lose everything, employees, friends, and family, before I *lend* you my wife."

"Sounds romantic but it's very stupid."

"You know what's stupid? Some creep asks to sleep with my wife and I'm supposed to agree? I know you from where, why are you obsessed with this, how many more questions must I ask to show you that this is mental?"

"How did you fall in love with her?"

Nicholas stared at the screen. "Why?"

"You fell in love the moment you saw her, and the same happened to me. So what is the difference between us?"

"There's a huge difference, she is MY wife."

"A little possessive are we? But be that as it may, you will eventually agree."

"NEVER,"

"What if I ask her?"

"You will not, do you understand me?" And Nicholas switched the PC off again.

The game of cat and mouse was in full swing. Sams knew that initially neither would want the other to know what he was asking and threatening with. His plan was to drive the wedge that would make them suspicious of each other, and for it to work, he had to make the threats beyond belief. Obviously, Dani knew it was him, but Nicholas hadn't yet caught on, so he wanted to keep it that way for as long as possible.

Every day, he made his presence known to Nicholas and propositioned Dani, and wondered what the mood at home was. Both must be nearing insanity as they struggled with lies, filth, threats, and blackmail. Just the way he liked it. What annoyed him most was that Nicholas was standing firm. He had bought and sold a couple thousand real shares, causing a slight downward shift, but it was having no effect. So far, Nicholas was immovable, therefore, it was time to change the game plan.

'Dani,' Nicholas called as he sat in front of his laptop one evening. 'Do you know what this is?'

She went to look. It was an out of focus picture, and there was no way to tell what it could possibly be right now. 'It's buffering. I'm going to shower, do you want to?'

He looked up at her and grinned. 'Yes please.'

Returning to close his laptop half an hour later, he stopped dead in his tracks as he saw the clear picture. It was a woman's bare chest. Then he froze, knowing that small birthmark very well, as he had been kissing it just minutes ago. 'What the...' He was about to call Dani when a message came up.

"Do you know what your wife is up to when your back is turned?"

"Who the hell are you and where did you get that?" Nicholas typed furiously.

"That would be telling."

"I know people like you, and Photoshop is wonderful."

"These are genuine."

"You have more? I want to see them, now." He felt unwell.

"So you are into pornography."

"I am not."

"I see your point; it's not really pornography if it is your wife. They are coming."

Nicholas waited until the file downloaded and then opened it. His hands flew to his head in disbelief. More pictures of a chest he knew well, and then, worse. These were of her back, legs, stomach, arms... "Where did you get them?" He demanded.

"I still have better, but maybe those will make you really angry."

"What do you mean?"

"You know exactly what I mean. A body has many parts."

Nicholas was raging now, feeling short of breath as he imagined other men gawking at her, lusting after her... "Who are you?"

"Okay, this is what I want to happen—"

"What do you think I'm going to agree to here?"

"Oh, you will agree to my terms if you want to keep your wife's body off the worldwide web, and I mean worldwide."

"When did this happen? I don't believe my wife would pose."

"The how is not important; what is, is what I can do with them."

"I'm going to go ask her to explain."

"The great ladies' man that you are, you believe women? They are full of crap, do whatever they want, and kick us in the teeth, there is not a one who can be trusted."

"I trust my wife."

"Is it? What if I tell you that she and a friend, who is not here, were lovers?"

"That is impossible."

"I'm not talking about a man, because you know very well that she was *pure* on her wedding night."

"Who are you and why are we discussing my personal life?"

"That college friend of hers is quite pretty, isn't she? They decided to stay virgins for men to marry, but both were lesbian sluts."

"I'll never believe it." Nicholas closed the laptop; refusing to look or read anymore. He paced the room close to a hundred times, then, went to look in the bedroom. There she lay fast asleep, her hair spilling onto the pillow, looking sweet and beautiful.

He paced the lounge again. He was angry and confused. Where had those pictures come from, because he could not deny that they were of her body, he knew it too well. There was however something strange about them, but he couldn't put his finger on it just yet. Furiously, he opened the laptop and deleted all the pictures, then, sinking into the sofa, he sat there, staring at nothing.

She came traipsing into the lounge and asked sleepily. 'What are you doing?'

He waited until she was within reach and pulled her onto his lap. 'I can't sleep.'

'I'll make you tea.'

'No, I'm fine now.' With one movement, he rose to his feet while still holding her, and her arms flew around his neck to hold on tightly. She threw her head back and laughed her pleasure as he swung her around. No, she was not what computer man was implying.

'Hello,' Sams greeted. He had wondered how long it would take her to call after that last run with the shares, and the daily badgering must be driving her mad.

'I beg you, stop all of this.'

'Unshakable, unmovable, that's me. One night, that is all I ask.'

'Do you not even realise that what you're asking is morally wrong?'

'Morally wrong,' he laughed. 'I love the way you speak.'

Her mind was in a mess. 'So I can't bribe you with anything?'

'You, bribe me?' He roared louder. 'No, there is nothing I want, except you for a night.'

'And after that...'

He took a few seconds to answer. 'I'll delete all your pictures, return all the shares, and never bother you again.'

'Is that a promise?'

'Are you actually considering my proposal?'

'Only if I see it in writing,'

'You mean a contract? This sounds interesting. How do you suggest we do it?'

She looked around; no one else in the courtyard, she went to sit down.

'So, let us get down to business.'

'Sams, please tell me this is a joke.'

'Oh no, no joke, I want you.'

'One time,'

'One night,'

'One time,' she reached the lift.

'I see this bargaining is going to take a while.' He said in good spirits. 'It's true what they say, huh? Everyone has a price.'

'And I am guessing you know how to write contracts. Write one and email it to me, I want to make sure it's worded correctly.'

'Via email, is my name stupid?'

'You decide because I'm not coming near you without one.'

'I'll see the wording is creative.'

'When would you want to do this?'

'I suppose as soon as possible would be best. Then we can all return to our lives and I will have a memory to treasure. Can I expect you today?'

'Huh, not today,' she needed to think about this, but what did she say? 'You have to prepare, get some romantic things, do the place up, candles, flowers, all the stuff we women like, and don't forget the condoms. Where should we go?'

'Obviously, not to your place. There is mine, a hotel, Anya's place, and there is also my mom's house. As it happens, she is away until next week.'

'Where is she?'

'Durban, she's doing a friend's beach house.'

How was it possible that she was having this loathsome conversation? 'I'll let you know. But Thursday it is.'

'I thought we agreed not to rush.'

She scrunched up her face, certain he was up to something again. 'I want this finished and you have more than enough time to get everything prepared by Thursday.'

'Thursday then,'

'What time?'

'Make it seven in the evening.'

'What must I tell my husband where I'm going at seven?'

'Two in the afternoon then, gives you plenty time to get back home. I'm guessing you are not telling him.'

'And if you breathe a word of this to anyone, but especially Nicholas, there will not be a place where you can hide, do you understand me?'

'Wow, perfectly, so a secret it will be, and your tough attitude is making me hot. Let me know where soon, and I'll go beautify the place.'

Nicholas sat staring unseeingly, then grabbed his jacket, keys, and went down to IT. She sat quietly, also staring out the window, suddenly looking so vulnerable that he felt his heart twist. 'Dani,' he called as he realised she was not aware of him.

She turned. 'Nicholas?'

'I can't work, so I'm stealing you away.' He raised his arm to Adam. 'I'm taking my wife, thank you.'

He took her to lunch, and afterwards to the Botanical Gardens. He just wanted to be in her presence without other people around, or at least with less people. They walked everywhere and then made a pit stop at the gazebo.

Pulling her into his arms, he kissed her; remembering that January day when she entered his life. That kiss had undone him, her sweet innocence knocking him over, which was why he always called her his sweet. Now, she knew some things but she still was that innocent girl, and would always be. How could he consider letting another man touch her?

Dani too recalled, he entered her life and made it complete. That day, he had come in with only one goal in mind but ended up staying. She loved him, adored him, worshipped him, and for all those reasons she could never let anything happen to him, or the company he loved so much. He believed in work, very hard work, so if she had to do this for him, even if absolutely despising it, she would.

'My sweet, what is wrong?' He caressed her pale face.

'Are you also going to tell me that I look sick?'

'Someone has told you already, who?'

'Margot, and the guys today,'

'How do you feel?'

'Tired, and I have a nasty headache, but I know it's stress.'

'What are you stressing about, my love?'

Imagine telling him that beauty of a proposal. 'It's all those weird viruses.'

'Forget those, it will be fixed. And I'll book us some weekend getaways so you can rest and relax.'

'That would be nice.'

Their lovemaking was different that night, an urgency neither could explain filling them, as if they had not seen each other in weeks, Nicholas running his mouth over every bit of skin, feeling as if he needed to assimilate her into himself.

She touched and caressed, as she had never done, tasting his skin and mouth, knowing there was nothing that could satisfy her as well as this, their passion burning and consuming until both were covered in a film of perspiration. Then they fell asleep, wrapped tightly in each other's arms, as if afraid that the other might disappear.

CHAPTER FOURTEEN

Dani awoke early Thursday morning; no, she barely slept, for today, she was to commit the most despicable act of her life. She wondered if what she had been mulling over was enough to get her out of it or if she still had to go through with it, but if Sams imagined her capitulating, he was wrong. She was going down fighting, but the very idea still made her sick. Perhaps that was what everyone saw on her face lately.

She went to work, and sat in silence for about ten minutes, merely staring out the window. She had done that most of Tuesday and Wednesday as well, except for the few things she had actually done on her laptop, which she had brought in to avoid being online on the Galfrey's system and have Sams discover what she was up to.

The guys threw her curious glances, not certain if they should approach and ask or just leave her alone because she was going through something.

Margot also watched and eventually could take no more. She walked straight to her. 'Dani, what is happening?'

Dani looked at her for a moment. 'I'm not completely sure yet, but I will have an answer before this day is done.' She opened her drawer, found paper, and started writing something. 'Does anyone have envelopes?' She asked.

Daniel gave her one.

Dani switched the PC on. 'I'm fine, Margot.' She smiled now.

'Okay, but please talk to me if you need to.'

'Thank you.' Waiting until her friend walked away, Dani slipped the paper into the envelope, and wrote on the outside. Then when she felt no one was paying attention, she grabbed her belongings, disappeared around the curved wall, into the lift, down to reception, and waited until someone arrested Simone's attention. Slipping out of the building, she glanced at the time. All she had to do was hurry.

She has probably forgotten to put it on, Nicholas thought. He had been trying to call her for the past half hour, and still no response. He dialled the landline.

'Hello.'

'Bruce, where is Dani? She is not answering her phone.'

'She's not here.'

'Is Margot there?'

Bruce looked up. 'In her office,'

'Okay, thanks.'

He called down to reception. 'Simone, have you seen Dani?'

'Huh,' she took a moment to answer. 'No.' The truth was, she was uncertain, because she thought she had caught a glimpse of her sneaking out earlier, but she couldn't just say that.

Nicholas got to his feet and went to peek in Samantha's office, then Catherine's. He walked into the boardrooms. He went down to the designing departments and walked through. Then past admin, HR, and down to financial, legal, and looked in the eating area.

Simone stared at him when he stopped at her workstation. 'Are you still looking for Dani?'

'Yes. Just call IT and check if she's there now.'

Simone did. 'Margot, is Dani there?'

Margot looked around. 'No, haven't seen her in a while.'

'Where is she?' Nicholas put a hand to his hair.

Simone took a deep breath and thought that she had better open her mouth now. 'I'm not sure because I was busy, but I think she went out.'

Nicholas stared at her for a second then went to the security guard outside the building. 'John, have you seen my wife?'

'Yes sir, the young madam left.'

'In what? She came with me this morning.'

'I got her a taxi.'

'Did she say where she was going?'

'No sir, she just got in and drove away.'

Nicholas stood there a minute, trying to figure out what she could possibly be doing or where she had gone. He went back into the building and all the way to IT.

'I'm guessing she's not here.'

Daniel looked up. 'Still looking for Dani?'

'What time did she leave, as she is apparently not in the building.'

'Sorry, I didn't notice that,' Daniel said now. 'But something strange happened these past few days, specifically this morning.'

'What do you mean strange?' Nicholas' brow furrowed.

'When she came in,' Daniel pointed to her chair. 'She sat there and stared out the window, as if she was working something out.'

'Are you sure?'

'How can I be sure what she was doing, she was just sitting there.'

'Margot,' Nicholas called as she stopped beside Tom. 'Do you know where Dani went?'

'Did she go somewhere?'

'The guard outside says so.'

'I came to ask what was going on because she was just sitting, but she said something I didn't understand.' She shrugged apologetically.

'What did she say?'

'I asked what was happening and she said *I'm not completely sure yet, but I will have an answer before this day is done*. And then I didn't see her again. Do you know what it means?'

Nicholas shook his head and ran a nervous hand through his hair. 'I'm going home to see if she is there, because she's not answering her phone either.'

He drove home as fast as he could chance it and noticed straight away that her car was gone. He went into the apartment and peered into all the rooms. Everything looked normal. Where was she, because he did not like how he was starting to feel.

Downstairs, he called the security guard. 'When did my wife come to get her car?'

'It was around ten o'clock, sir.'

'You wouldn't happen to know where she was going.'

'No, but she had a small suitcase.'

Nicholas' mouth opened. What could this mean? He ran into the apartment again and opened her closet. He could not remember all her clothes, but it seemed as if a few items were missing. What the hell; where would she go without telling him? He grabbed the phone.

'Hello Nicholas,' Carol greeted.

'Hi, have you seen Dani or have any idea where she might have gone?' He asked.

'No, is she not at work?'

'No, or home, and it seems she took luggage.'

'Whatever do you mean? She can't possibly have gone somewhere without telling you.' Carol didn't like how this sounded.

'Well, she's not here, and I have no idea where she is.'

'She must be somewhere, doing something. I'm guessing you can't get hold of her.'

'I've been trying for ages.'

'We will just have to wait then, what else can we do? I'll also try to get hold of her and then let you know. Are you staying home or going back to work?'

'She left from there, so I'll go back.'

By one o'clock, the sense of dread at Galfrey's was palpable. From top to bottom, no one could work, everyone phoning each other, all trying to remember where they had seen her last, what she had been doing, who she had spoken to...

Simone burst into Margot's office and closed the door.

Margot saw the wild look. 'What's wrong?'

'This,' Simone stuck an envelope in her hand. 'DHL just brought it in, it's addressed to you. It's Dani's handwriting.'

Margot took the thing immediately, tore it open, and casting her eyes over the note, she went deathly pale. 'Oh hell,'

'What does it say?'

Margot's voice shook. 'She has gone to fix this mess all by herself.'

'You mean Sams?' Simone chewed her lips. 'What does she say?' She pointed to the note.

Margot looked at it again.

'Margot,

Tell everyone to stop worrying, especially Nicholas and Simone.

I figured out what to do, I just couldn't tell anyone because you would try to stop me.

This stupid thing needs to be over, once and for all.

Thank you for being my friends,

Dani,'

'Should we tell Nicholas?'

'We have to, or he will go ballistic.'

'About the pictures...' Simone asked nervously.

'No, not that. I wonder where she went, though. Simone, get back to reception and do not breathe a word of this to anyone. I'm going to see Nicholas.'

'Mr. Galfrey,' the secretary's voice called. 'Margot Becker to see you,'

'Send her in.' He looked up as she entered his office.

'Nicholas,' she said. 'Please don't worry about Dani, she is fine.'

He jumped to his feet. 'You have heard from her?'

Margot nodded. 'Yes.'

Nicholas grabbed the phone and pressed repeat. It rang non-stop, nobody answered.

'She didn't call me, she wrote me a message.'

'Where is this message?'

'Huh... she's fine, that is all that's important.'

He narrowed his eyes. 'Margot, what are you hiding?'

'Nothing, so just leave it at that. She's okay.'

'No, no no no,' he waved a finger. 'My wife is doing something crazy, everything is not okay. I also realise that you are close friends and obviously, you do not want to violate her trust, but I can see you know what this is about and it does not look like a good thing to me. And why didn't you tell me this earlier when I was in IT?'

'I still don't know where she has gone, she just said she's fine and that we should stop worrying.'

'Can I see the message?'

'I'd prefer you didn't.' If she could keep his mind at peace but oblivious to the pictures, then she would have helped her friend right.

'This is my wife we are talking about, if she is in trouble I want to know.'

He had a point because heaven knew what kind of plan Dani thought she had. What if it backfired?

Nicholas' phone rang. 'Dani, where the hell are you,' he said angrily as relief flooded him. 'What are you doing?'

'I'm sorry Nicholas, but I have to.' She had meant not to call him until this insanity was over, but just hearing his voice was giving her the courage she needed.

Nicholas' gaze fixed on Margot's face. 'You have upset us all; Margot is standing in my office with tears in her eyes, trying to hide what you are doing but by hell I'm going to wring it out of her.'

Margot turned. If that wasn't a clue to get out of there then she was daft.

'Nicholas, please don't make her do anything, because she doesn't know what I am doing. When everything is over, I will explain.'

'Where do you think you are going?' Nicholas walked across quickly and put his back against the door. 'Right,' he said into the phone. 'Now, between the two of you I am getting an answer.'

Margot's phone rang. 'Can I answer it?'

He made a gesture to go ahead.

'Margot, something terrible is happening,' Simone spoke too quickly. 'Sams just called me, he's looking for Dani too. She was supposed to meet him at two for something but didn't turn up. What must I tell him?'

Nicholas was studying Margot as she listened, the look of dread on her face was quite something to behold.

'Huh, give me a minute, I'll be right there.' She ended the call. 'Nicholas I have to go.'

'Not before you tell me what is going on.' He spoke loud so Dani could hear it, then realised she had cut him off. He was raging. 'Do you love your husband?'

'Of course I love my husband.'

'Then, explain to me how I feel.'

'That's just it Nicholas, it is because of love that we do things like this. Please let me go, I need to help with something.'

'Who was on the phone, and don't lie because I saw that whole *what do we do now* look.'

She closed her eyes. 'It was Terence.'

'Wow,' he said sarcastically. 'I should make lying reason for dismissal, because you are blatantly lying to me.'

'Nicholas, we are wasting precious time, please let me go.'

Seeing her eyes shine tearfully, he stood aside, opened the door, and let her out. She ran to the lift. He went out as well, watching as numbers changed on the panel. He climbed in and came out in reception, making sure Margot didn't see him. There she stood trying to calm down Simone. Right, Margot was tough, Simone... he wondered how many minutes it would take to break her. Then Simone asked someone to stand in for her, and he saw the two disappear to the courtyard.

He followed them at a distance. What if Dani was putting her life in danger? Fear gripped him.

'What did he say?' Margot asked.

'He asked to speak to Dani. What could I say, she's not here. But he started shouting at me, saying I was hiding her. I said why would I do that? He told me she was supposed to meet him somewhere. He was raging, I was afraid so I told him that we have all been looking for her since this morning too. He was very surprised at that. He said how can that be? I told him that she went home, took her car, and went somewhere, but we don't know where. I told him Nicholas is frantic and he laughed at that, as if he was enjoying himself. How could I think he was nice?'

'Did he say why she was supposed to meet him? Why am I asking? But she called Nicholas while I was in his office, so he knows she's okay. Now, he's trying to figure it all out.'

'Oh no Margot, you can't tell him.'

'I know and Dani would kill us both. She loves him too much to hurt him like that. I just don't understand how she is trying to do it now, when she has failed for so many years already.'

'I just thought of something,' Simone said suddenly. 'What if she made an appointment to see him somewhere, and while he is there, she went to his place?'

'Oh lord no, I hope not. If he finds her there he could become unpredictable and hurt her.'

'Should we go check?'

'Do you know where he lives?'

Simone nodded. 'I have never been there but I got his address when I looked on his phone.'

'You are a genius, girl. Give me five, I'm just getting my things.' Margot flew out of the courtyard, through reception and up the lift.

Nicholas did not move. He had a choice; confront Simone or follow them, perhaps discover where Dani was, and then confront all at once, he thought angrily. Then he became angrier, sure they were talking about Sams.

They left in Margot's car, and he tried to hang back as far as he could so they wouldn't notice the white Audi following them. Eventually, they stopped somewhere and he knew they were doing the same thing he was, looking for Dani's Beetle. They sat close to half an hour but nothing happened.

His phone rang, seeing the number he took a deep breath. 'Hello,'

'Did you find her?' Carol asked nervously.

He was not going to worry any more people. 'She is fine.'

'I haven't been able to get hold of her at all.'

'I know, there is something wrong with her phone.'

'Is she with you?'

'Not right now, but everything is okay.' He hated lying to the people he cared about, but he couldn't tell the truth either because he didn't even know it himself.

'That's a relief. Tell her I want to speak with her when you see her.'

'I will do that, bye.' He saw Margot's car move. Obviously, realising Dani was not here, they were going home. He would have loved to be in that car, to hear what they were discussing.

He wondered if he was supposed to go home. But no, never, not without her. He sat up, that was Sams driving into the property, and he was alone. Nicholas fought the urge to get out and go beat him into a pulp, because whatever was happening was his doing. Sams' place was near the gate, so he parked quickly. Nicholas found himself opening and closing his hands into fists.

Hell, but he needed to know what was going on. He looked at the back seat; his laptop was there. Pulling the thing, he opened it and went to his email. That stupid conversation was still there, making him angry all over again. He opened a file... His laptop made a sound and a message flashed.

"What are you doing?"

"Trying to work", he answered.

"Get off that file."

"Who are you and why am I listening to you?" He could barely think.

"Be glad I am telling you to get off, because I have a little surprise in that file."

"What do you mean?"

"What don't you understand about surprise? And remember, some are pretty nasty."

"I'm sick of you; can you leave me and my wife alone now?"

"Sorry, have to go, phone call."

Nicholas closed the laptop when he saw computer man was off. He sat there wondering what he should do, his anger growing towards Dani as well. Why couldn't she have told him what this was about? Why hadn't she wanted his help? Did she believe there was something he could not handle about her?

Sams was outside again, going to his car. This time, Nicholas found it quite difficult to follow in rush hour, and every time he got stuck behind a red robot, he could only guess where Sams had gone, as he could turn at any time and Nicholas would lose him completely. But eventually, Nicholas thought that he recognised where they were headed, and as he did, he became angrier.

They drove down a street full of two-storey houses and eventually Sams pulled into one and parked in the garage. Nicholas stopped a distance away as he watched Sams go to the front door, take out a key, and let himself in. The family home. Trying to think what to do, he froze in shock as he saw a white Beetle come up the road from the other side. His heart pounded, his gut hurt, and he felt bile in his mouth. Dani!

He watched her get out of the car and lean against it, as if she were having trouble breathing. He wanted to get out immediately. But now, not only was he concerned but also beyond mad. What in hell's name was she doing here? He decided to wait a few minutes and then march up to that front door and demand to know what was going on.

She looked worried as she glanced around, put her hand up, took a deep breath, and rang the bell. The front door opened, Sams leaned towards her to kiss her, and Nicholas thought his stomach would explode. She turned her face sideways, not letting him touch her lips. Nicholas started a deep breathing, heavens, but he did not feel well.

Dani walked into the house and the front door closed.

As he reached to open the car door, he realised a woman was standing there. 'Excuse me,' he said and wondered where she had come from.

'Nicholas,' she bent to look at him and offered her hand. 'Bianca Strauss, Sams' mother.'

He took her hand automatically, but had no doubt that there was a stupid expression on his face. 'What is going on?'

She made a gesture with her head. 'My son is being taught a lesson in accountability.' She moved from the door and let him get out. 'I am impressed, Nicholas, how did you figure this out?'

'I followed her worried friends to Sams' place and then followed him. I still don't know what is going on, but it is time I find out.'

She arrested him with her hand. 'You can't go in there yet, Dani needs this. She has been waiting for this truth for years.'

'I don't understand.'

'Nicholas, what do you know about my son?'

He was at a loss.

'I am his mother but I know what kind of person he is, not a very nice one. He is quite the incredible liar, very mean, extremely vain, and far too smart for his own good.' She announced sadly.

'I don't know much about him at all, except that Dani feels very uncomfortable and fearful in his presence.' Nicholas told her.

'The poor baby, he has been terrorizing her for quite some time, over six years, if I'm working it out right. How she kept sane with the things he did, I can't tell. But she is a strong one.'

Nicholas felt his rattled nerves. The more this woman spoke, the more afraid he became for Dani.

Bianca's hand gave him a reassuring squeeze. 'Don't worry, I won't let him hurt her. We just have to give them time so he can finally tell her what he did at and after the dance.'

'Doesn't she know?' Nicholas asked.

Bianca shook her head. 'He drugged her, so she recalls nothing. He has to confess and finally give her peace.'

Nicholas did not like the sound of that. 'Do you know what he did?'

'If I had not walked into his bedroom that night, you would not have married a virgin.'

'But... you said she was drugged.'

'Now you see what my son is. He does not ask permission for anything, he thinks he can just have, by fair means or otherwise.'

'She is in there, alone with him.' He pointed to the house.

'And it's all right,' she touched an earpiece. 'I will know when to go in. Dani and I spent the day working this out. Remember, there is more than one story unravelling here tonight.'

'But why didn't she tell me?'

'Because she loves you and didn't want you to lose the company.'

Alarm bells went off in his head. 'Excuse me?'

'That was his threat to her. He has been quite mean again, threatening to annihilate you if she doesn't sleep with him.'

He ran a hand through his hair. Of course Sams, the computer genius. How stupid was he? 'She can't, I won't let her.'

'Nicholas, she is not going to do anything of the sort, and that is why I am here. Do you know where your wife went today?'

'Well, she came to see you.'

'Do you know where I was?'

He shook his head. 'I know nothing, where were you?'

'Durban.'

'You mean... she flew to Durban?'

Bianca nodded. 'She tracked me down yesterday, to inform me of this most sordid tale. Then she flew down, we met at the airport, spoke for a while and flew back. Do you know how much that girl loves you?'

He dropped his head, feeling shame for how close he had been to the edge of doubt. 'I know she does.'

'Good, so don't ever forget it. And you know love is like that, sometimes, you hide things from the one you love because you want to protect them.'

Nicholas nodded, shocked that she had flown to another city because she wanted to stop Sams from hurting him. A lump sat in his throat.

Bianca patted his shoulder. 'I know, sometimes, we feel so stupid.'

'May I go in with you or is there something else you have worked out?'

'No, you can come in. Just promise that you will not try to hit him.'

'What if I can't control myself?'

'Nicholas, I am not asking for his sake, I am asking for yours. He will pummel you because you have no idea how strong he is.'

'I'm not that weak either.'

'Please leave all bravado at the door. Then take your wife and go home.'

'Just like that; and he answers to nothing?'

'Believe me, I know he needs to be taught a hard lesson, but not everything we know can be proven. And that is what the law requires, proof, evidence.'

'He chats to people on computers, can't those conversations be used?'

'Did he do it to you as well?'

'Some, I just didn't realise it was him.'

'What was he going on about with you?'

'Threatened to ruin me, and asked to sleep with Dani.'

Bianca shook her head. 'I see how he was doing this, threatened you both with the same thing and got the desired results. You love her, so you are willing to lose everything. She loves you, so she tries to save everything.'

CHAPTER FIFTEEN

Sams was still congratulating himself that he had finally found the one thing that made her yield to him. Perhaps he should have let her get married sooner, because this love business was a great playground for blackmail.

He had already asked for the explanation as to why she was so late and she told him that she got a flat tyre on Rivonia Road and then realised that she had forgotten to pump the spare since she did not know when, so she had to call a tow-truck to take her to a tyre shop. People at work didn't know where you were the whole day, he told her, and apparently, your husband is having quite the fit, he watched her face go paler, because hell, she was pale already.

'Why didn't you answer your phone,' he asked darkly.

She told him she had switched it off so she wouldn't be interrupted and to stop everyone from trying to dissuade her from going through with the plan.

He liked that answer, but that still did not explain all the other hours, what had she been doing?

'Do you think adultery is easy, especially for me?' She asked angrily.

He saw her point. She had apparently gone to movies so she could calm herself, and then went to sit at some lake so she could relax. He believed that. She had done that many times before, always liked large bodies of water when she was troubled.

'Have you eaten?' He asked again.

'When did you know me to eat when I'm upset?' She asked.

True, he knew that too. Then, she divulged what she wanted out of this encounter, the truth about their Graduation dance. He showed her the contract he had drawn up as requested.

She gave it a dismissive glance then said she would sign it after hearing the story of September 2008. 'Afterwards,' she closed her eyes to say it, 'I'm yours.'

He felt an erection right there, then cast his mind back and recalled...

Dani had always been quite the health nut and he thought it provident because of his rugby regimen. When they finally got together, she would make sure he stuck to those strict menus and supplements. So when he slipped her Roofies at the dance as the evening wound to its end, he knew that she would probably be out within minutes because it was quite possible she had the cleanest blood in that school. He was not wrong, it happened the instant she sat in the car.

He carried her upstairs to his room, dropped her on the bed, and undressed her. As he took the pictures, he felt the heat rise in his body, but first... He went to the bar and grabbed the first two bottles his hands could find then returning upstairs, he started on the liquid as he continued clicking; he turned her on her side, lifted her arms, propped her like this, then that, and the flaming liquids cascaded down his throat.

Leaning towards her, he touched her breasts, and felt his pants tighten. If he was going to do this, he had to do it now. He removed his jacket, tie, shirt, and lay on the bed beside her. Leaning over, he kissed her but hated the non-response mode. He kissed one of her breasts and felt things happen in his groin area again. Off went the pants and shorts.

He snapped a few shots of himself now, then going to her, pulled her to the edge of the bed, turned her properly, and—

'What the hell,'

Someone familiar dashed into the room, but he wanted this so badly that he could not think, or focus. He felt himself being dragged away and the phone flew somewhere. Then he felt a small cold hand slap him three times. He opened his eyes and looked straight at her. 'Mom,'

'What the bloody hell did you do?' Bianca screamed at him. 'What did you do,' she cried hysterically. 'Tell me you didn't.'

He was still recovering so he wasn't sure.

'Stay there.' She commanded and ran to Dani. 'What did you give her?'

'Huh...' he blinked his eyes hard. 'I'm trying to remember.'

She returned to her son and slapped him again. 'Focus and recall, that's all I ask, focus and recall; what did you give her?'

'Huh... we call it Roofies, but there's a bunch of names.'

'What is it?'

'Sedative.'

'What else,' she demanded. 'Because she is like the dead,'

'It's a... potent hypnotic sedative and...' he slurred. 'A skeletal muscle relaxant.'

'Oh god... Did you hurt Dani?'

'I don't remember.'

Bianca slapped him again. 'You want to be a rugby champion? She is seventeen, moron, seventeen! You are eighteen; do you know how the courts view this? You will be a rapist and go straight to jail. Do you have any idea how long jail feels? Of course you don't, so you toy with things you should leave the hell alone. So, focus and recall; did you hurt her?'

'I... I think I didn't have time.'

She closed her eyes. 'Why were you going to do this? And to Dani of all people, she is sweet, innocent—'

'I want her.'

'And so you make this decision without her consent?' She queried angrily. 'When, oh when will men stop using that thing as a weapon?'

'I couldn't help myself.'

She glared at him. 'If I pee in my pants because my bladder is full while I'm stuck in traffic, I couldn't help myself. This... it is called premeditation. You worked this scenario out in your head, you drugged her, it is a crime. Get dressed,' she commanded. 'Did you people have alcohol?'

'Not Dani.'

'Was there any seafood on your menu?'

'The starters,'

'Did Dani have any?'

'We all did.'

She looked around the room for all of Dani's things, brought them to the bed and carefully dressed the girl in her pretty party clothes. She sat there a few minutes, trying to think what she was supposed to tell this child when she came to. Getting to her feet, she began pacing the room then stopping, fixed her cold gaze on Sams. 'Go downstairs and bring me the box of laxatives, and a glass of water.'

Bianca went to her son's computer, turned it on then ran to her bedroom and grabbed a pill from her bedside table. She got back to Dani, just as Sams also entered the room. Opening Dani's mouth, she pushed the pill from her bedroom and a quarter laxative to the back of her throat and forced her to swallow some water. She turned to her son. 'Drink this,' she gave him two full laxatives.

'Mom…'

'Drink them.' She pushed the glass of water into his hand and watched him swallow the tablets. 'Now, go online and look up antidotes for the crap you gave her.' She turned to Dani. 'I'm sorry, my baby. Maybe you didn't need the other pill but I'm not taking any chances that he may have caused more damage than even he knows.' Then, she too went to the computer. There wasn't much information, except that the effects of the drug could last up to seven hours. But the girl could not stay here all that time, she had to go home; her parents were expecting her.

'This is what is going to happen.' She grabbed Sams' shoulder and shook him, so he could focus on her words. 'You are going to wake Dani, and she is going to ask why she is here, as any normal person would. You will tell her that she had an adverse reaction to the seafood, and that you are sick too. That you brought her here because you needed the toilet urgently, as you could not go to a strange place. She fell asleep on your bed while she waited because she wasn't feeling well either. Do you understand me?'

He nodded.

'Now that your brain is clearer, did you hurt her?'

He shook his head. 'No.'

'Okay, but Sams, know this.' Bianca told him with a withering look. 'What you saw me do here tonight was for Dani's benefit, not yours. Because what you were about to do to an innocent is quite abhorrent. And let me tell you my feelings on this so you are never confused; if you ever try or do hurt another woman and I find out, I will turn you in. Either you learn to be accountable, or you are going to run into a lot of trouble in the future. Now, wake that girl, and I will be downstairs to drive her home.'

Sams watched her leave the room, then turned to Dani. He sat on the bed's edge. Was he supposed to feel bad or guilty about what had just happened? He didn't. And hell, he still wanted her. He reached for one shoulder. 'Dani, Dani, wake up.'

It took five long minutes to get her to open her eyes. She looked spaced out and drunk.

'Sams,' she said groggily as she moved an arm. 'What... why...'

'We are both sick, it was the seafood. I have been running the whole time. You just passed out on my bed. Are you feeling okay?'

'Not really,' she tried to sit up but felt dizzy. 'I must go home.'

'Yes.' He helped her to her feet.

'Thank goodness we only have one Graduation dance.'

They walked downstairs to the lounge.

'There you are,' Bianca said with a smile. 'Are you two kids okay? Both of you look rather green around the gills. Let me guess, they fed you junk again.'

'Maybe.' Sams said.

'You,' Bianca pointed to him, 'are not driving anywhere looking like that. Come Dani, let me take you home.'

Three days later, sitting in the school's courtyard, he was looking at the pictures he could not pry his eyes away from, as she sorted out her art folder.

'How are you feeling?' She asked. 'Has your stomach settled down?'

'Huh... what,'

'Your stomach, I'm feeling better, are you?'

'That's good.'

'Sams, why can't I remember anything after the middle of the dance? I feel woozy and confused.'

'Food poisoning works differently on everybody.' He said absentmindedly.

'What are you looking at?' she asked suddenly, aware that he was paying no attention whatsoever.

'Huh?'

'You are looking at something you are not supposed to, right? You do know that pornography is not only illegal on school grounds, but in general, quite yuck.'

'Only ugly old ladies say so.'

'Do I look like an old lady to you?'

'You don't count, because you're just different.' He shifted in the seat.

'Do you have to do it in my presence?' She couldn't look at him. 'And, just a reminder, you are the head boy, supposed to set an example.'

Something cruel filled him. Why did she think she was better? Why did she sit on this moral horse she rode everywhere? Why couldn't she just be normal? Why wouldn't she drink, take drugs, or have sex? Maybe it was time someone contaminated her a little. He stuck the phone under her nose.

It took five seconds for her to burst into tears. 'How could you?' She cried. 'I didn't ask to participate in your rubbish. Now I have things in my head I did not need. You are disgusting.'

Complete insanity flooded him and he had never felt anything like it. The malicious sneer stretched across his face as he told her. 'It's not rubbish, it's you.'

The art folder fell, spreading her work on the ground. She grabbed the phone and looked at the picture. All colour draining from her face, she made a sound, as if something had ridden over her and pressed the life out of her.

'When,' she jumped to her feet. 'When did you take this?' But the background was one she knew well and the date on the screen spoke volumes. She slapped him and then tried to delete the thing as she cried.

He took the phone from her shaking hand. 'My phone, my property.'

'Delete it.' She commanded.

'What is in it for me?'

She looked at him as if she had never seen him before. 'You are going to blackmail me?'

'Life is not fair. So my question stands, what do I get?'

She took a breath, wiped her brimming eyes, and went down on her knees to gather her art from the ground. 'You are despicable. And nothing, you get nothing from me.'

The way she looked at him, made him feel a smidgen of guilt. 'Fine, I'll delete it.' He pressed the buttons on the phone.

'It doesn't matter, does it?' She told him furiously, as she grabbed all her things together and looked at him with those eyes that could just see things. 'You have more. I hope they burn a hole in your head.' She walked away from him.

He ran after her and touched her arm.

Swinging around, she hit him with the art folder. 'You told me you were sick, you told me I was sick, and yet you had time for this,' she pointed disdainfully and then slapped him again. 'If that's what you want, fine. But pictures are not me. When you do grow up and become a man then maybe you will be able to do the right thing.'

Nothing was ever the same again. He had phoned to apologise countless times, even told her that he had deleted them. It was creepy how she just knew that he hadn't...

'Why are you crying now?' Sams asked when he saw the tears as she sat in his lounge.

'You don't get it, do you?' She shook her head sadly. 'We were friends and you did all this. I wasn't in love with you, but I liked you. Why couldn't you have just been my friend?'

'Why couldn't you have been my girlfriend?'

Dani shook her head again. 'I don't know what to say.'

'No more words,' he grabbed the contract. 'Just sign, and let's do this.'

'Tell me something, what is going to happen after this?'

'Maybe I'll be happy then.' He said.

'Do you still have Galfrey shares?'

'A few thousand,'

'You must return them.'

'Says who?'

'I say. Sams, do not imagine me a little girl anymore. One who is scared of you, because I'm not.'

He looked at her. 'I have been noticing this change. I don't know if I like it, but it does make me hot.'

Dani wondered if he had ever grown up, because she felt as if he were still eighteen. He had talked like that back then too, and his acceptance of other people's rights was still non-existent. 'Can I ask you to delete the pictures before we go upstairs?' She had no doubt that he had already replaced them.

'I don't know if we will make it up there.' His thumb hooked into the belt. 'Do we have to talk about all this stuff?'

'This is how people get into the mood, they talk. They get to know each other first, not just rush for the first bed they see.'

'Who is thinking bed right now, the sofa looks quite decent to me, and the carpet is rather plush.'

'Sams, do you date often?'

'Why would I, I want you.'

'And Simone? Do you realise that if you are in some kind of relationship with her, you are actually cheating on her?'

'So are you on Nicholas.' He grinned his pleasure. 'I like the thought of that, I despise your husband.'

She shrugged. 'Nicholas is a different subject altogether. What about Simone?'

He looked at her for a second. 'Tell me this, did you ask Simone to delete the pictures from my phone?'

She looked surprised. 'When did she do that?'

'You had nothing to do with it?'

'That would involve revealing things I don't like, to people I like.' She was becoming excellent at lying to Sams. 'Does that mean they don't exist anymore?'

'They do. The little idiot didn't know I had them on the PC too.'

'Do you have them upstairs as well?'

'No, I took them off here. My mom uses the computer and I didn't want her to find them. And peculiar, I haven't had time to replace them on the phone.'

'You will have to break up with Simone.'

'Why?'

'You can't date her and be involved in this.' She made a gesture.

'Dani, are you offering a longer tryst than just today?'

'No, I'm gone after this. But when I go, things will be right.'

'I don't know what needs to be right with you, but I know I will be right. So, sign on the dotted line please,' he offered her the contract.

She took it this time and perused over it. 'Where is the pen, you made a mistake.'

He had an amused look as he passed her a pen. 'What are you changing?'

'I told you, one time, not one night. I could not possibly survive all that energy.' And as she felt right now, she was not lying. She would probably not survive anything with Nicholas either. Why was she feeling like this?

'You do look rather wan.' He agreed. 'Is everything else to your satisfaction?' He pointed to the paper in her hands.

'I suppose.' She licked her lips, but felt awful. She needed to speed this up. 'Where is my copy?'

'There.' He pointed. 'And please sign.'

'When and how will I know the pictures are deleted?'

'I'll let you look on the PC.'

'And flashes, and what about the shares,'

'I'll dump them tomorrow. Now sign.'

'Sams,' Dani got to her feet. 'Why did you think that all this was actually going to happen?'

'What do you mean?'

'Did you really believe that I was going to cheat on Nicholas?'

'But you are here. And if you renege on the contract I can still exact my payment.'

'That is what you think you can do. But that is not how it works.'

He went towards her and for a moment, she felt fear. Then she stuck her chin out in defiance, one hand went into a pocket, and she pressed the alarm panic button Bianca had given her.

'What the hell,' Sams covered his ears. The alarm stopped screaming and he stared as the front door opened, and in walked his mother and Nicholas. 'Mom... What... why are you here?'

'Because of you,' Bianca turned to Dani. 'Did he tell you everything you needed to know?'

Dani nodded as she welcomed Nicholas' embrace.

'Are you okay my sweet?'

'I will be.'

'Right,' Bianca said and pointed. 'Everything you have done; you are going to fix. Give me your phone.' She turned to Nicholas and Dani. 'Unfortunately, I did not know the pictures existed until you told me about them today. Had I known, he would not have terrorised you for so many years.'

'Mom, you do know that I am a man.' Sams told her.

'No, you're not; you are a mean teenager in a large body. Oh, just in case you don't know what is happening. Right now, someone is entering the townhouse and confiscating your computer.'

'You can't do that, it's my place. And it's called breaking and entering.'

'It's in my name, that makes everything inside my property, and he has my keys, so he is not breaking anything. No matter how fast you drove, you would never get there in time, so that is that problem solved.' Bianca shook her head. 'And did you honestly believe that you could blackmail Dani forever, that she wouldn't be able to figure out a way to stop you? You are smart, but you are an idiot too. I believe that was your challenge, was it not, may the best mind win?' She threw him an inquisitive glance. 'It seems we have a winner. By the way, Nicholas is pressing charges, so perhaps you should quit the rugby club now.'

'You can't do any of this, and my PC... my life is in there.'

'Sorry, but I am not leaving it for you to manipulate more people. That computer is out of our lives.'

'You can't do this.' He shouted.

'Can't I? I just did. And by the way again, your father is arriving tomorrow. You can explain to him why you thought this was so entertaining.'

'I am over eighteen, why do I care what he's going to say?'

'When he shrinks your fortune from this,' she made a measure with her hands and then with her fingers. 'To this, I think you will listen to what he has to say.'

'This is unfair. I am almost twenty-five, when I'm supposed to get my money. No one has a right to take it from me.' He walked towards her, made a fist, and leaned threateningly into her.

'Excuse me,' Nicholas said as he patted Sams on the shoulder.

Sams turned to look at him, and felt a fist squarely on his face. He raised his arm to strike back but Nicholas struck him again, twice. Dazedly, Sams sunk onto the sofa.

'Don't you ever speak to your mother like that again,' Nicholas told him furiously. 'Or any other woman.'

Sams glared at him through a very foggy brain, then getting to his feet stumbled up the stairs.

Soon, there were things breaking against walls and on the floor.

Bianca's eyes filled with tears. 'I am so sorry for what he has done to you all this time.'

Dani came to her immediately. 'I know, and it's not your fault. And I am so grateful that you always looked out for me.'

Bianca wiped her eyes and then fixed her gaze on Dani's face. 'Are you all right, honey? I noticed the whole day how pale you are.' She touched Dani's cheek; it was cold.

'I haven't been feeling well.'

'I can see that. How do you feel now?'

'Very tired,'

'Dani, smile for me.'

Both Dani and Nicholas thought it a strange request, nevertheless, Dani tried.

'Oh lord,' Bianca said as she watched Dani's facial muscles inability to perform the natural task. 'You look poisoned.'

'What?' Nicholas turned Dani to look at her. 'Smile my sweet.'

Dani tried. 'I'm just tired,' she said.

'How long have you been feeling like this?'

'A couple of weeks,'

'The hospital is a few blocks from here; you have to take her there immediately. Dani, have you eaten anything exotic recently?'

'Nothing I can think of,'

'Do you remember touching anything?'

Dani shook her head.

'How do you know she's poisoned?' Nicholas asked with concern.

'I'm an interior designer; I remember the old lead paint and what that poison did to people. I can't be sure if it's a heavy metal she's contaminated with, but it looks similar. She is not well, Nicholas; take her to hospital now, and tell them what I said. And insist on it because heavy metal toxicity is one of the least looked into problems.'

'Thank you, thank you for everything you have done.' Nicholas picked Dani into his arms. 'Come sweetheart; let's get you to hospital.'

CHAPTER SIXTEEN

'Nicholas,' Dani fluttered her eyes open slowly.

'You're awake, my sweet.' He gave her a tender smile. 'How do you feel?'

'I don't like these tests.'

'Neither do I and I would take your place in a heartbeat if I could.'

The tests had begun and as Bianca suggested, the doctors had started with the heavy metal toxicity tests. Hair, nail, blood, urine, and skin samples were taken. No, there were no heavy metals in her system, no lead, no mercury, no lithium, no cadmium. Yet she remained poisoned.

Almost every evening she got better, but some mornings something strange happened. Within two hours of waking, she was worse. She would have muscle spasms, dizziness, weakness, sweating, and even loss of speech. Numbness concentrated on her face and throat, and sadly, Nicholas noticed every day, that it was burying her beautiful smile. No one understood it, and doctors scratched their heads in frustration.

Just about everyone from Galfrey's had already been to see her, and Dani thought that she could easily open a flower shop for the thousands of blooms that had come through the hospital's front doors in her name.

Between Carol and Nicholas, one of them was always first at her side in the morning. Nicholas was staying in Bedfordview for the duration, as he could not bear the thought of being in their apartment. Without her, it was vacant, and he definitely could not sleep in their bed alone.

Nicholas was beyond worried; he was scared. He knew doctors could figure out things, symptoms, analysis, diseases, but this had them dumbfounded and it frightened the very life out of him as he thought of the possibility that no one could help her.

He had also contacted Anya, and the poor girl was probably damaging more than she was doing right at Gurggle because he could feel her anxiety every day when she called to hear of Dani's progress.

A week after the continuous loop that had everyone worried sick to their stomach, Margot, Terence and Simone came to visit. The women chatted softly and the two men went for a walk down the corridors.

'I am going mad,' Nicholas admitted. 'No one understands it and her heart is taking a beating. She gets better and worse throughout the day, every early morning she looks better then at around eight, she starts feeling sick all over again.'

'Is that so?' Terence's interest was pricked.

'And you know what the strangest thing is, I feel as if I'm getting sick as well.'

Now, Terence's interest was definitely aroused. 'You mean you are developing the same type of symptoms?'

Nicholas nodded. 'It feels like it. Every now and then, I feel this odd tightness in my face, as if I'm losing my expressions. I haven't told her, don't want to worry her more.'

'This sounds fascinating, and it reminds me of a case during an expedition to Nepal. One of our members fell ill, and he went into just such a cycle, he would get better and worse every day. Then a second member started with the same symptoms. We eventually discovered they were eating a local weed at approximately the same time every day, as they had taken a liking to the bitter taste; it's somewhat similar to olives. What they didn't realise is that it was toxic.'

'Did they get better when they stopped?' Nicholas asked curiously.

'Not right away, they had to be airlifted. But after a detoxifying treatment, they did recover.'

'So Dani could be poisoning herself daily?'

'It's possible. The question is with what. You said it happens at around eight every morning, what is it she does then?'

'It might either be when she gets ready for the day or breakfast, because what else is there that she can do at that time in a hospital?'

'This bears looking into, Nicholas. We'll just have to find out.'

Both turned on their heels and returned to the room.

Nicholas went to her side immediately and took her hands. 'Dani what do you do every day before eight o'clock?'

'You mean here? I wash, get dressed, and have breakfast. Why do you ask?'

'Terence and I have been talking and it seems it's an odd coincidence that you feel worse every day after eight o'clock.'

She digested his words carefully. 'You think I'm poisoning myself.' She looked at Terence.

'It seems that way,' he agreed.

'I was poisoned before I was admitted so it can't be the food.'

'I'd say so too.' Terence found the girl interesting. She was young, but no fool, with an ingenious sense of humour so he understood why Margot liked her so much. And amusingly, Dani seemed to think his wife was some type of goddess, which he personally had always believed. No, he was not going to pretend this case didn't intrigue him. 'Someone has to watch and record everything you do, then wait for the reactions. And since at IRC we have the right facilities, I will make arrangements to send someone tomorrow.'

Inter-nations Research Centre sent two female lab assistants the following morning, looking very much the medical scientists that they were. There were hundreds of packets, containers, and bags; so every time Dani used something, it was bagged, tagged, stored, and reactions, if any, recorded.

By the end of the day, there was hardly anything left in the room. What was, was equally bagged and tagged. She did get sick again after eight o'clock, and they recorded her symptoms with serious interest, although they couldn't tell what had caused it because she had not reacted to anything instantaneously.

Finally, the scientists returned to the laboratory to deposit the assortment they had gathered during the day. Now the work began to unravel the mystery of Dani's poisoning. Soap, toothpaste, hair brush, lip-ice, deodorant... the list was long, but it was there, being broken, cut up, torn apart, and analysed.

It took five days for IRC to discover what had poisoned Dani, and then they stared at the culprit item, wondering how it had become contaminated with Tetrodotoxin. The toxin was known to exist in some toads, newts, sea stars, angelfish, and puffer fish.

And perhaps not strangely, Dani had been recuperating somewhat during those five days, as the contaminant was conspicuously absent from her room. Although, her heart was still not quite what it should be.

Terence stood now in the room facing them.

'I'm so thankful you finally have it, what was it?' Nicholas asked eagerly.

Terence took two plastic bags from a container and dangled them from his hand.

'My lip-ice. But… why are there two?' Dani frowned.

'You didn't know you had two?'

She looked pensive. 'I kept getting confused about it. The one is shorter than the other, right?' She saw Terence nod. 'Which one was poisoned?'

'The newer one, so of course every time you used that one, you would get worse. Which also explains why you felt as if you were being poisoned too,' Terence looked at Nicholas. 'Every time you kissed her, it was being transmitted to you.'

'Is there a treatment?'

'There is no antidote, but the good news is that it works itself out of the system. There are a few things we can also do to expedite recovery, but it seems Dani is doing quite well on her own since she hasn't been spreading this on her skin.'

Nicholas sighed with relief and grabbing Dani's hand, kissed her fingers in thankfulness. 'Thank you Terence, you have no idea how wonderful your words are.'

'I have an idea.' Terence said as he saw Dani's brimming eyes.

A serious look paused on Nicholas' face. 'What about her heart? This thing has hurt her badly. And my other question, how did this happen?'

'That is obviously the mystery we have now. Is it an isolated case or is there a poisoned batch of lip-ice out there that we need to recall? We have already contacted the company and they are looking into it very seriously, tracking the numbers and we will soon know where that merchandise was delivered. It is odd though, because merchandise sells around a time frame and we haven't heard of any other poisonings.'

'If it is an isolated case?' Nicholas queried.

'In that case, we have someone out there who meant serious harm. What we do not know is if it is personal or a random attack. Am I guessing right that both of you would like to know the truth?'

Both Nicholas and Dani nodded.

'Although only one is contaminated, I am sending both to forensics.' He waved the bags. 'I am just sorry that fingerprints and evidence are probably beyond retrievable. Do you recall where you got them?'

'Where I always do,' she named a store. 'But I still don't understand why I have two. I'm not saying it's impossible, it's just odd because I don't recall getting one recently. And I didn't think I needed another one.'

Dani stayed with her parents in Bedfordview through her convalescence, which was not as fast as everyone hoped. The doctors needed to monitor her recovery as her heart and low blood pressure had become problematic, and Nicholas did not want her to be home alone during the day lest she need emergency help.

When he thought that she could have been taken from him, he wanted to scream, punch walls, and kick heavens knew what. So he thought, churned, and flipped things over in his mind.

'What are you doing?' She asked as she turned in bed one night.

'Thinking,'

'About what,' she queried.

'We should sleep.'

'Nicholas,' she sat up against her pillow. 'You are already doing nothing of the sort. What is bothering you?'

He also sat up. 'I want to ask you something but I don't know if it's too soon or if you want to tell me.'

She considered his words. 'You want to know what Sams did and how he was blackmailing me.'

He nodded. 'I want to know everything, so I can help you. He caused you anguish and I don't want to see it on your face anymore.'

Years had passed, but she still felt the helplessness Sams had dragged her through, and she watched Nicholas' face go from shock to anger as she opened her heart and let it all go. 'So there you have it.' She felt emotional, upset, and was sobbing as she concluded the sad mess.

He reached out and held her against his chest, caressing her face and hair. 'That is horrible, and I wish you had told me right at the beginning, I would have—'

'And that is precisely what I wanted to avoid, you trying to sort it out and he getting upset and leaking all that rubbish. He would have shamed us all, not to mention the media ripping us apart. It wouldn't have been fair on Galfrey's, your parents, mine, but especially you. And not just that, I was so ashamed of those pictures, they made me feel dirty.'

'They were not your fault.' He kissed the side of her face. 'And I think we must press charges.'

'You do know what kind of spectacle we might start if we do.'

'I know, but someone has to stop him. We will talk to our parents and tell them we have to do this. He cannot just be given chances to redeem himself, learn nothing, and then continue unhindered.'

'I will speak to his mother and then we'll go see whoever we have to and hope that this is going to help put him right.'

Figuring out who had poisoned the lip-ice proved impossible. The forensic lab gave them the hard facts. There was no way of knowing who had done such a thing as there was no evidence, and no traces of foreign DNA save Dani's and Nicholas'.

Dani wondered if it had been a random act, but instinctively knew that it was not. Someone out there disliked, perhaps even hated her, and it was an uneasy feeling knowing it. One thing she did not know, Terence and Margot were taken with the notion that they needed to find the perpetrator, so an investigation of sorts was taking place in their home every evening.

'This may sound cliché, but if we had to write a list of suspects, whose name would we place on top?' Terence asked.

'Sams, and after that it would be empty.' Margot told him. 'The most obvious is often the correct answer. We could badger him a bit and see what falls out.'

'This need to hurt the people one purports to love is quite insane to me. Because if he wants her this much why would he also harm her?'

'Considering I am the one in psychology I could write you a thesis. To the twisted mind, it makes perfect sense. Either I have you or no one else will. And Sams is no idiot, he knows he will never have her, so why should Nicholas?' She looked up from a book she was perusing. 'And the fact that it was aimed at her face, where that gorgeous smile just makes people fall in love with her... I say it is Sams.'

'The problem is how do we prove it?'

'I'm going to do a bit of snooping around his mother and see where it leads.'

It became the expected nightmare. They were well-known people, of a certain standing in society and it included an up-and-coming sportsman; of course people wanted to know, read, leer, discuss, and gossip about.

Sams' PC was confiscated and perhaps not too unpredictably, the problems started. Everything they searched for was gone. If anyone had imagined Sams stupid, they made a mistake. He was flippant about allegations. He spoke clearly, concisely, and softly. He was talented, he became the media's darling. Dani... everyone forgot that she had been the *it* girl just months previously. And everyone wanted to know what kind of resentment drove a beautiful young woman to make such allegations.

Nicholas raged as he saw the case disintegrating even before it got to court. He wanted Sams to admit that he had done wrong, to feel regret for the distress he had caused, and to pay for it, so he could learn that people did not do what they wanted without a care in the world. He seethed as he recalled deleting those pictures from his laptop the night he had seen them. If only he had guessed at all of this and kept them.

There was the dilemma. No proof existed, so what was it that they expected to prove? As for Terence and Margo's suspicion that he was responsible for Dani's poisoning... How did anyone substantiate such a claim? Where had Sams found the poison? How had he contaminated the lip-ice? When and how had he planted it on Dani that she had not become aware of it? There was a mountain of questions, and hardly a molehill of answers.

Nicholas worried about Dani's health, she was stressed and barely ate. Sometimes, he could see she wished she could stop the insane loop she had created by agreeing to press charges. That she felt persecuted every time she opened a newspaper and read some stupid remark Sams and his defence team had made. They were running on public sympathy, and getting it freely. Sams was a strapping boy, a diplomat's son, of considerable means, had been a head boy in school, achieved distinctions in every subject, was a phenomenal sportsman, and was still studying for his MBA... the list of accomplishments was long indeed.

There was one question the media asked constantly too. Why was Sams accused of being some fantastic computer genius? He did not look the type. Didn't all those guys look like geeks, nerds, whatever the term was nowadays? True, he had some fancy hardware and software, but he had the money to afford it. And Dani was purported to be close to genius as well? One of the newspapers printed a comic strip with a woman in skimpy attire, pouting lips, long flowing brown hair, and long red nails pressing enter on a keyboard, and a door opening in the background.

Nicholas threw the thing into the wastepaper basket angrily. What was wrong with people? Did they think she was having fun? Did they imagine that she could sleep at night? Did they realise she could not step out the front door and people murmured and pointed? Did they know she was wasting away under the tension? He couldn't care less what people said about him or Galfrey's, but he detested it when they mumbled about her. One night, he almost punched someone in a restaurant, when he had been sitting with Andrew and heard someone call her a spiteful socialite.

How he regretted having pushed her to do this. He had erroneously imagined Sams learning something. Sams was learning nothing, because he was still manipulating everything and everyone.

'Mr. Galfrey,' his secretary called.

'Yes,' he said tiredly.

'Margot Becker is here to see you.'

'Send her in.'

Margot entered carrying a file. 'How are you today, Nicholas?'

'As you see. How I despise this pandemonium.'

'Me too.' She sat in the chair. 'But I have some good news for you.'

'Really,' he leaned forward on his desk. 'Concerning what?'

'How Sams got the Tetrodotoxin.'

He was interested now. 'How did you discover that?'

'Terence did.'

'That's amazing, tell me.'

After she had spoken with Bianca, they knew a few new things about Sams. They had drawn a special questions list and she had filled it in as she spoke with the other woman. When sushi came up as Sams' favourite food, Terence made it his personal quest to visit every restaurant in the Bedfordview area that sold the speciality. Terence said there was a connection and he was going to find it. So he eventually ran into a chef who told him an interesting story. Someone had come in once and asked questions concerning fugu, the Japanese dish that contained puffer fish, the best-known carrier of the poison.

The young man wanted to sample the dish, but they didn't sell it. The last thing the restaurant needed was to have someone die at their dinner table because they did not have trained chefs.

The chef explained that although he had never done it himself, he knew how the puffer fish were dissected, cleaned, chopped, and prepared. That most of the poison was in the organs, especially the liver, but specifically in the bile. That if the knife nicked any of those, well... disaster was assured, which was why no restaurant in South Africa wanted to take the risk. And although most puffers were poisonous, not all were, and there were different levels of toxicity, but how anyone knew that, was a different question.

Terence asked if a pet puffer could be poisonous and if it was possible to determine the potency of the poison. Chef told him that it all depended on the algae and bacteria the fish fed on. The answer was that a person had to be able to do some research into a few things. It was also possible to ask anyone on the internet, and some crazy person would have no problem in mailing something like that to anyone in the world. What it looked like when it arrived, he had no clue.

Terence asked chef if he recalled what the young man looked like. No problem, chef told him, he's a regular customer. Terence got a good description from a complete stranger.

'That sounds promising, but it's not evidence or proof that he did it, even if we know it.' Nicholas told her. 'Thankfully, it seems he did not want to kill her outright, still... lord she is ill. And with the media frenzy she is not getting better as I hoped she would.'

'I know and I wish I could do more.'

'Margot, you have no idea how your concern has supported me.' He rose to his feet. 'Does Terence have any ideas how it got onto the lip-ice?'

'Well, when I visited Dani the other day we were just talking and something occurred to me. She started getting sick after the Galfrey ball, so I asked her to try recall that day minute by minute. So she is writing me a list of everything she did that day, from the moment she opened her eyes until she closed them again.'

'Huh...' Nicholas actually blushed.

Margot laughed. 'Not that; and you can tell her when you see her this evening.'

It took Dani three days to remember the entire ball day, and she faithfully wrote all she had done from brushing her teeth in the morning until throwing the bedcovers back that evening.

Margot sat reading that list as if she were about to write an exam. She had coloured pens, with which she circled the times Dani used her lip-ice, and everything seemed normal until she got to the dance.

There, she realised Dani's nervousness, she was applying lip-ice just about every ten minutes. It still didn't mean anything. Then she arrived at the meeting with Sams outside.

She read the conversation carefully, and saw disturbing things. Sams was a peculiar mixture of narcissist and self-hating individual. Doggedly, she continued until they were all inside dancing. Tiredness made her throw the papers aside and go make tea.

She glanced at Terence, who was in front of the PC, having a conversation with a Japanese scientist, a virologist, and they were discussing the puffer fish, both trying to work out lethal dosages of powerful toxins, and compiling a list. What she could make of it was that there were a lot of snakes on it already. She heard the name taipan, tiger snake, and death adder. She knew the puffer was already somewhere on it, just didn't know if it was near the top or the bottom as they were going for the top ten.

Margot grabbed a box of pretzels and proceeded to spread them all over the kitchen floor. Going down on her hands and knees, she picked them all up and dropped them onto a plate.

'What are you doing there?' Terence queried as he walked in. 'Oh, thanks.' He took something from the plate.

'Don't eat it, I've just picked it off the floor.'

'First of all, the floor is clean, so the five second rule applies.' He grinned. 'Second, I don't think I should eat my flash. I didn't know where it had got to and you picked it up now with the pretzels.'

Margot got to her feet and looked at him, a strange expression on her face.

'Is there something stuck to my hair?'

'No,' she turned around and walked out.

'Your tea,' he called after her. Then he took the cup and went to her. 'What happened in the kitchen?'

Margot waved the list at him. 'The answer is here, but where?'

He took her free hand, pulled her to him, and dropped a kiss on her lips. 'You'll figure it out.'

She did, at three in the morning. She jumped out of bed and almost ran to the list and giggled as she stared. 'Oh my goodness, there it is.'

The mystery was out. When Dani's clutch purse had gone flying onto the ground at the dance, Sams too went down on his knees to help her pick her things, and dropped the contaminated lip-ice into it. He knew her well to choose the right brand and type. But that they knew it was not going to help them much. Because knowing and proving were two very different things altogether.

'It's all very exasperating.' Margot was saying.

Simone took a bite of her sandwich, chewed for a few seconds and then asked. 'So what do we need to prove?'

'Everything, anything, otherwise, he will get away and go make someone else's life a misery if he is not brought to book. That is how those people are. They are always a disturbance, and get away with a lot.'

'So they can't find all the stuff he used to do on the computer?'

'No, nothing. He either deletes it right away, or there is some code to open something no one has yet seen, or there is a completely different computer where he does all his creative work from, and he is laughing his head off because no one can find it.'

'What about the photos?'

'Same thing, completely gone. As much as we are glad about it, it is extremely frustrating because there is nothing to prove that Dani is telling the truth. As for her poisoning, it is all fiction to everyone but the doctors, the lab at IRC, and those closest to her. We are the ones who saw her sick.'

'So, if you had the pictures...'

'I don't know, Simone.' Margot took the drink to her lips.

Simone grabbed her phone, searched for something, and then said. 'Margot, what if I told you that Sams will pay for everything he has done?'

'I would ask how?'

Simone passed her the phone. 'Remember when I deleted the pictures off his phone? I still don't know why, and I have never looked at them, but I sent them to my phone first.'

There was juice all over the table in front of Margot. She started coughing and then she thought she was going to have an anxiety attack as she started hyperventilating. 'Good god, you are brilliant.' She choked out of her mouth. Then jumping up from the chair, she grabbed the phone, grabbed Simone by the hand, and they were running to the lift.

For once in her life, Margot did something crazy. She did not walk, she ran to Nicholas' office, she did not knock, she stormed in. Thankfully, he was alone.

He looked up in surprise and noticed Simone coming towards them quickly. 'Margot, what's wrong?'

'We can get him. It is all here.' She waved the phone in her hand.

'What's there?'

'The pictures.' She passed him the phone. 'Just scroll down, every blessed disgusting one is there.'

He stared at the one that was on and made a face. 'Everything?'

'Yes. It's my phone.' Simone said as she walked in. 'Don't ask why I did it, I don't know.'

'But...' Nicholas placed the phone on the desk. 'How are we going to prove wrong-doing on his part? It's on your phone.'

'Well,' Simone said. 'I see it like this. He sent them to me from his phone, the number is still registered there.' She pointed to the phone.

'Okay,' Nicholas nodded. 'A link to him, but his crazy team is going to say she posed for them. And they do look posed.'

'Even if she did,' Simone continued again. 'There is something people don't know about Sams' phone.'

'And what is that?' Margot asked.

'Sams has had the same phone for years. First, because it is absolutely amazing, and I don't think anyone else has one like it in South Africa. His dad got it somewhere overseas and Sams adapted it. Second, it's a military marvel, that's what he called it. Every picture he takes is instantly dated, including time. See for yourself,' she pointed to her phone. 'And that is the worst thing that could have happened to him.'

Both Nicholas and Margot looked at her uncomprehendingly.

'The technology he loves so much is bringing him down. Those pictures are dated 2008. Guess how old Dani was? Seventeen, underage. As far as I know, there is a law against pornography involving minors. So you see, Sams is in a lot of trouble.'

Shock spread on both Nicholas and Margot's face.

Finally, Nicholas understood why he had thought those pictures strange, he had been looking at her seventeen-year-old body, not how she looked now.

When confronted with the evidence, Sams admitted the truth, sat down, looked Dani and Nicholas in the eye, and tried to explain. He wished she had come alone, but she wanted her husband to be there. Even things no one had thought about asking were revealed. He had infected the computers at Galfrey's, through Simone's flash, to spy, alter and delete files at will, which was really no news to any of them anymore.

He offered to settle the matter by compensating Dani. She looked furious when he said that, as for Nicholas... Sams could swear he meant to pulverise him. No, they wanted no money. What Nicholas wanted was a public apology. He wanted people to know that Dani was not the silly socialite the papers had labelled her.

Was that the end of it, Sams asked. No, Nicholas said. You have to answer about underage pornography, blackmail, and whatever else the police see fit to charge you with. All sorts of things happened then. Eagles Rugby Club dismissed him, Harris International fired him, and the university expelled him.

Bianca went to see him as he sat in a lonely cell awaiting bail. With tears pouring down her face, she told him how much she loved him, but refused to pay it, and then added that she hoped his father would do the same.

Richard Strauss listened to his ex-wife, agreed with her, but told her that the silly boy needed one of them to get him out of there so he could be feeling miserable at home, as he considered what he had done to his life. That he felt responsible for how Sams had turned out as he had left him without a father at fourteen. But he had been so very angry with her for having cheated on him, that he had found it impossible to stay anywhere near her because he still loved her.

Bianca cried pitifully and asked if he saw it possible to forgive her, because she had hated herself for the past ten years like no one else possibly could, because the strange thing about her cheating had been that she was avenging herself, because he had cheated on her first. She had never seen that man again, in fact, he had been a complete stranger, and she didn't even know his name.

'I cheated? When? Never Bianca, even when women draped themselves all over me, and there were a thousand opportunities for that. Where did you hear this?'

'Sams told me.'

'Sams?'

So Sams was questioned by both parents this time, and a dreadful truth emerged. He had lied to Bianca to test her, because he did not believe that women were trustworthy, and she proved everything bad he had ever imagined. Dani... well, he liked her and when the divorce proceedings began, he finally achieved what he had been unable to until then. She was a sweet girl, with a good heart and she reached out to him. Going home with her every day brought them together. He had thought about coming clean about the lies but the more they fought the closer he got to Dani, making it the best time of his life. Why would he change that? Yet, look at her now, even though she had been a good girl, she too had eventually dropped him and married someone she shouldn't have.

Richard and Bianca were shocked to their roots. This was something neither had considered. Obviously, Sams was not well because what child did something like that to his parents, and then sat through the divorce watching as they tore at each other in anger and distress, without ever opening his mouth to stop them, or explain. Putting himself through something that neither parent had wished for simply to be near a girl.

Bianca called Margot and begged her to come to the house.

Margot heard the sad story, and asked what it was they expected her to do. Nothing, they said, they understood she was Dani's friend and she was obviously supporting her, but could she suggest a good therapist, psychologist, psychiatrist... anyone who could help because as she could plainly see and hear, Sams needed more than to just be taught a lesson. Somewhere, he had lost more than mere social skills and they needed to get him the help he desperately needed before he became something much worse than this.

After medication that could have kept a small hospital running smoothly for months, stress that made her more ill, depression, and constant worry, Dani finally started improving and the doctors happily declared her fit and healthy.

No one was happier than Nicholas was, as she announced that they were going home. She was sick and tired of cowering at her parents' house in Bedfordview and now she wanted her life back, and that included returning to work.

'Do you want to return to IT or do you want to move to one of the designing departments? You can pick whichever one you want. And don't think I told them anything, the heads of departments decided when they saw your designs.' Nicholas told her with a smile as he sat on their bed and rested his back against the pillow.

'I'm glad that I am getting the chance to move, but I'll stay in IT until the end of the year, and how many weeks of that are left? Then we will have a wonderful holiday, and in January I'll decide where to go.'

He smiled. 'And that way, you make sure your followers adore you forever. Those guys are crazy about you. They would visit every day if they could.'

'Do you go see them often?'

'I walk past there every morning to report on your health. Oh, and I have to tell you. I think something is going on between Tom and Simone.'

'Ah, so it is the Englishman. At least he is a great rugby enthusiast, if not a player. Her father is quite the aficionado apparently. He'll have a mate now.'

'I'm so glad we are home.' He extended a hand to her.

'And who would have guessed,' she teased as she jumped onto the bed and kneeled beside him. 'That Nicholas Galfrey was actually yearning to be domesticated.'

'Yearning, no, and domesticity had never entered my mind, but you...' he gazed at her adoringly. 'You keep me firmly planted and I love the sense of security I have when we are together.'

She leaned in and kissed him, then, her hands ran over his chest, starting a path of heat.

'You need to rest, my darling,' he said unconvincingly. Goodness, but he missed her.

'The doctors have declared me fit. They also said that my heart is strong enough to run a marathon.' She grinned. 'So, is it a marathon?'

'Yes,' one hand cupped her face. 'Although... There is a sprint in there first.'

She giggled as her hands went to the waist of his pants and started sliding them down. 'I missed you so much.'

He made a sound and reaching for her camisole, pulled it off. 'I missed you more.'

She breathed deeply, her eyes like smouldering emeralds; her mouth going down to his. 'I love you.'

'But never more than I love you, my sweet.' He whispered as they became lost in each other.

Athina Paris lives in South Africa but spent her formative years in Mozambique, where she was born. Years in convents and boarding schools prompted a deep curiosity, which quickly developed into an avid interest in reading and storytelling and led to a lifelong obsession with the written word and books. By fifteen, she had discovered ancient civilizations and became fascinated with various mythologies; a love she has kept to this day.

She studied Interior Design then turned to Creative Writing and followed that with Scriptwriting.

She became a spectator of human nature, quiet and shy, she preferred recording conduct and so built a treasure-trove of observations from which she drew the plots and settings for her romantic novels.

Set in faraway and exotic places, Athina's romantic works take her characters on voyages of self-discovery while dealing with catastrophic love lives in an imperfect world.

A stint as a high school English teacher polished her skills, a position she has vacated to concentrate on her professional goals of writing, editing, and proofreading.

If you enjoyed reading this book, please leave a review and let Athina know.

Here are more titles by Athina:

 Love & Madness

 All I Ever Wanted: Jessie

 Knight Kisses

RockHill Publishing LLC

There are some lessons that only time can teach, but you do not learn talent, you only perfect it over time.

www.rockhillpublishing.com

9 781945 286537